IN THE GARDEN OF SORROWS

KAREN JEWELL

MINDSTIR MEDIA

Published by Mindstir Media, LLC
45 Lafayette Rd | Suite 181| North Hampton, NH 03862 | USA
1.800.767.0531 | www.mindstirmedia.com

Printed in the United States of America
ISBN-13: 978-1-958729-32-8

For David, Gabe, and Zach.

And for my father,
the great storyteller.

CHAPTER

1

ULLER KNEW MEN WHO WOULD HAVE KILLED HER FOR what she'd done.

It was the summer of 1923 when the Pentecostals held their revival on Fuller's land. He had no use for their religion, never wanted to be washed in the blood of the lamb. But it was no surprise they came to Isabel for the favor. Sharecroppers and sawmill workers came often enough to the Fullers' door when there was someone sick or a birth not going right. Asking her to come.

Fuller married Isabel when she was barely sixteen. It was rumored she was part Cherokee and had the sight like her mother. He never knew nor cared about the Indian blood, but the sight – that was true. Like knowing when their oldest boy Carl left for the war that he would never come back.

A few months after Carl left, Isabel woke to the sound of his footsteps in the hall. Carl entered the room and sat down beside her, the four-poster bed creaking, and put his head on her shoulder.

"Do you want some supper?" she said, rocking him gently.

"No, Mama," he said. "I'm just passing by." He kissed her on the lips like he did when he was a boy. Then he was gone. The telegram they got from France said that was the night he died.

There were other things, like knowing where lightning would strike, or that her sister-in-law's baby wouldn't be right. One year she knew the cotton crop would fail before Fuller finished putting the seed in the ground. She never spoke much about it, never tried to change things much. She just seemed to know life with terrible clarity.

It was almost dark on that evening in late July when Fuller first heard about the revival. He had already sent the boys in to help their mother with the washing. Fuller was heading to the barn with the mules when off to the south, against the last light of the sun, he saw a figure walking slowly his way. The gravel road in front of their place led to town, and he wondered what mission might lead a man there late in the evening in the middle of the week.

He unharnessed the team, watched the man turn into the dirt lane that led to the house. He could make him out now – it was Everitt Wilson. Wilson made his way along the side of the house to the back porch, took off his hat, and nodded in the direction of the barn.

"Evening, Mr. Fuller," he shouted.

"Evening, Everitt."

Wilson worked as a hired hand for Fuller on occasion, picking or chopping cotton, or whenever he needed extra help, and Fuller bailed Wilson out of jail every so often on Monday mornings after Saturday night brawls at the pool hall. Riding back to the farm, Fuller would say a few words about how drink can make a man shirk his responsibilities, wisdom with which Wilson always solemnly agreed. Wilson lived with his wife and six children in a run-down shotgun house at Floyd's Landing, five miles south of the Fuller place. His house, one in a row of now half-abandoned houses built by the lumber company, looked out over the river at a cluster of shanties and tents on the other side, sheltering men and families looking for work at the sawmills or in the fields.

Wilson raised his fist to knock, but Isabel had already appeared, the light from the kitchen outlining her silhouette against the wood frame of the screen door. Fuller couldn't hear their conversation. He saw his wife gesture as she invited Wilson in, the halting shake of the man's head as he declined, and Isabel stepping out onto the back porch. She would think it discourteous to carry on a conversation, even with a hired hand, through the screen door. Fuller turned back to the task of bedding the mules for the night. When he thought to look again, Wilson was gone.

It was dark now. Fuller saw Isabel's figure through the kitchen windows, bending in and out of sight as she worked on supper. He wished for rain or a breeze, anything to break the heat. Shirt stuck to his skin with dirt and sweat, he turned toward the house, the long hours of hard labor in the fields settling in on him, legs heavy, arms and back aching, the weariness burning in his muscles and seeping into his bones.

He pulled off his shirt and stopped at the pump to wash up. Isabel's murmured conversation with the three boys, who were in the kitchen waiting for their father, rose and fell over the sound of the crickets. He put his head under the rushing water of the pump and closed his eyes in relief.

The screen door slammed. Isabel had sent their boy Samuel out with a towel and a clean shirt. Samuel swatted the towel at the moths hovering around the porch lantern and took the steps off the back porch in a single jump.

"Boy, you'll have the devil to pay with your mother if you break that lantern or get that shirt dirty," Fuller said. Still bent at the waist with water running down his neck, he reached for the towel.

"Not if I tell her you did it."

"Then you'll have the devil to pay with me."

Samuel, just fourteen but already taller than his father, grinned. "Not if you can't catch me, old man."

Fuller straightened. It was an invitation to go after the boy, likely ending with Samuel's two younger brothers joining in and all of them on the ground wrestling while the supper got cold. He smiled wearily and pulled on his shirt. He was too tired tonight.

"I would take you up on that, but I don't like to shame you before supper."

They went into the house together. Ben, eleven, and James, ten, were seated at the kitchen table, James complaining that he was hungry and Ben telling him to be quiet. Fuller nodded at his wife in greeting, but she avoided his eyes and turned away. He took his place at the head of the table while Samuel held his mother's chair. Isabel said grace, and they ate.

Fuller pushed his chair back when he finished eating, excused the boys, then looked down the table at Isabel.

"Someone sick down at Floyd's Landing?"

"No."

"What did Wilson want?"

Still eating, she paused, then lowered her knife and fork.

"A little group at Floyd's Landing have started a church. Pentecostal. Wilson's taking his family there now."

He snorted. "That is news. I've known Everitt to see Jesus, but it was always at the end of a bottle. He in some kind of trouble, thinking he'll be a holy roller and repent?"

"He didn't come to discuss his conversion, Edward, nor did I think it my place to question him about it. His church is planning a revival and they're looking for some place to have it."

"I've seen his church," he said. "More tarpaper shack than house of the Lord."

"He asked about the pecan grove on the northeast corner – would we mind if they held the meetings there. The trees would help with the heat, and it's close enough to Little Creek for baptisms."

"You don't suppose they'd be looking for snakes in the creek, would they?"

"I've never heard of any snake handling around here." She got up to pour him coffee.

"Singing and shouting in tongues and such," he said. "I doubt there's a landowner in the county would want that on his property."

Isabel poured his coffee then returned the pot to the stove. "No. And there's few landowners in this county that pay any respect to people who have nowhere to go."

He rested his elbows on the table, bent over his cup, picked up his spoon and stirred. "They don't have a preacher at that church. They make do with their own learned study of the scriptures. Hard to imagine they could attract much of a crowd."

Isabel stood by the stove, her face flushed with the heat. She turned her head to look out the window, though what she could see looking into the dark from the lighted kitchen was hard to say. "They've got a preacher coming. Been in his ministry three years, mostly in the hill country. A young man, on fire with the holy spirit they say."

"Who is he?"

"His name is Kane. Reverend Micah Kane."

Fuller sat for a few minutes without speaking. "Well," he said finally. "If you think it will be all right."

Isabel bent closer to the window, peering into the darkness. This morning when she went to the pump to draw water, a crow had flown in a circle over her head, cawed once then perched on a low-hanging branch of the elm tree at the corner of the house. She waved her arm to shoo it away, but the crow didn't move – just ruffled its glossy black feathers, cocked its head and looked at her. It was then she knew with certainty what had been lurking about the outer edges of her mind in the past few days.

Trouble was coming. Maybe already here.

She dropped her gaze to the dirty dishes in the sink.

"Yes," she said softly. "I think it will be all right."

CHAPTER

2

I SABEL ROSE BEFORE DAWN ON SATURDAY, BUT SHE'D BEEN awake long before. The night Carl came to her – the night he died – she had glanced at the clock when she heard his footsteps and seen that it was a little before two in the morning. Since then, on more nights than not, she would wake around that time, alert, feeling she should get up, that something needed to be done. Realizing what time it was, she would take a drink of water from the cup on the nightstand and lie back down, images of Carl filling her mind. She would settle finally on a particular memory, different ones on different nights, wrapping her thoughts around it as she had wrapped her arms around him as a baby and as a boy. Sometimes she went back to sleep. Other times she waited the night out.

She slipped out of bed and into the hall, closing the door gently behind her. She passed the boys' room and went to the bedroom at the back of the house, where she kept a few clothes so she could dress without disturbing Edward. In her mind, it would always be Carl's room. They had offered it to Samuel, now the oldest, but he had refused and still slept with his two younger brothers. She supposed there would come a day soon when Samuel changed his mind.

The narrow bed Carl had slept in was pushed against the wall. A washbowl, pitcher and a kerosene lamp sat on top of the bureau, a bathtub in the corner of the room. Except in winter, Edward and the boys bathed on the back porch; the bathtub was for her. Edward and Carl had carried it in after a trip to town, putting it in Carl's room because the room opened into the kitchen as well as the hall and hot water could be carried in easily. Edward fitted a drainpipe from the tub through the floor so the water would drain, promising Isabel as he worked that she'd have a real bathroom with running water someday.

She closed the doors and slipped out of the cotton shift she wore to bed. She poured water into the bowl and bent down to wash, then straightened and went to the mirror hanging over a shelf on the wall. Her blue eyes were still a startling contrast to her hair, which, except for a few gray strands, was as black as it had been when she was a girl. She ran her fingers through it, drawing it away from her face and shaking her head so that it fell across her shoulders and down her back. Then she turned away and pinned it up without looking in the mirror again.

She heard Edward cough, then rise, and when he paused outside the hall door, reached quickly for a dress hanging on the door, pulling it over her head and beginning to button it.

"Isabel?"

"Yes."

"Are you all right?"

"Yes. You go on. I'll wake the boys."

Edward went out the back, headed to the outhouse and then to the barn to start milking. She finished dressing, then woke the boys and sent them to help their father with the livestock while she made breakfast. They would quit work early today because on Saturday afternoons they went to town.

After Edward and the boys left for the fields, Isabel sat at the kitchen table to make a list of a few things to pick up at the store that evening. Baking soda, cocoa powder, and castor oil. She stared blankly at the list, pushed it away, and looked out the screen door and kitchen windows at the morning sun already hot on the back of the house. She raised her coffee cup to her lips and, despite the heat, felt a slight chill run down her spine. She might have imagined it. But the visions often came unexpectedly, with only the slightest warning. She set the cup down and sat as still as she could. Mockingbirds called from the trees by the road, hens clucked softly in the chicken coop. But there was nothing else. She rose and set about her chores.

That afternoon Samuel drove them to town. Their 1916 Ford Sedan had caused quite a stir when it arrived from the factory in Detroit, fully equipped, with a $740 price tag. They had bought it for Carl. Edward refused to learn to drive, but Isabel drove occasionally with Carl in the passenger seat beside her. On her second outing she clipped the side of the porch, shouting "whoa" instead of putting on the brakes. Carl grabbed the wheel before she hit the house, and when she finally managed to stop, he collapsed in laughter.

"It's not a team of mules, Mama."

The night before he left for the war, Carl parked the car in the barn, polished it, and checked the engine one last time. No one paid much attention to it in the first few months after he was gone. Dust and cobwebs settled on it like a shroud. Then one morning Edward came back to the house when Isabel thought he had left for the fields. He didn't say a word, just went to the cabinet where she kept the cleaning rags, pulled out a few, and went back to the barn. Every evening after that, he ran a rag over the car and turned the engine. From the house Isabel would hear the faint sound of the engine sputtering to life and after a few minutes, as twilight settled in, the sound would fade to a murmur then die.

Samuel laid claim to the car a year ago, running occasional errands during the week and driving them all to town on Saturday nights and then again on Sunday mornings for church. Isabel sat in the front seat beside him, and Edward climbed in the back with the two younger boys.

The town of New Caney, population 399, was four miles north of the Fuller place. They pulled into town a little before three o'clock and parked in front of Lambert's General Store and Hardware. Edward bought gas while Isabel shopped, then helped her carry the purchases to the car before returning to the benches outside the store for his weekly discussion of current events with Sheriff Dennis. He would collect the boys later for supper at Etta's Café. Isabel gave Ben and James a dime each to spend as they roamed Main Street with their friends to taunt the girls they saw, hoping one would turn around and give it right back. James would spend his dime on a Hershey Bar and a Coca-Cola; Ben would tuck his in his pocket, careful not to lose it, and store it in the Mason jar of coins under his bed. Isabel suspected Samuel was headed for the pool hall but didn't ask.

Isabel, as she usually did on Saturdays, went to Doc Walker's house. It was a short walk. She passed the café, the post office, the bank, the telephone office and the school. Behind her, on the east end of Main Street, were the pool hall, the barber shop, the blacksmith, and the jail. An ice factory and a cotton gin sat on the outskirts of town. There were two churches, Baptist and Methodist, whose members tolerated each other quite well except for occasional heated discussions on immersion as opposed to sprinkling or other theological issues of importance.

Doc Walker's white frame house sat under huge oak trees at the end of Third Street, in the northwest corner of town. Just beyond Doc's house, Third Street turned into a narrow dirt lane that in a few hundred yards trailed out into cotton fields. The grass in Doc's front yard was patchy and brown from the summer heat, but roses grew on lattices around the front porch in a wild riot of pink and red. Isabel had planted them years ago.

She waved as she turned into the yard. Doc's aging hound Shep napped in the shade and made a half-hearted attempt to rouse himself when she stopped to pat him. Doc sat on the porch swing, waiting for her.

"Isabel. How are you?"

"Fine, Doc, and you?"

"All right for an old man. Let me get you some lemonade."

"I'll get it, Doc."

"No, no. You sit."

She sat and rested her head on the back of the swing, the fragrance of roses heavy in the still evening air. Doc returned in a few minutes with two glasses of lemonade and a small plate of cookies.

"Edward and the boys all right?"

"They're fine, Doc. Your roses sure are pretty."

"Unusually pretty this year."

She smiled. He had thought those roses were unusually pretty every year she could remember. They fell silent, swinging together as the sun set. Since losing Carl, Isabel often sat with Doc without speaking for a long time. He never hurried her, never questioned the silence that had fallen over her or the sadness that was always just below the surface.

Doc had known her since she was a girl and still remembered the first time he saw her. He had set up practice in Painted Tree, a one-street town in the hills, and was the only doctor for miles in any direction. One night in the early fall he went to see two elderly patients at the end of Holland's Holler and stayed later than he expected. Tired and still miles from home on horseback, he rounded a bend and saw a small house with a light burning a hundred yards or so up the slope. He tied his horse to a tree about halfway to the house and went the rest of the way on foot.

Before he reached the house, the door opened. A girl, no more than six or seven, stood watching him. He stopped, not wanting to frighten her.

"My name's Israel Walker. I'm a doctor, been making my rounds up the holler, and I'm wondering if I could trouble you for a drink of water."

"There's a bucket on the porch. You can come up."

Doc stepped onto the porch. The girl reached over her head for a dipper hanging from a nail by the door, lowered it into the bucket, then handed it to him. As he drank, he looked at her more closely. Her black hair fell to her waist in a tangle of curls; she wore a faded cotton dress, several sizes too big, that hung below her knees. Like most children in these parts, she was barefoot. Unlike many, she was clean. He looked at her face and was startled to see that she was examining him just as intently. She lifted her eyes to his and gazed at him without blinking.

"Hope I didn't scare you, stopping this late at night," he said.

"You didn't scare me. I saw you coming across the ridge. My name is Isabel."

He looked back in the direction he had come. "It's awful dark out there. I don't know how you could have seen me that far away."

"Not tonight," she said. "I saw you this morning. On your horse. I knew you were coming, and you wouldn't hurt us."

He smiled, certain that the child was confused. He was nowhere near that ridge this morning. Only later would he learn that, like her mother, she saw things others did not.

She invited him in. Her father was Arthur Johnson, and he died the year before, she explained. Her mother was in the back putting her two younger brothers to bed.

Doc stood just inside the door, removed his hat, and surveyed the front room. To his left was a kitchen, lit by a single candle on a rough-hewn table, and to his right a sitting area with an assortment of rockers and odd chairs grouped around a stone fireplace. A handmade braided rug covered the pine board floor.

"We should tell your mother I'm here."

Isabel disappeared through a door in the middle of the back wall, then returned a moment later, followed by her mother. When the woman stepped into the light of the fire, Doc's breath caught in his throat. She was tall, almost as tall as him, and slender. She wore a man's white shirt, the sleeves rolled up to her elbows, trousers, and round-toed boots. Her hair, like Isabel's, was dark, but it was straight, and she wore it in a long braid. Her eyes looked almost black. Light and shadows from the fire danced across her face – a face that was one of the most intelligent and one of the most haunted he had ever seen. She extended her hand, and when he shook it, he could feel the calluses on her palms.

"Israel Walker, ma'am."

"Mary Clara Johnson."

"Isabel was kind enough to offer me a drink of water."

"Yes, she told me. I have to get back to the boys, but you're welcome here. Isabel will fix you a bite of supper."

Mary Clara returned to the back room. Doc helped Isabel ladle beans from a pot on the kitchen stove. She selected a piece of cornbread for each of them from a plate covered with a cloth napkin and set the food on the table.

"There isn't much, you know," she said.

"I shouldn't eat then."

"Yes, you should."

He sat with her on a bench at the table, insisting that she take half his cornbread because he couldn't finish it all.

"It's like the loaves and fishes," she said, her feet dangling from the bench.

"Your mama read you that story?"

"No. No time for her to read to me now, what with Papa gone and the boys. I read it myself."

"You can read?" He was surprised. "You've read stories from the Bible?"

"I've read the whole thing."

Doc left soon after supper. He stayed in Painted Tree seven more years before the lumber company asked him to set up practice in New Caney. Any time he was near Holland's Holler, he stopped by. Mary Clara farmed a few acres, took whatever sewing work she could find, and Doc worried at times how the family would survive. Mary Clara always insisted, though, that he come in and eat something. In return, he would examine the children and let them search his bag for the candy he'd brought. His visits often stretched into late evening conversations with Mary Clara by the fire. When he left, he'd pull a bit of medicine from his bag, and a book or two for Isabel. It was a constant source of wonder to him that at such a young age she would pore over his anatomy textbooks and greet him on his next visit with questions about what she had read. He worried that the subject matter and illustrations were inappropriate for a girl her age.

"If she's reading it, she must be ready for it," Mary Clara said.

Mary Clara died eighteen years ago, but Doc still talked about her. A most unusual woman, he'd say, and Isabel would smile. Now, swinging beside him, Isabel looked out over the darkening sky and watched as the first stars appeared.

"Tell me what you did today, Doc."

He set his empty glass and plate on the porch and turned slightly toward her. "I doctored a broken arm and saw two widow women with nothing wrong but lonesome."

She laughed softly. "That's what you get for being the most eligible bachelor around. Lots of widow women in this county wouldn't mind keeping company with you."

"Oh, I suspect they'd tire of my company pretty quick."

"Could be they would tire of comparison to Mary Clara."

"Well." That was all he would say. When Doc talked about her mother, Isabel often wondered what he left unsaid.

"Got another bad case down at Floyd's Landing," he said. "Woman took a knitting needle to herself. Five children already and all of them hungry. Says she can't have another one."

Isabel shook her head. She wasn't shocked, having heard similar stories from Doc on more occasions than anyone would suspect. "How is she?"

"Bad. I got most of the bleeding stopped, but she's real weak. Told her I'd be back early tomorrow morning. I'd like you to come with me if you can."

She thought for a moment. Edward would have to see to breakfast and that the boys cleaned up for church, but it was likely she'd be back in time for services. "All right. I will."

Shep raised his head, looked in the direction of the road, and growled. They stopped swinging and heard footsteps on the gravel coming in their direction. There were no lights on the road, and they wouldn't be able to see who it was until he was almost to the house.

"Isabel?" It was Edward.

"Yes, Edward."

"Evening, Edward," Doc said.

"Evening, Doc." Edward stopped at the gate. "It's late, Isabel."

"I'm coming."

Doc looked in the direction of the gate, then at her, a question in his look. She turned her head, patted his hand, and said good night.

"Watch that step, now," he said as she rose from the swing.

"Yes, Doc. See you in the morning."

"It's on the south side of the river," he said. "Second row of tents after you cross the bridge. You'll see my car."

"Good night, Doc."

"Good night."

Isabel and Edward walked back to the car without speaking. The boys were waiting for them, and they all piled in for the ride home. When they were getting ready for bed Edward asked what Doc meant about seeing her in the morning.

"He's got a patient he wants some help with. A woman down at Floyd's Landing. I said I'd go."

He pulled down the bedspread and sat on the side of the bed.

"Sheriff Dennis got wind of it," he said. "Things are getting bad down there, likely to get worse as the lumber company lays off more men."

She lay down and dropped her head wearily on the pillow. She knew jobs at the sawmills were getting scarce. Most of the raw timber in the area was gone, the lumber company having cleared the land for miles around as fast as it could.

"It's hard to understand doing that to your own child," he said.

She stiffened. "Yes. It's hard to understand what people are willing to do to their children."

If he heard the bitterness in her voice, he chose to ignore it. He turned down the lantern and stretched out beside her. All the windows in the house were open but sweat beaded on her forehead and on the back of her neck. She moved restlessly, trying to find a place on her pillow that wasn't damp, listening to the crickets and the shrill intonations of the bullfrogs calling each other. Something, a fox or a raccoon, rustled in the bushes outside. She stared at the ceiling, saw nothing but ripples of darkness.

"I don't think you should go to Floyd's Landing in the morning. It's best you not go down there anymore."

She didn't answer. After a while he began to snore and she finally slept, tossing fitfully in the heat. After a few hours, she woke with a start. She knew what time it was but glanced at the clock anyway. A few minutes before two in the morning.

She lay in bed without sleeping again until 4:30, then rose and went down the hall to Carl's room to dress. She went from there into the kitchen and picked up a basket and a loaf of bread she had made the day before. Leaving the house quietly, she stepped out onto the back porch and eased the door shut behind her. She lit the porch lantern and carried it with her to light her way to the barn. She stopped at the storm cellar, raised its heavy wood door and, brushing aside a cobweb, stepped down into cool darkness and the smell of damp earth. Shelves filled with jars of herbs, tomatoes, corn, beans, okra, pickles, apples,

peaches and jelly lined the walls. Burlap sacks of pecans, walnuts, potatoes, onions, and dried peas sat in the corners. She selected a few jars
of fruits and vegetables and put them in the basket with the bread, then
stepped out of the cellar.

Standing in front of the barn, she pushed the door open. The car
gleamed black in the light of her lantern. She put the basket in the
passenger seat, then walked to the front of the car and cranked the engine. Settling herself behind the wheel, she stepped on the clutch and
flipped the ignition switch like Carl had shown her. The car lurched
forward as she released the clutch awkwardly and stepped hard on the
gas. Heart pounding, she slowed to a crawl, steering carefully around
the barn, into the dirt lane, and up onto the road. Then she drove off
to Floyd's Landing.

She gripped the wheel tightly as she drove, keeping the car in the middle
of the narrow gravel road. The ditches that ran alongside were cracked
and dry. She could have walked New Caney Road blindfolded, having
been alone on it after dark on foot or on horseback hundreds of times,
with nothing to light her way. But sitting behind the wheel of the car,
following the path of the dim light cast by its headlights, she had a
dizzying sensation that she was navigating foreign ground. She shook
her head and the moment passed.

She drove through flat, familiar farmland, interrupted only by occasional fence rows and sloughs. It was the time of morning when
dark slowly gave itself over to light, a gentle easing in the night sky.
She decided she could see well enough to drive without headlights and
turned them off.

There was a light on at the Coggins' place, their nearest neighbors,
half a mile to the south. The Coggins' dogs barked as she drove past but
didn't follow her. They were getting old, and one of them had walked
with a limp since Carl shot it. Carl had gotten good and tired of those
dogs coming after everyone who passed by, he'd said. They were the
meanest dogs in the county, and you took your life in your hands getting
anywhere near the place. One Saturday night on his way to see a girl

he was courting, Carl had been ready for the dogs with a good-sized rock in each hand and his pistol in his pocket. He knocked the first two senseless with well-aimed throws and shot the third in the hind quarters for good measure. Old man Coggin always suspected it was Carl that did it – Carl being known for having the best arm and truest aim around – and spread the word in town that he knew who shot his dog but couldn't prove it. Everyone agreed that the dogs were much better behaved after the incident.

The sky to the east had taken on a reddish glow, and Isabel began to make out the faint outlines of Floyd's Landing in the distance. A few hundred yards to the south of the row houses, tents, and shanties, just over the county line, was Smitty's grocery store and saloon. Not far from that was the Pentecostal church, its weathered boards and tarpaper something of an eyesore, the cross on its roof slightly crooked and giving the entire structure the appearance of sagging to one side. Isabel thought the choice of location for the church a little strange. Smitty swore he hadn't sold any liquor since Prohibition, but everyone knew he was lying.

Edward and Sheriff Dennis had led the crusade to make their own county dry, shutting down stills whenever they found them, satisfied, for now, that most of the drinking went on across the county line at Floyd's Landing. Edward wasn't opposed to the notion of a man having a drink now and again. He was opposed, however, to drunken men passing in front of his place, shouting and swearing after late nights in town. More than once, he had leaped out of bed and run from the house in a rage, slamming the front door behind him and stooping to gather a few rocks as he charged into the night.

"Get on out you damn sonsabitches!" he would yell, slinging rocks at the offenders. "I'm raising a family here and it ain't right you come around cussing and carrying on."

Lying in bed with the windows open, Isabel heard every word he said. So did the boys, giggling and whispering "damn sonsabitches" to each other until their father returned. She used to think Edward would get himself shot one day, but he never did. No matter the size of the group, the men would fall silent and mumble their apologies as they headed on. Edward's strength was widely known, his wrath, seldom seen, considered something to avoid.

She braked and slowly crossed the narrow, one-lane wood bridge at Floyd's Landing. Once safely past the river she looked to her left and saw Doc's car in front of a tent down the second row as he had described it. She turned into the packed dirt yard of Smitty's saloon and parked, then collected the basket of food and walked across the road. Doc must have heard her coming; he came out of the tent and stood waiting for her in front of it.

She raised her hand but, not wanting to disturb the occupants of the other tents, didn't speak. She heard a baby crying and an occasional cough or murmur from inside the tents she passed. She waited until she was only a few feet from Doc, then asked in a low voice, "How is she? Any better?"

"No. She's dead. Man in the next tent came to get me, but there was nothing I could do."

She heard soft sobs inside.

"Are the children in there with her?"

"The two little ones are, but they're asleep. The neighbor's wife came to get the three older ones. They were awake through most of it."

He nodded in the direction of the sound. "That's the husband. I thought I'd give him a few minutes alone with her, but we'll go in."

He lifted the flap of the tent and held it up for her. Stooping slightly, she stepped inside. To her right were two cots. The dead woman lay on the nearer one. Her husband sat on a small stool by her side, elbows on his knees, head hanging in his hands. Doc had covered the woman with a blanket, but she could see bloodstains, darkening from red to brown, scattered on discarded bedding and on the floor of the tent. To the left, three thin mattresses lay on the ground, two of them empty. On the third, a baby, eight or nine months old, slept next to a child that she guessed to be only a year older, if that. The baby was restless, sucking its thumb and fingers. Whimpering, but still not waking, it turned its head and sought out the other hand.

Behind her, Doc spoke. "Mr. Piggott."

The man didn't move.

"Mr. Piggott. Mrs. Fuller is here."

Isabel waited a few moments, and when the man didn't speak, said, "I'm sorry for your loss, Mr. Piggott. I've brought some food for the children."

At that he looked up at her, and she drew back slightly. There was a darkness about him, something that almost made her shudder. *What else could you expect,* she told herself. *Death and so much grief in the room.*

"Thank you, ma'am," Piggott said. "There's only a little money left, and it'll have to go for milk for the babies. They weren't weaned, and they'll both be crying for her soon."

She recognized the familiar twang of the hill country in his voice. "Have you been here long?"

"No, ma'am. We come a few months ago. I got work at the sawmill, but it didn't last. I ain't been able to find nothing since."

He turned to look at his wife.

"I have to get back to town," Doc said. "I can send a man with a wagon to get your wife, and we'll help you bury her."

He didn't answer.

"You go on, Doc," Isabel said. "I'll stay here with Mr. Piggott for a while."

Doc looked at her.

"It'll be fine," she said. "Stop at the house on your way back and tell Edward to send Samuel with milk for the babies."

She stayed with the Piggott family the rest of the day. A neighbor woman brought sugar water for the babies, who woke up shortly after Doc left. Isabel held the older one while Piggott fed the baby, the girl thrashing in her arms, crying and reaching for her mother. Hearing the commotion, the three older Piggott children, all of them between the ages of four and seven, crept into the tent. They sat silent and wide-eyed on the mattresses, turning their gaze from their mother to Isabel and back again. Samuel arrived mid-morning with milk and reported that Edward wanted to know when she was coming home. She sent him back with the car, keeping Blue, the horse he had ridden, with a reply that she didn't know and instructions for fixing Sunday dinner.

The wagon Doc sent arrived late morning and Isabel was relieved to see it, knowing the effect the afternoon heat would have on the dead woman's body, the tent already smelling of graying skin and dried blood. She took the children for a walk down by the river while their mother's body was moved, then fed them and put them down for a nap. While they slept, she took the blood-stained bedding to the river and washed it as best she could. The sun was setting when she finally left the tent and headed for home, her back and arms sore from bending and lifting the children. She turned to Piggott as she mounted her horse.

"Come see Mr. Fuller after you've buried your wife," she said. "Our boys are back in school until the October harvest, and it's likely he'll have work for you."

"I will, ma'am. I thank you for your kindness."

She smiled sadly, and turned Blue in the direction of New Caney Road, letting him walk until they were over the bridge. As she passed the last houses at Floyd's Landing, someone called her name. It was Everitt Wilson, sitting on the front porch of his ramshackle house. She stopped her horse and waited as Wilson walked hurriedly toward her.

"I just wanted to let you know, Mrs. Fuller. We heard from the Reverend Kane, and he'll be here in two weeks. If it's all right with you, we'll be at your place Wednesday next to start getting ready for the revival."

"That will be fine."

She kicked Blue into a gallop. For just a moment, she had the dizzying feeling she had experienced when driving the car that morning – of watching herself riding on unfamiliar ground. *I must be tired,* she thought. The feeling passed.

CHAPTER

3

EDWARD WAS WAITING FOR HER ON THE FRONT PORCH, furious. She stopped Blue in the road and slipped down from the horse when she saw her husband coming to meet her.

"It's almost bedtime and the boys haven't had supper," he said, his voice even and low and crackling with anger. "We're starving to death."

"You couldn't cut some ham? Fry some eggs? There's four loaves of bread on the counter."

"We had eggs for breakfast."

"Spoken like a man who's starving."

He slammed the gate open. Blue snorted and reared back. She held the reins and stroked the horse's neck to calm him.

"We agreed that you wouldn't go down to Floyd's Landing."

"No, we didn't. You said it was best I not go there anymore. I didn't agree."

"And you pay me no mind?"

She sighed and looked at him, framed by the house she hoped to paint in the winter once the hogs were butchered, lamplight in the windows, hydrangeas and marigolds crowding the walk. An owl hooted from high up in the limbs of the oak trees, which looked black as they reached for the evening sky. She saw Samuel winding the Victrola in the front room, heard the rhythmic scratching of a record and the first strains of "Back to Dixieland," one of his favorites. Edward wore work clothes but was clean-shaven, his hair, sprinkled with gray, slicked back with pomade. She caught a faint whiff of bay rum.

She handed him the reins. "You take Blue. I'll see to supper."

Samuel was stretched out on the living room rug when she went in, James lying next to him, his head on Samuel's shoulder, a second record on the Victrola. Samuel smiled as she came through the front door, gave her a little wave, then closed his eyes and sang. "Pack up your troubles in your old kit bag and smile, smile, smile!" Isabel hated the song; it conjured up images for her of grinning skeletons in military garb, caps set jauntily on their skulls, bones rattling as they marched in time to the music. She was tempted to tell them to turn it off but went into the kitchen instead to find Ben buttering uneven slices of bread that he had cut and set on the table. She rubbed his head with her knuckles and kissed him.

"How about some plates for that, Benny?"

Ben, absorbed in his task, didn't look up. "I don't really need a plate. Samuel and James might need a plate."

She set plates on the table, sliced ham, scrubbed a bowl of carrots. The Victrola ground to a halt, and Samuel and James soon appeared in the kitchen. Samuel took a plate and grabbed two pieces of the bread Ben had buttered.

"Just one," Ben complained. "Jesus Christ."

The screen door creaked open. "What did you say, boy?"

Edward stood in the doorway. The three boys froze. Isabel shut the icebox and turned to Ben.

"You know we don't talk like that, Benny." She set a jug of milk on the table. "Everyone sit down and eat."

She poured milk, Edward and the boys stabbed slices of ham and slapped them on the bread. They ate in silence, Ben staring glumly at his plate. Samuel munched carrots and watched him with amusement. Finally, when Ben could stand it no longer, he rose and asked to be excused.

Edward looked up. Isabel spoke quickly. "There's pencil and paper in the desk in the front room. When you've written 'I shall not take the Lord's name in vain' a hundred times, you may go straight to bed."

"A hundred?"

"There's only one whipping waiting for you in the barn," Edward said. "I suppose you can take your pick." Samuel snickered. Edward turned to him.

"You find this funny, son?"

Samuel shook his head. "No sir."

Ben took his plate and glass to the sink and disappeared into the front room. Edward and the other two boys soon followed, and Isabel washed the dishes in solitude. When she had finished, she went to inspect Ben's work. He was bent over the desk in fierce concentration, pencil gripped tightly in his hand. She leaned over his shoulder, and he handed her the pages without looking at her. He was at seventy-nine, the paper covered front and back, the sentences a smudged jumble of capitalization, emphasis, and size.

I SHALL NOT TAKE THE LORD'S NAME IN VAIN. i shall not take the Lord's name in vain. I SHALL not TAKE the LORD'S name in VAIN.

Then further down the page: The Lord's name in vain I shall not take. IN VAIN I shall not take the LORD'S Name. Vain in name lord's the take not shall i. Vain vain vain vain vain. Name name name name name. Shall NOT, shall NOT, shall SNOT SNOT SNOT.

Isabel bit her lip, determined not to laugh. Edward looked up from his newspaper. She folded Ben's list and put it in her pocket.

"Good, Benny. Time for bed." She turned to Samuel and James, engrossed in a game of Old Maid. "You too."

"We weren't cussing," James said. "Why do we have to go to bed?"

"Because your mother told you to," Edward said.

James threw down his cards in disgust. Samuel picked them up and put the deck in a desk drawer. When the boys had left the room, Edward shook his head.

"Cursing and back talking," he said. "Samuel suspended from school for a week for playing hooky. I don't know what they're coming to."

"Samuel's done his suspension. You don't need to keep reminding us. They're boys. If that's the worst they get up to, I wouldn't worry."

He folded his newspaper carefully, set it on the floor beside his chair. He reached into his pocket and pulled out his knife. "They could use a little more attention from their mother." He snapped the pocket-knife open and began to pare his nails.

On the table next to him were three framed photographs. The first was of Edward, Isabel, and Carl, taken shortly before they'd left the hills. Edward, in his Sunday suit and bowtie, stood straight and stiff facing the camera. Isabel, solemn, bent slightly over Carl, who stood on a chair in front of his parents, an expression of sheer glee on his face, in leggings and a long shirt that his brothers later insisted was a dress. The second photograph was of the six of them, taken shortly after James was born. The third was of Edward and the four boys at the train depot, as Carl was leaving to report for the army. The boys all looked as if they were about to cry, but Edward was smiling, so sure Carl had done the right thing to enlist. And, above all, proud of his son the soldier, the way only a man could be proud. Isabel had refused to be in the picture, not wanting the strain of sleepless nights that showed so visibly on her to be captured for all time, but mostly because she wanted to spend those last few moments with Carl looking at him, not posing for the camera, to memorize every detail of his face, the light in his eyes, the dimple in his chin, his long slender fingers.

She went to the table and picked up the photograph of a smiling Edward and his suffering sons. It turned her stomach. She would have torn the photo to bits and thrown it in Edward's face long ago if it weren't one of the few photographs she had of Carl. She traced Carl's image with her finger. "My shortcomings as a mother haven't gotten any of our sons killed."

He closed his pocketknife with a click, and they stared at each other for a few moments. She set the photograph back on the table and went to the Victrola, straightened the short stack of records next to it, then stepped around his chair and bent to retrieve her darning basket from under the sewing machine. When she lifted it, she felt a hitch in her lower back, then a sharp stab of pain. She dropped the basket and grabbed her knees, bent over again, unable to stand straight. Edward jumped up. She waved him away.

"I'm fine." But she started to sweat and for a moment thought she might faint. She walked, stooped, to the open front door, rested her right arm on the door frame to support herself, her face inches from the screen, and took a few gulps of fresh air.

"Is there anything I can do for you?"

"If you could just bring me the liniment. It's in the cabinet to the right of the sink."

He went to the kitchen and came back with the liniment. She held out her hand for the bottle.

"No. Let me. You won't be able to reach."

She hesitated, then pulled her shirttail out of her trousers. He shook a few drops of liniment onto the palm of his right hand and set the bottle on the windowsill. Standing behind her, he lifted her shirt higher, then began to rub. She felt the rough calluses on his fingertips as he moved methodically across her lower back, the cool sting of liniment that warmed as it penetrated her skin. She rested her head on her forearm, closed her eyes, and sighed in relief as the soreness began to subside.

"More?"

She nodded. He shook more of the liquid onto his palm and massaged her again, back and forth, and then slower, more rhythmically, his right hand slipping under her belt towards her tailbone, his left hand coming to rest on her side. He increased the pressure from his fingertips, his breath deepening to match, and for just a moment she wanted to lean back, to yield to him, to see if the past could be forgotten for a while, if only briefly, temporarily.

She opened her eyes and stepped away from him. She pulled down her shirt and tucked it in and took the liniment bottle from the windowsill.

"It's much better now. I overdid today."

She went towards the kitchen to put the liniment away, stopped when she heard him speak.

"A man has needs, Isabel."

She turned and looked at him. "I guess that gives you another reason to fault me, then. Not paying enough attention to the boys. Not paying enough attention to you. Is there anyone or anything else I'm not paying enough attention to? Maybe you should write it down, Edward. Make a list of just what it is you want me to do and tell me when I'm supposed to do it."

He ran his fingers through his hair and shook his head. "I believe I'll take a walk before bed." He opened the screen door and was gone.

Isabel went to the kitchen and put the liniment away. She pulled out a chair and sat at the table, put her head down on her arms and closed her eyes. She rested for a while, then rubbed her eyes and looked up. And there was Mary Clara, sitting in a chair in the corner, watching her.

For a year or so after Mary Clara died, Isabel often had the sensation that Mary Clara was watching the world through her eyes – enjoying the sunrise over the rim of her coffee cup, taking stock of the garden, listening to the boys bickering, savoring the taste of jam cake at Christmas. Sometimes when Isabel spoke, she heard her mother's voice, the precise inflection, the husky laugh. The feeling that Mary Clara inhabited her body eventually passed, but then Mary Clara began appearing in Isabel's dreams. Not long after that, the visits began. There was no regularity to them. Mary Clara might come several times in one week, then not appear again for years. She had spent a good amount of time with Isabel when Carl died, not always visible, but Isabel could feel her mother's presence even when she couldn't see her. Sometimes Mary Clara looked as she had shortly before she died; other times she appeared as she must have as a new bride. Today she wore the white shirt, trousers and boots she had favored as a young, but mature, woman, her hair black again and braided down her back.

"Mother?"

Mary Clara smiled.

"It's been a while, Mother. How's Carl?"

"Carl is fine."

Isabel's eyes filled with tears. There were so many questions she wanted to ask, details she wanted to hear, but she knew from their past encounters that Mary Clara wouldn't, or couldn't, say anything more about Carl.

"He would have turned twenty-three this year," Isabel said. "Graduated from college and married, most likely, with a baby – a girl, I think. She'd be just like you."

She wiped her eyes and nose with her shirt sleeve.

"If I could just see him," she pleaded. "Talk to him. Know that he's all right."

Mary Clara didn't respond.

"Well," Isabel said. "Nothing you can do, I suppose."

Mary Clara pointed her finger toward the living room. "I heard that conversation between you and Edward."

"It's a low blow, Mother. Accusing me of not paying enough attention to the boys."

"True. But on the other hand, I don't think he was really talking about the boys."

"Don't tell me you're taking his side."

"I'm not here to take sides."

"No, you never did."

They were quiet for a moment.

"It's good to see you," Isabel said. "After all these years, I still think about you every day."

Mary Clara leaned forward in her chair. "You take care, Isabel. You take care."

Isabel heard Edward's footsteps on the front porch and turned in that direction. When she looked back again, Mary Clara had disappeared.

CHAPTER

4

ILSON CAME A WEEK FROM WEDNESDAY AS promised. Edward had left at dawn after loading a crate of dynamite into the wagon and setting a coil of fuse and an old jacket with blasting caps tucked in its pockets on the seat beside him, the words "Danger Explosives" stamped on the crate faintly visible as he drove off in the morning darkness. He spent most of July and August every year dynamiting stumps and burning brush. When he bought their land from the lumber company twenty years earlier most of the trees had been cut down, leaving an almost impassable tangle of undergrowth and brush. New Caney Road had been nothing but a wagon path then. Arriving after a three-day journey from the hills with all their possessions, they had camped until Edward built a makeshift shack. They cleared the first few acres of land by themselves, Isabel working beside him and keeping an eye on Carl. He often labored through the night by the light of the fires he built to burn the stumps and brush. Isabel would lie with Carl on a mattress on the floor of the shack, singing him to sleep, firelight flickering through the cracks in the walls.

One night when Carl was asleep, not long after they had moved from the hills, Isabel rose and went outside to where Edward was working. She watched him bury his axe in the root of a stump with a heavy thunk, raise it over his head and bury it again, his shirt discarded and skin glistening in the heat, the muscles in his arms and back rippling with effort.

"Rest a while," she said. "You need some rest."

He pulled the axe free again and looked at her, panting.

"I'll give you everything you want someday," he said. "Then I'll rest."

She went to him, slipped her arms around his waist and ran her tongue from his sternum to his belly, tasting sweat and smoke and rich Delta soil.

"I have what I want," she said.

He set the axe aside, reached down and pulled her dress over her head, drew a deep breath at the sight of her breasts and hips, full and ripe like the moon that hung low on the horizon, every inch of her familiar to him now but still as intoxicating as the first time he was with her. He picked her up and eased her to the ground, then lost himself in her, putting his finger gently on her lips to shush her cries.

Afterwards they lay half-drowsing, and Isabel thought or dreamed for a moment that it was Carl lying on the hard ground beside her. He was older, his fair hair turned dark but still curly. He was asleep and she tried to rouse him, pressing her hand against his cheek and turning his face toward her, where she saw blood and mud and that his lips were cold and gray. His eyes stared blankly, lifelessly, at her efforts. A scream whistled in her throat as she woke with a start. She sat up and scrambled frantically for her dress.

"We're going to lose him, Edward."

"Lose who?"

"Carl. Something terrible is going to happen."

He rose and put his arms around her, felt her heart pounding against his chest.

"Carl's big and strong. No need to worry about that boy. He'll bury both of us some day."

She squeezed him hard. "I'm afraid for him, Edward. I'm afraid."

"I'll look out for him. I promise."

They had built the house after the first year's crops came in and added onto it with a new kitchen and Carl's bedroom after the three younger boys were born. Sometimes at night she would go to Carl as he lay sleeping, put her hand up his shirt, press it to his heart and pray that he never be taken away from her. But the passing years brought more prosperity, more happiness, and the terror of her dream faded. On the few occasions that she thought of the dream, she tried to dismiss it as the natural fears of an overworked young mother with her first child. Until the war came.

Standing now at the sink washing breakfast dishes, Isabel looked out the open window to the north. The cotton fields came within forty feet of the house on the south side, but on this side Edward had left a wider expanse of land. The dirt lane skirted the house between the road and the barn and beyond it lay her garden. There was a slight breeze this morning, the old scarecrow's sleeves rising every now and then in mute protest as he stood guard over her string beans and tomatoes.

She heard Wilson's approach before she saw him. He looked in the window as he passed in front of her, raised his hat slightly in greeting, then disappeared around the corner of the house and reappeared at the back door. Drying her hands on her apron, she stepped out onto the porch.

"It's another hot one today, Mrs. Fuller."

"It is, Mr. Wilson."

"Not too hot for serving the Lord, I reckon." Wilson grinned, displaying his few remaining tobacco-stained teeth. His shirt and overalls looked and smelled as if they had seen a number of hot days since their last washing. He peered at her expectantly, and she looked away. The scarecrow's arms hung limply at his sides, as if fatigued by his earlier efforts.

"The Lord made the day, didn't he," she said. "He seems to keep making them, over and over again."

Wilson appeared confused. Then he nodded sagely and opined, "His will be done," and moved on to the subject of President Harding's death the week before. Isabel wasn't interested in his political opinions.

"Tell me about your Reverend. You're still expecting him?"

"Yes ma'am. First meetin's set for Saturday night. Got a couple of the boys coming soon with a wagonload of timbers. We'll be building a brush arbor if that's all right."

"That'll be fine." She had seen these primitive structures before – posts driven into the ground to support a roof of crossbeams woven with limbs and brush. No money for a proper tent, she assumed.

"Don't reckon Mr. Fuller will mind if we clear some brush off the fence row for him."

That was true, although she knew Edward would have an opinion about a man with a family to feed using a workday to clear brush without getting paid for it.

"He won't mind at all," she said.

"I'll be on my way then. We're surely obliged, Mrs. Fuller."

"My pleasure."

Wilson tipped his hat and, with another grin, backed away. She watched his retreat, resting her head for a few seconds on the door frame, then went back to the dishes. From the kitchen window she saw him walk north on New Caney Road until he came to the fence that marked the boundary of their property. He jumped into the ditch on the east side of the road and clambered up the other side, disappearing from view when he sat down on the edge of the cotton field to wait for his companions to arrive.

Isabel turned her attention to the washtubs of tomatoes she had set on the kitchen table. A bumper crop this year had her struggling to keep up with the canning, but summer's bounty was their winter food supply, and nothing could go to waste. Samuel had hauled water for her and brought in extra wood before setting off for school, and the pots on the stove were boiling. She poured boiling water over one washtub of tomatoes to loosen their skins, then refilled the pots to sterilize her Mason jars while she skinned and quartered the tomatoes and tossed them into a kettle. When the kettle was full, she set it on the stove, added a little water and skimmed the tomatoes as they cooked. She packed the cooked tomatoes into hot jars, ladled cooking liquid to fill them, then sealed them with rubber bands and covers. She set the finished jars on one end of the table to cool. Then she started on the next batch.

By mid-afternoon the kitchen was a steam bath. Isabel was soaked in sweat and tomato juice, and hungry. She cut cornbread and green onions and went outside to get milk from the buckets standing in a trough of water by the pump. Before filling her cup, she drained the trough to refill it with cool water. While waiting for the water to drain, she looked to the north and saw Wilson and his band of assistants. The skeleton of the brush arbor was well under way, and she could tell even from a distance that the structure was large. She was amused at Wilson's ambition and hoped their traveling preacher was good enough to fill it.

She turned back to the trough and saw that it was almost dry. She refilled it, then scooped a cup of milk from the nearest bucket and sat on the porch to eat. She was almost finished eating when the boys came home. They dropped their empty lunch pails on the porch and sat down beside her.

"How was school?"

James clutched his hair with both hands and shook his head.

"Terrible," he said. "I had a terrible day."

"What happened?"

"Miss Moxley. She's downright crazy."

Miss Moxley, their teacher, was generally even-tempered and well-liked, and despite the efforts of a few of the boys in her class, seemed to be an effective educator. Isabel sometimes wondered how the young woman kept her wits about her.

"She paddled Cordie Overman three different times," James said.

"Well," she said. "If I know Cordie Overman, he had it coming."

"Of course he had it coming," Samuel said.

"But then she whacked Elizabeth Brickell with a yardstick for missing one long division problem when it was her turn at the board," James said. "Elizabeth Brickell! Teacher's pet Elizabeth Brickell, who gets almost everything right all the time!"

"That is unusual," she said. "But why was your day so terrible? Did she paddle you?"

"No. But I just sat there all day thinking, Elizabeth Brickell? Elizabeth Brickell? If this can happen to Elizabeth Brickell, what's next?"

Samuel, laughing, reached across Isabel and grabbed the front of James's trousers. "Did you wet your britches? Did mean old Miss Moxley make you wet your britches?"

"Stop," she said as James lunged across her lap at Samuel, and she pushed them apart. "It sounds like Miss Moxley was having a bad day. Let's get you something to eat and maybe you'll feel better."

James rose with a heavy sigh, opened the screen door, and stopped. "Good Lord have mercy," he shouted.

She jumped up and pushed by him into the kitchen. There was blood everywhere. Dripping from the table, pooling in the sink, streaming down the walls. Puddling on the floor, bubbling on the stove. Curdling in tubs, clotting in row after row of glass containers on the sagging table. She looked down and saw that it was on her clothes, spattered on her boots, drying under her fingernails. She closed her eyes. "So much blood," she whispered. "So much blood. How could any of them have survived?"

"Mama? Mama?"

She opened her eyes. James was watching her anxiously.

She looked around the kitchen. Steam rose from the kettles of boiling water on the stove. Tomato juice dripped from the table. Plops of cooking liquid and pulp were scattered on the floor, even on the walls in a few places. Quart jars of canned tomatoes lined the table and counters. There were mounds of discarded skins in the washtubs, a pile of stained dishtowels in the sink.

"You're such a jackass," Samuel said to James.

"No, Samuel," she said. "I'm such a messy cook. And don't call your brother names."

She gave them sugar cookies to eat outside while she cleaned the kitchen, then relented on a short game of baseball before chores. She sent them to do the evening milking when she realized that the baseball game had stopped for a newly discovered wasp nest. High sport, the boys were swatting wasps with their caps and a two-by-four, counting the kill and the number of stings.

It was almost sunset when she thought to check on Wilson's progress again. The boys were gathered around the kitchen table finishing their homework and she went outside to collect okra and cucumbers from the garden for supper. It appeared that the frame for the brush arbor was completed, but she couldn't tell how far they had gotten on the roof. There was no sign of activity there now. Turning back to the house, she was surprised to see Piggott emerge from the fields on the far side of the barn, waving as he approached. She recoiled slightly, as she had on their first meeting, and thought briefly of Mary Clara's admonition. "You take care, Isabel. You take care." She shook her head. *He's a grieving widower and father, nothing more.*

Piggott came closer. "I wanted to thank you again for your kindness, ma'am."

"I'm glad we can help, Mr. Piggott. You've been working with Mr. Fuller today?"

"Yes, ma'am. I thought we cleared near a quarter acre, but Mr. Fuller said it weren't that much. Didn't hardly stop to rest and Mr. Fuller, he's still out there."

"He works very hard. He always has. And how are the children?"

"Missing their mama real bad. My sisters come on Sunday and took the four youngins home. They'll take care of them 'til I get back. But they could only take two each, so I ain't got nowhere to send my oldest girl."

"Caroline, isn't it?"

"Yes ma'am, Caroline. She'll have to stay with me."

"I wish things had turned out differently for you and your family."

"It surely weren't what we expected." His voice broke.

She nodded in the direction of the storm cellar. "You'll find empty jars in the cellar there. Help yourself to some milk, and I've got a pot of stew on the stove. There's plenty for you and Caroline."

"I cain't take no more from you, Mrs. Fuller."

"Yes, you take it. Get the milk and I'll be right back."

Returning a few minutes later, she held out a covered tin pot wrapped in rags. Piggott tucked it under one arm, and with a jar of milk in the other, said that he thought he could make it back to his place with the load. Then, knowing that Floyd's Landing was no place for a young girl to be left alone all day, she told him to bring Caroline to her. "She can help me here while you work with Mr. Fuller."

He thanked her again. "Tell Mr. Fuller I'll see him in the morning."

Isabel walked slowly toward the garden, arms crossed in front of her, and watched until he reached the road. He nodded back at her, and she raised her hand slightly then looked away, staring across the horizon, where the setting sun glowed red against the cornstalks. Bits of the boys' conversation drifted from the kitchen windows. *I should get back to the house,* she thought. But then she saw it – something dipping and gliding in the sky just over the rows of corn, with what looked like a tail dangling behind it. She blinked her eyes, thought maybe it was gone, but there it was again, rising, falling, and shaking its tail in some mad dance across the sky. A kite. A kite like the first one Edward and Carl had built together one rainy Sunday afternoon, Edward so patient and Carl insisting on doing everything himself. Carl painted designs on newspaper and was reduced to tears when twice he ripped the paper tacking it onto the frame. Edward had cut strips from an old sheet for the tail and waited while Carl clumsily tied each one on. The rain stopped but the wind still blew and the three of them went out to the road. Edward held the kite high above his head and ran, Carl trailing after him, until the kite was finally aloft. Isabel clapped and Carl shrieked in triumph, then Edward handed him the ball of string and told him to hold on tight.

Where could it have come from? The air was still, not even a hint of a breeze. The kite floated closer and, with it, echoes of a small child's laughter. She heard peals of unabashed joy, a sound that Edward had once long ago described as the sound of angels singing.

"Carl?" She stepped closer to the road. "Carl?"

Suddenly, from behind her came the faint sound of an explosion. Edward dynamiting stumps. The laughter stopped. "Don't," she whispered. "He's come looking for us, Edward. Don't do that, you'll frighten him." A second explosion followed, louder this time, the windows in the house rattling slightly, acrid smoke drifting toward her. The kite plunged into the field and disappeared as the third blast hit her. The ground shook under her feet and she dropped to her knees. She heard panicked screams, the loud wheezes of someone running, boots thudding, the jangle of metal on metal. The ground shook again, and a blinding jolt of pain shot through her head. She gasped and leaned forward to catch herself on her hands. Looking up, she saw a faint shimmer in the cornfield, as if someone or something hidden behind a wave of light was moving rapidly across it, the stalks closing behind him to conceal his passage. She shuddered. Then the vision stopped.

CHAPTER

5

ILSON AND HIS MEN FINISHED THE BRUSH ARBOR
Friday afternoon. Isabel and Edward, at Wilson's invitation, walked over before supper to see it. Built partially under the pecan trees, it extended beyond the trees to the east toward the creek. Tall posts planted every six feet or so supported the rafters, and a thick canopy of brush and branches laced through the rafters formed the roof. The ground under the shaded interior was covered with sawdust.

Edward stood outside while Isabel, accompanied by Wilson, walked up the center aisle. Makeshift benches of split logs sat in rows on each side, turned slightly inward to face the crudely constructed pulpit at the end. Wilson sat down in the front row as she stepped behind the pulpit and surveyed the otherwise empty congregation.

"You've done a fine job, Mr. Wilson," she said.

He grinned, but before he could respond, a smooth, deep voice came from the back of the arbor.

"The sinners in the back are waiting for the word, ma'am. But you'll have to speak up to reach us."

She peered in the direction of the voice but the setting sun and shadows from the trees made it difficult to see the tall figure at the end of the aisle.

Wilson jumped to his feet. "It's the Reverend Kane," he whispered excitedly. "He come this morning. Got four or five others with him, too."

Isabel watched Kane from behind the pulpit as he walked slowly toward them. Despite the heat he wore a black suit and a white shirt buttoned at the collar. He was clean-shaven, but wore his hair long, brushed straight back from his forehead and curling slightly where it rested on his shoulders. His eyes, dark and intense, appeared to be fixed only on her during his journey down the aisle, but he paused and greeted Wilson as he passed, then stopped a few feet in front of the pulpit. He was young, in his early thirties, she guessed. *He looks proud,* she thought. *He is not a humble man.*

"You must be the kind woman Brother Wilson told me about," he said.

"Yessir, Reverend," Wilson chimed in. "This here's Mrs. Fuller. That's Mr. Fuller out walking the fence row." He pointed but Kane still looked at Isabel. "This here's their property."

"Pleased to make your acquaintance, Mrs. Fuller." Kane stepped forward and extended his hand across the pulpit. "I'm Micah Kane."

She looked down at the offered hand. It was tanned and rough, the nails uneven but clean.

He went on. "Your hospitality is widely known, ma'am. I have already found comfort under your pecan trees, resting in the shade and preparing for the meetings."

She took his hand and smiled slightly. "I'm glad to hear it, Reverend. Usually all we find under there is pecans."

A look of mild surprise crossed his face, but before he could say anything, Edward's voice came from the back.

"This the preacher?"

Isabel leaned slightly to look around Kane. She tried to withdraw her hand, but he gripped it more tightly. Startled, she looked in his face again. She was even more startled by what she saw, the wide-eyed boldness of his stare a look she knew well enough but hadn't noticed from a man in a long time. She pulled her hand away again and this time, he let go.

"Yes, Edward," she said, stepping out from behind the pulpit. "Come meet Reverend Kane."

Wilson joined the circle as Edward approached. The men shook hands and Kane thanked Edward for the use of his property. Edward asked a few questions about where Kane had been that summer on the revival trail, then asked, "How long you plan on this one lasting?"

"It's hard to say. Sometimes the power of the spirit is so strong the meetings go on for months. We go as the Lord leads us."

Isabel knew Edward would have something to say about that. Quickly, she inquired, "Have you found a place to stay, Reverend?"

"Yes, ma'am. Brother Wilson showed us where to set up camp."

Wilson explained that Kane and his followers were camped on the river down by Floyd's Landing. They arrived in wagons filled with tents, musical instruments, song books and Bibles. They had already posted flyers in town about the revival and done some visiting.

"Well," Edward said. "You're a busy man, Reverend. We'll let you get back to work."

Looking at Isabel, Kane shook Edward's hand. "I hope we'll be seeing you at the meetings."

"We may stop by," Edward said. "But you start without us if we're not here." He turned to Isabel, who said goodbye, and the two of them walked down the aisle and out of the brush arbor. Isabel could feel Kane watching her, but she didn't look back. They walked along the fence row to the road, Edward examining, as he always did, each row of cotton they passed.

"We need rain," he said.

They walked the rest of the way home in silence. Isabel paused at her garden before going inside, bending to pull a few weeds in the last light of the day. Edward had chores to finish in the barn, but he stood with hands in his pockets, rocking on his heels, watching her.

"I'd be willing to bet the young Reverend Kane puts on quite a show," he said.

She straightened and wiped her forehead with her arm, bits of dirt from the roots of the weeds in her hand falling on the front of her shirt. She looked out over the cotton field to the brush arbor. It was dark and silent.

"Yes," she said. "I'm sure he does."

Saturday was the first night of the revival. On their way to town the Fullers passed several wagons parked on the side of the road, their teams tied to makeshift tethers. Because it was still early, Isabel supposed they belonged to Reverend Kane and his followers. When they got to town, she did her weekly shopping. She felt a tug at her dress as she lifted the sack of groceries into the car.

"Mama," Ben said.

"I'll get your dime in a minute, Benny. Just let me finish here." Standing on the running board, she pushed the sack further into the car, then rested for a moment, one hand on the assist handle, the other on the driver's seat, her head drooped forward and shoulders aching. Another tug on her dress, and she pushed herself up and reached into her pocket for her coin purse.

"I was thinking, Mama," Ben said.

"Thinking what, sugar?"

"Thinking why you never eat supper with us in town. You can keep my dime and have enough money to eat supper with us."

Still standing on the running board, she looked down at his upturned face. Her throat tightened. *My babies are growing up,* she thought. *Soon they'll all be gone.* She touched Ben's cheek. He had such beautiful eyes, blue like hers, and Edward's light brown hair. Glancing up, she saw the hopeful look on Samuel's face, a look that tore her heart and then turned quickly to a scowl.

"Money's got nothing to do with it," he said.

She turned back to Ben.

"You buy yourself something, Benny." She handed him the dime and stroked his hair. "It's not the money – Mama's just not hungry tonight."

"Appetite's got nothing to do with it either," Samuel said. "It's just a place to eat dinner, Mama, with good food and folks we know. There's no reason you can't."

She attempted a smile for Samuel, but he looked away. "I'm sure you'll all have a good time. I'll see you after a while."

Isabel usually hurried past the café on her way to Doc Walker's, but tonight she slowed, then stopped on the sidewalk outside. "Etta's Cafe" was painted in large, slightly peeling red letters on the storefront window to the left of the door, "Real Home Cooking" on the right. A worn menu was propped against the glass on the windowsill inside. Looking through the glass, she could see the scarred wood tables and chairs arranged neatly on the cement floor and, at the back, the table where she had sat the last time she ate at the café. A Saturday night in 1918, the night before Carl left for the war. She could almost see their images in the glass, as Edward and the boys joked and laughed over supper and she sat silent, afraid. She remembered that all through supper she kept repeating in her head, please don't take him, Lord, take me instead. And all the while she knew he was gone.

She shook her head and blinked back tears. She turned away from the café and headed for Doc's house. He was inside when she arrived, standing at the sink washing his supper dishes. He turned to greet her as she came in. She kissed him on the cheek and pulled a towel from the drawer.

"You don't have to do that," he said.

"I know."

They finished washing the dishes and put a pot of coffee on. She found a tray under the sink and loaded it with cups and a piece of chocolate cake a neighbor had brought. When the coffee was ready, they went outside to sit in the porch swing.

"I'm surprised you're here. Thought you'd be at the revival tonight," he said.

"It's early, Doc. You know the party won't get good until about midnight."

He shook his head. "Edward's a tolerant man. There's not many would put up with that on his property."

"It's my fault. I can't seem to say no to anyone looking for the Lord – whether I think they're looking in the right place or not."

"Then I say what I've said many times. Edward's an unusual man. He takes your decisions on things most men wouldn't even hear of."

She didn't respond. Doc waited a few minutes, then patted her hand.

"I met the Reverend Kane," she said.

"Don't say. What do you think of the traveling man of God?"

"I don't spend time thinking about men of God. They usually have a lot to say about how women should act. And it seems they think it's their mission to put women in their place. I don't find that very interesting."

He chuckled. "You're so much like your mother, Isabel."

"Pigheaded?"

"More like a natural force. If there's a man alive thinks he could put you in your place, I'd like to meet him. Just so I could tell him he's a fool."

She gave him a wry smile. "Eat your cake. Before I eat it for you."

While Doc ate his cake, he told her he knew some Kanes years ago up in the hills. He recalled there might have been a boy that would be about the age of this preacher, but he wouldn't have expected any of that bunch to turn out a man of the cloth. All of them smart and good looking, but you never could quite trust them. "He might not be from that Kane family," he said, "but it's something to keep in mind."

She nodded thoughtfully. "I don't plan on seeing much of the Reverend Kane," she said. They sat in companionable silence and finished their coffee, then she said good night.

She made her way downtown and found Edward smoking a cigar with Sheriff Dennis outside the jail. James soon wandered by, and she sent him to find Ben and Samuel. As they drove home, they passed dozens of wagons and horses tethered along the fence row that marked their property and cars parked by the side of the road. Campfires blazed at the revival site and the faint rhythms of drums and guitars drifted across the field. The boys wanted to stop, but Edward said no.

Isabel thought Edward was asleep when she slipped into bed beside him after saying prayers with the boys and tucking them in. She sighed and closed her eyes.

He reached over as if to touch her hair, then hesitated. "The boys need you, Isabel. You can't go on grieving Carl forever."

He moved closer, stroked her cheek with the back of his hand, ran his finger down her neck to the top of her nightgown.

She opened her eyes. "Stop. Just stop." She pushed his hand away and sat up. "It's not up to anyone else to tell me how to grieve. Especially not you." She was sweating, thoughts whirling angrily in her head.

"I would take his place," she said. "Do you understand that? I would give anything to take his place."

"Carl's?"

"Yes. I wish it had been me instead of him."

"You have three other boys. You'd do that to them?"

She took a drink of water from the cup on the bedside table. "They'd turn out all right without me. Carl would look after them."

"You don't know what you're saying, Isabel."

He rolled to his side. After a while, she fell into a restless sleep. She woke in the middle of the night as usual and rose quietly, closing the door as she left the bedroom. She checked on the boys, who were sprawled across their beds, and closed their door as well. She paced through the kitchen and the living room then stepped out onto the front porch. A full moon lit the yard. She eased into one of the rocking chairs, leaned her head back, and began to rock.

She was almost asleep when she heard the scrape of boots on the gravel road, someone walking toward their place. Startled, she leaned forward in the chair and looked in the direction of the footsteps. She had no intention of saying anything, but the bright moonlight and her white nightgown must have given her away. The traveler stopped at the front gate.

"Good evening, Mrs. Fuller." It was Reverend Kane. He still wore a dark suit, but had unbuttoned the collar of his shirt, rolled up his sleeves, and slung the jacket over his shoulder.

"Reverend. You're out awfully late. And on foot – it's a long walk to Floyd's Landing."

"It was a good night. Many souls were brought to the Lord. I was in such a state of the spirit that I needed to be alone for a while."

She was amused, although she couldn't say exactly why. "That must be quite a state. It being three in the morning and all."

He must have taken her conversation as an invitation. He turned into the walk and took a few steps toward the porch, but she stopped him.

"I'm afraid I'm not dressed for company, Reverend. I don't get many visitors this time of night."

She made out his smile in the moonlight. "Oh, I think you do, ma'am. The only question is, are you visited by angels, or by demons?"

She was taken aback. "Whatever they are, Reverend, I don't think it's any of your business."

"It's not if you don't want it to be, Mrs. Fuller. But we sang a song tonight that made me think of you. 'There is a balm in Gilead, to make the wounded whole. There is a balm in Gilead, to heal the sin-sick soul ..."'

Isabel, breathing heavily, began to rock. "We're not in Gilead, Reverend. In case you haven't noticed."

"No, ma'am, you're right about that." His voice was low. He turned to go, took a few steps toward the road, then looked back at her with such intensity that she crossed her arms instinctively, feeling she should cover herself.

"This isn't Gilead. It's where you live – with all your sadness."

That was all he said. She watched as he disappeared into the night.

CHAPTER

6

I SABEL AVOIDED GOING NEAR THE BRUSH ARBOR FOR THE next few days. Sheriff Dennis and other visitors who dropped by kept her informed about the progress of the revival. The crowds increased in size each evening. Piggott told her there were reports of healings and other unspecified miracles.

"It's peculiar, though," he said. "The Reverend don't hold much with speaking in tongues. There's some that's done it on a couple of nights, swept away by the spirit. But the Reverend Kane, he don't seem to encourage it."

"Maybe the Reverend likes to hear himself talk in English," she said. "Speaking in tongues might distract him."

Piggott didn't seem to know what to make of that. He stood on the back porch with his daughter Caroline, whom he had brought to Isabel for the first time on Monday. Isabel wasn't sure what to do with the child. She suggested to Piggott they send her to school, but he explained that Caroline hadn't said much since her mother died and, anyways, he was planning to take her back to the hills as soon as he got a little money together. True to Piggott's explanation, Caroline hadn't spoken at all on the first day. She sat in a chair in the kitchen watching Isabel bake pies then trailed along quietly behind her to the barn, the henhouse, the smokehouse and the cellar. The second day Isabel killed a rattlesnake in the garden with her hoe. The boys were excited about the dead snake when they got home from school, but it didn't seem to interest Caroline.

"You sure she ain't no trouble?" Piggott inquired.

Isabel assured him she wasn't. A neighbor had brought her a bushel of peas yesterday evening, she told him, and Caroline could help with those.

After Piggott had gone and the breakfast dishes were done, she directed Caroline to a chair on the porch and showed her how to shell the peas. They worked side by side, Isabel lost in her thoughts and Caroline mute, peas pinging into the bucket between them. Isabel was surprised when Caroline spoke.

"Miz Jenkins says it was the will of God Mama died."

Isabel, bent over the bucket with her elbows on her knees, examined the shelled peas carefully for a few moments before responding.

"Who's Mrs. Jenkins?"

"She stays in the tent next to ours."

Isabel straightened in her chair and rubbed the back of her neck. Looking out over the fields for a moment, she then turned back to Caroline, who sat very still, her bare feet poking out from under a worn pair of overalls and her eyes fixed on Isabel.

"I don't know that the will of God has much to do with it. There's only one sure thing about life. And that is that we're all going to die."

She felt the harshness of her words as she spoke. She leaned toward Caroline and stroked her hair. "But maybe dying's easier," she said softly, "than being left behind."

Caroline looked at her, stricken, and pushed her hand away. She flung the peas she held in her hand into the dirt and, with her bare foot, kicked the bucket with the fruits of their labor off the porch. Disregarding the steps, she jumped to the ground and disappeared at a run into the cotton field.

Isabel rubbed her eyes wearily, then got up, retrieved the bucket and picked up the peas, one by one, that were scattered in the dirt. She didn't go after the girl. She would be fine wandering around the property by herself and she'd come back when she got hungry.

It was almost time for the boys to be home from school when she decided she should look for Caroline, wanting to be sure the child was clean and fed before her father came. She walked along the rows of cotton, didn't see Caroline anywhere in the field, made her way past the barn and down toward the creek. When the boys went missing, she usually found them swimming. But there was no sign of Caroline.

Standing on the bank of the creek, she shaded her eyes with her hand and turned in a full circle, stopping when the brush arbor came into view. Caroline had attended the revival on a couple of nights with her father, so she set off in that direction, walking north along the creek and then turning west along the fence row. She called Caroline's name, but there was no response.

She entered the brush arbor, glad for the shade, calling Caroline's name again as she walked past the empty pulpit and log benches, and out the other end into the pecan grove. She stopped short when she saw Reverend Kane sitting on the ground, leaning against the trunk of a tree.

"Mrs. Fuller."

"Reverend."

He didn't move from his position. She looked at him for a few moments, then turned to survey the rest of the pecan grove.

"Did you hear me calling for Caroline?"

"I did. But Caroline, whoever she is, is not here."

"Well, I see that now." She crossed her arms and looked around again. She explained she was looking for Caroline Piggott, who'd lost her mother not long ago, and she was watching her for a few days until her daddy could take her back home to join the rest of the family.

"Ah, yes. Such a sad child. I think I could help her, but she won't talk to me."

Isabel thought the Reverend had an irritating way about him. "Apparently not everyone appreciates your powers, Reverend. Nor shares your convictions."

He pushed himself to a standing position and promptly bent over to brush his pants, Isabel wondering as she watched how it could take so long to get a little dirt and grass off. He finally looked up at her, and she was startled, like the first time, by the raw openness of his stare that made her want to look away.

"I don't know how to appreciate my powers myself – if you want to call them that. And sometimes I don't know about my convictions either.

But I can listen to what makes her sad." His voice was soft, pained. She flushed and felt her throat tighten. He took a step toward her, then another, until she imagined she felt his breath on her throat. She turned away and saw something move under the honeysuckle bushes.

"Caroline?" She went to the bushes and bent down to look under them. "Did you hear me calling you? Come out of there."

She waited, bent over and peering under the bushes, until the girl finally crawled out and pointed to her hiding place. "It's my playhouse."

"That's real nice," Isabel said, glad that something drew Caroline's interest and glad she didn't have to think of what to say next to Reverend Kane. "I've got some things you can play with. We'll make you a tea set for your playhouse."

Caroline's face lit up and she took Isabel's hand. Isabel turned back to Kane. "I hope the rest of the revival goes well, Reverend." He reached out his hand to her, but she put both of hers on Caroline's shoulders.

He lowered his hand and spoke so softly Isabel wasn't sure she heard him right. "I'm still waiting for you to come."

She flushed again. "Say goodbye to the Reverend Kane, Caroline." They left him to his meditations.

On Friday night Edward and the boys went to the revival. The boys had been to enough camp meetings over the years to know there were likely some sights to be seen at this one and they pestered Edward at dinner until he relented.

"Go wash your faces," he said.

They whooped and jumped up from the table.

"Clear your plates," Isabel said. "And comb your hair."

The dishes clattered into the sink and the boys, pushing and slapping at each other, banged out the screen door to wash up on the back porch.

Isabel rose. "I'm surprised you're taking them."

Edward poured his coffee from cup to saucer to cool. Pouring it back again, he shrugged. "Been a long summer. We're playing Riverton tomorrow night and Sunday. Figured we might as well go see the

Reverend tonight." Edward and Sheriff Dennis were captains of the New Caney Bombers baseball team.

Isabel, her back to him, scraped the remains of dinner into a bucket of apple peels and cornbread scraps, then dropped the dishes back into the sink, lifted a kettle of hot water from the stove, and poured it over the dishes. Looking out the window, she could see a crowd beginning to gather at the brush arbor. She added a handful of soap powder to the dishwater.

"I don't think you should be giving the boys the idea it's just entertainment going on over there," she said.

Edward snorted, pushed back from the table, and brought his cup and saucer to the sink. "I won't give them that idea. I reckon they can figure it out themselves."

He joined the boys on the back porch, the boys fighting over the comb and splashing water on each other until he yelled, "That's enough now. Let's go."

"Don't stay too late," Isabel called out the kitchen window, but she didn't know if they heard her. She watched them shortcut across the field and disappear from sight.

She finished the dishes and wiped a damp towel over the table. She swept the floor and pushed the chairs back into place, spread the wet dishcloths over the windowsill to dry, then lifted the bucket of table scraps and took it out to the hogs.

She came back inside, sat down at the table, and surveyed the kitchen. There was nothing that couldn't wait until morning. The lantern on the table sputtered light around the room, but the rest of the house was dark. She bent down, pulled off her shoes, crossed one leg over the other, and rubbed her bare feet. She longed for a cool bath but was too tired to pump water for one. Looking around the kitchen again, she eyed the icebox. She got up and rummaged through a drawer, found the ice pick, then opened the icebox and chipped a small piece of ice off the block inside. Holding it carefully in her hand, she sat back down, pulled a second chair out from under the table, and propped her feet up.

She sighed as she rubbed the ice gently across her forehead, down her nose and around her lips, then drew it down her throat and around the back of her neck. The melting ice joined her sweat and ran in small rivulets down her chest and back. Her dress was loose-fitting, but it was damp and stuck to her skin. She unbuttoned the top two buttons, pulled the skirt up over her knees, and fanned herself with it with one hand, pushing the loose strands of her hair up off her neck with the other.

It wasn't long before the momentary relief of the ice was replaced by the hard jab of the wood chair against her shoulders and buttocks. She lowered her feet to the floor and, still holding the dress bunched up over her knees, padded restlessly around the kitchen, opened the door to Carl's room, and stepped inside.

A faint glow of white sheets on the bed was the only break in the darkness. She turned back to the kitchen and lit a match from the lantern on the table. Cupping her hand over the match, she returned to Carl's room and held it to the lantern on the bureau. The wick sputtered. She watched as the flame grew, then blew out the match and sat on the bed.

Carl hadn't left much in the room when he went off to the war. She had given his clothes to Samuel a year ago. She hid his baseball, a prized Christmas gift, among the mementos of his childhood stored in a small chest in the hall closet. Maybe she would give it to one of the boys someday. She didn't know, nor care, where the medals were. They had arrived in a neatly wrapped brown package one day and she had handed them to Edward, saying, "These are for you. I have no use for them."

Carl always had a stack of books on the table beside his bed – for her to read to him when he was little, and then to read for himself late into the night until she got out of bed and scolded him for still being awake. On top of the stack was the last book he had bought from a drummer: stories by Mark Twain. Not long after he left she had opened the book to find that he had written on the inside cover, "For you, Mama. But I get to read it first. Love, Carl."

She picked up the book and held it to her chest, then lay down on the bed, turned over onto her side, and drew up her knees. She lay there for a while, huddled into a ball on the worn white sheets. Then she turned over onto her back, opened the book slowly, and began to read.

It seemed she had been reading for only a few minutes when Edward and the boys came home. She heard laughing and singing, the heavy clomp of boots on the porch, the screen door slamming, shouts of

"Mama, is there any pie left?" She closed the book, rose from the bed, and went into the kitchen.

She helped them cut the pie and poured glasses of milk. Leaning against the counter, she listened to the account of the revival as they sat around the table. The Reverend Kane was something, they said, he could talk more Bible than anyone they ever heard. People were struck down by the spirit, falling right on the ground when the Reverend laid his hands on them, crying and waving their hands and confessing their sins.

"And dancing," James said. "They were playing that music and people were whirling and dancing. You never saw anything like it, Mama."

"Yes, she has," Ben said, his mouth full of pie. "Mama knows how to dance."

"She does not," James said.

"Does too. I saw her."

They all stopped talking and looked at her. She flushed. She would have thought Ben was too young to remember the last time she danced.

It was her birthday, seven years ago. She had baked a coconut cake and her brother George had come. They'd gathered in the living room after supper, and she had opened her present from Edward and the boys – a necklace of colored beads and little earrings to match that dangled just below her earlobes when she put them on. She'd laughed, delighted, and said she didn't know what she'd wear them with or where she'd wear them because weren't they just a little too flashy for church? George had pulled out his fiddle, Carl played the harmonica, and while Edward held James, she danced with Samuel, then Ben, until she was out of breath and said she couldn't dance any more.

Then George had winked at Edward and, pulling the bow slowly across his fiddle, struck the first few notes of a slow waltz. Edward put James down on the floor and stepped across the room to take Isabel by the hand, led her to the middle of the room, slipped his hand around her waist, and pulled her to him. After a few faltering steps, they began to dance, her arm pressing the muscles in his back as they moved slowly together like they had when they were courting.

"You can wear that necklace and earrings for me," Edward whispered, his mouth covering her ear. "And no need to wear anything else with them." His boots shuffling quietly on the floor, they danced until George finished the song, and she stood with her head resting on his shoulder as Carl and Samuel whistled and clapped.

Edward looked across the table at her now. She looked away. Then back at Ben, forcing a smile.

"You're right, Benny. I used to dance. But I've forgotten how."

CHAPTER

7

ISABEL DECIDED TO SKIP THE SATURDAY NIGHT BASEBALL game. She'd wait until Edward and the boys left, then take her bath and do a few things to get ready for Sunday dinner. The boys' church clothes needed pressing, she told Edward.

Edward let the boys quit work earlier than usual that Saturday so he and Samuel could get in a little practice before the game. Isabel made a fresh pitcher of sweet tea and sat on the front porch watching the four of them play baseball in the front yard. They took turns at pitcher, batter, catcher and fielder, Isabel worried every time James got up to pitch that he would get his head knocked off by a line drive. The ball came close a couple of times but being the youngest and fearless, at least when it came to baseball, James seemed unfazed.

"You might want to rest up before the game," she told Edward on one of his trips to the porch for a drink.

"These boys don't need rest."

"It wasn't them I had in mind."

She went in to fix a picnic supper for them to take to the game. She cut cheese and tomatoes, wrapped up some cold chicken and rolls, and added a tin of cookies she'd baked that morning. A few dried apples and she decided that was enough. They left late in the afternoon.

Waving goodbye from the front porch, she watched the car, dust cloud trailing, until it was out of sight. She stood on the porch for a moment, arms crossed, staring absently at the corn field across the road, then walked slowly to the chicken coop and collected a few eggs. Back in the kitchen, she put the eggs in a bowl and stored the things she had used to make the picnic supper. She set up the ironing board, put the flatirons on the stove to heat, then gathered up the boys' church clothes, kicked off her shoes and stood in the kitchen, barefoot, ironing until dusk.

When the ironing was finished, she returned the boys' clothes to their room then pumped water for her bath. She put two pots of water on the stove to boil, enough to make the bathwater warm but not too hot for an August night. It took a number of trips to fill the tub, a job she would have had the boys help with if they had been there. When the bath was ready, she put the latch on the screen door, then went to Carl's room, leaving the door that led from the bedroom to the kitchen open behind her.

It was not quite dark; she didn't bother to light the lantern. Standing beside the tub, she unbuttoned her dress and pulled it over her head. She stepped out of her bloomers and into the bath, settled into the water with a groan, leaned back, and closed her eyes. She lay in the water for a while, half awake and half asleep, until finally she roused herself and sat up, reaching for the soap. She lathered the back of her neck and her shoulders, unpinned her hair, rubbed soap into it, then, drawing her knees up, lay back in the tub and put her head under the water to rinse.

She stayed underwater for as long as she could hold her breath then pushed herself up to sitting position, water and soapsuds sloshing around her. She splashed more water from the tub on her face and, with both hands, pushed back her dripping hair. Arms stretched behind her head, she suddenly froze. She wasn't sure she had heard a noise, but she sat completely still, certain someone was there.

"Mrs. Fuller."

She gasped.

A soft knock on the wood frame of the screen door. "Mrs. Fuller."

It was Reverend Kane.

Collecting herself, she replied. "Who's there?"

"It's Micah Kane. I'm sorry to bother you. I'm on my way to the meeting, but I'm wondering if I could trouble you for a spoon of honey if you have it. I seem to be losing my voice."

Honey, she thought. *Losing his voice.* "It's no trouble at all, Reverend. If you'll wait right there, I'll be with you in a minute."

Grasping the sides of the tub, she raised herself slowly out of the water, trying not to make a sound that would reveal to Reverend Kane that he had interrupted her bath. She cautiously lifted one leg over the side of the tub, then the other, and stood dripping water onto the floor. Looking around the room, she realized she must have carried her towel, the last clean one in the bureau, to the kitchen and left it there. She panicked for a few seconds, then pulled the top sheet off the bed and used it to dry herself quickly. She threw her dress over her head and stepped into the kitchen.

Kane was standing on the back porch. She lifted the latch, opened the screen door and invited him in. He removed his hat and coat as he came inside and she wondered how, living in a tent down by the river, he kept his white shirts clean and pressed. He apologized again for disturbing her.

"I was just finishing up a few chores."

His eyes moved down her dress. "Yes, ma'am."

She was suddenly aware of what she must look like, barefoot, hair falling to her waist and still dripping, her dress thrown on hastily and wet in spots. *If he shows any sign of amusement,* she thought, *I'll send him on his way.*

He didn't. His eyes lingered on the spots where her dress clung to her skin, and when they met hers again, his expression was solemn. "A woman's glory," he murmured. She reddened and raised her chin slightly.

"I beg your pardon?"

"'But if a woman have long hair, it is a glory to her.' First Corinthians."

"Eleventh chapter as I recall," she said. "Right after that nonsense about woman being the reflection of man." At a loss, she reached for his coat and hat and hung them by the door.

"I'll fix a cup of mint tea to go with that honey. It's the best thing for your throat."

He sat at the table and she put the kettle on to boil. She set a small jar of honey and a plate of cookies on the table. He watched as she steeped the mint and poured the tea, but she avoided his eyes. She carried the cup to the table, bent over slightly, and spooned a large portion of honey into it. She stirred gently, placed the spoon in the saucer and set the tea in front of him, then retreated to stand by the sink. For just an instant, she thought she caught a glimpse of Mary Clara sitting in the corner, but when she turned to look, no one was there.

"Thank you."

"You're welcome."

He took a few sips of tea.

"Help yourself to some cookies."

"Thank you."

"You're welcome."

He smiled at her. "My mama would say we're being very polite. Although I doubt she'd be proud I came calling unannounced after dark."

He took a few more sips of tea. "I'm feeling much better already."

"Glad to hear it."

He took a cookie and finished his tea. "I need to go. I'm sure they're wondering where I am." He pushed back from the table but remained seated. "It didn't look like much of a crowd gathering tonight."

"You've got competition, Reverend." She told him about the baseball game and said she wouldn't be surprised if most of the town was there. "Although from what I hear you've made quite an impression on folks."

He stood and shoved his hands awkwardly into his pockets. "I believe the Lord's been with us. Then I get to doubting myself, although I try not to let anybody see it."

She picked up his dishes and carried them to the sink, set them down, then turned around. "If it is a gift you have, then maybe doubting is the first step to using it wisely."

"Maybe so." He walked to the door, retrieved his coat and hat, looked around the kitchen again and back at her.

"So your menfolk are at the baseball game. You're all alone?"

She gazed at him coolly. "Why, no, Reverend. You know we're not alone. God is watching every move we make."

He smiled slightly and put on his hat. "Amen," he said. "Amen."

The town of Riverton was twenty miles or so up the river, a rougher place than New Caney, its baseball team hard-knuckled and not above a dirty play every now and then. But the Bombers held their own and lost the first game by only a run. Semi-pro teams came through New Caney occasionally and their players were always surprised by the local talent. More than one game had ended in a fight when the visiting team beaned a batter deliberately in frustration, or both teams cleared the benches and had it out when tensions ran high. Edward never started a fight, but he was happy to help finish one, and Carl had followed suit when he joined the team. Isabel had been known to take the little boys home in the wagon, leaving Edward and Carl to walk home after the fight or the game, if it resumed.

Isabel went to the Sunday afternoon game. Samuel pitched well and one of Edward's hits was a triple, but they lost, four to two. After the game she spread blankets on the grass and they sat with a few other families eating picnic suppers at dusk. Ben and James and the younger children played their own baseball game on the empty field, while Edward and Samuel lay half asleep on the blankets. When it got too dark to see the ball, Isabel rounded up Ben and James and they went home.

"Looks like slim pickings for the Reverend tonight," Edward commented as they passed the brush arbor. "Another night or two like this and I expect he'll be moving on."

"You think so?" she said.

"The Lord may be leading him where to go, but I imagine the collection plate has a lot to do with how long he stays."

She looked back at the revival site. "I hadn't thought about that."

She sent the boys to bed as soon as they got home, then unpacked the picnic basket. Edward came in from the barn and told her he was going to bed.

"I'll finish up here," she said. "Then I may go over to the revival for a while."

He looked at her in surprise. "I didn't think you were much interested in it."

"I was thinking I should stop by at least once."

"See you in the morning then."

She waited until she heard him get into bed, then left through the front door and walked north on the road to the fence row. She stepped down into the ditch and up the other side, thinking she should have brought a lantern, and made her way along the fence row, keeping the fires at the brush arbor in sight.

The crowd was smaller than it had been on previous nights, the rough-hewn pews only half full. She stopped in the pecan grove, just outside the light of the brush arbor, and stepped up onto a large root for a better look, steadying herself against the trunk of the tree. She saw a few faces she recognized, but most were strangers, likely from the camps and Floyd's Landing.

The revival was in full swing, the congregation standing, hands raised, swaying side to side, and there was Kane in front of them. He had unbuttoned a few buttons on his shirt, which was soaked with sweat, and rolled up his sleeves. He paced back and forth, jabbing the air with a Bible for emphasis as he spoke, and slamming his fist on the pulpit each time he passed.

"John 6:63. Jesus said it is the Spirit that quickeneth, it is the Spirit that gives life."

Slam.

"Psalm 119. David prayed, quicken me after thy lovingkindness. Give me more life, more abundant life."

Slam.

"We should never fear anything that lovingkindness does."

Slam.

"It is like honey to the mouth, water to the soul, fulfilling in you all the good pleasure of His goodness, from glory to glory."

Slam.

"Halleluiah!"

Slam.

"Halleluiah!"

Slam.

The worshippers responded with shouts of "halleluiah" and "yes, Lord" and "amen." A woman on the front row stepped haltingly toward

Kane, palms up, fingers twitching, panting a rhythmic hunh-huuh, hunh-huuh, hunh-huuh. A man behind her babbled, "jo lo kindela, shan da shan da, bo bo bo radela, raysake. Shatta bakara, shatta bakara, baka. Ha ha la la, ha ha la la la." Isabel watched in sick fascination as others jumped and stomped forward and took up the chant. Kane put his hands lightly on the heads of some, and each person he touched fell back in a faint into the waiting arms of the crowd.

I don't know that I'd call that quickening, she thought. *Jabbering like a baby and falling to the ground like the dead.* She watched a while longer until the congregation finally tired, and Kane nodded to his guitarist and announced the final hymn.

"Number 14 in your Triumphant Songs book. 'Let Him In.'"

Their voices were subdued and hoarse as they sang. "There's a stranger at the door, let him in, He has been there oft before, let him in." Kane said a short prayer at the end of the hymn, stepped into the center aisle embracing and shaking hands as people began to leave, and looked directly at the spot where Isabel was standing.

Surely he couldn't have seen me, she thought. She slipped behind the tree and edged her way to the far end of the grove to wait until they were gone.

Kane and some of the other men put out the fires. There were torches stuck in the ground around the arbor and they took those to light their way to the road. Isabel waited a few minutes, until the sound of the group's murmuring voices and quiet laughter faded, then stepped out from behind the tree. The moon came out for a moment, just enough so she could see the fence row, then disappeared again behind the clouds. She had gone only a few steps when she tripped over something, a vine or a rock. She almost screamed when a hand reached out to catch her.

"You're the one who's out awfully late this time, Mrs. Fuller."

Heart pounding, she recovered quickly.

"Yes, Reverend. I'm sorry I was so tardy to the meeting. I promised Mr. Wilson I would attend at least one evening, but I just haven't had the time."

"I understand." Letting go of her arm, he walked slowly past her to one of the smoldering fires. He kicked at the logs a few times, sparks flying, then bent down and blew on the dying embers. A small flame. He blew again and the fire started.

"Come sit down," he said. "I'll tell you what you missed."

"You don't have to do that, Reverend. I'm sure it loses something in the retelling, especially without an audience."

Kane, still squatting before the fire, looked down at the ground and shook his head. She thought she heard him laugh.

"I would say you're a hard woman, Mrs. Fuller." He looked up at her. "But somehow I don't think that's true."

She crossed her arms, walked past the fire and up the center aisle of the brush arbor, and sat down in the front row. He followed her, hesitating as he approached and standing uncertainly in the center aisle. He stepped around her to sit down.

"No, Reverend. Your place is behind the pulpit."

He hesitated again, then went behind the pulpit, leaned forward, and rested his arms on it.

"You sure seem nervous for a man who does this all the time."

He wiped his forehead and laughed. "I'm not used to a congregation of one."

"Then don't think about it like that. We're two or more gathered in His name. Now tell me how it goes."

He laughed nervously again and cleared his throat. "I've thought about things I might say to you. But now I don't know what you want to hear."

There were popping sounds from the dying fire, a loud sigh as a log fell away.

"I want to know why you do this. I want to know why you say the things you say."

"Why I do this," he said in a low voice. He seemed to struggle with his emotions before going on. "I felt the Lord calling me when I was just a little boy. If you knew where I came from, you'd understand what a strange thing that was. My mama scrubbed us up once in a while and took us to church, and folks would turn and whisper when we walked in and sat in the back pew. My brothers hated it, but I'd sit and listen to the music and the preaching, and I'd feel like I was home. I said something to that effect one time and my two oldest brothers whipped me for being stupid."

He looked out into the night. "So, I stopped thinking about it. Ran from it. Did a lot of things too young and a lot of things I should never have done. Then life just started to go wrong, I guess. I lost some people I cared about." His voice broke.

Isabel thought of Carl and her eyes welled suddenly with tears.

Kane swallowed hard then shook his head ruefully. "I was a sinful man, in the belly of the whale like Jonah. I was lucky the Lord wouldn't let me go."

"So the whale spit you out here," she said, gesturing at the empty pews. "You sure know how to get folks excited."

"I'm not what gets folks excited, Mrs. Fuller. It's the mystery. The longer I do this, the more I believe in the mystery. And this is only part of what I do. My greatest calling is to be with people, wherever they are, whatever their circumstances. To break bread with them and remind them that God is always with them."

She watched him as he spoke, although she could hardly see his face in the darkness. He spoke well, but there was more to him than that. Something that drew you in.

"Always with them?" she said. "I've been with people too, Reverend. In all kinds of situations. About a year ago we got word there was a family in bad shape – migrant workers who'd come to town a few days earlier, pitched a tent down at Floyd's Landing. I took them some food and I saw something I don't think I'll ever forget. They looked like skeletons. All of them – the mother, the father, the children. They were starving. Starving to death."

She shuddered. "Where was the presence of God in that place, Reverend? Do you think God was in that tent that day?"

He was silent for a moment. "So much suffering in the world," he said softly. "Poverty and killing and greed. I don't pretend to understand it. But yes. I think God was there. I think in that moment, in that place, God looked like Isabel Fuller."

The night suddenly went still. She felt his eyes locked on her, heard the short, rasping sounds of her own breathing. She shook her head slightly and looked away.

"I don't know about that, Reverend."

"What happened to the family?"

"They moved on. I went back the next day and they were gone." She stood and stepped into the aisle. "I imagine you'll be moving on soon, too."

He walked around the pulpit and stopped a few feet from her. "My time here is short. But I'm not finished yet."

She flushed. She met his eyes briefly then turned away. "It's time for me to go."

"I'll walk you home."

"No need."

"Please. I want to."

They made their way to the road, stumbling a few times in the dark. He stopped at the end of the fence row to untie his horse. She stroked the animal's neck and he offered to let her ride while he walked, but she declined. They walked side by side in the middle of the road, Kane pulling the horse behind him, its hooves clacking on gravel the only sound. When they were almost to the house, he stopped.

"Why are you so sad, Mrs. Fuller?"

She walked on without answering, opened the gate to her front walk then clicked it closed behind her. He followed her but stopped just outside the gate. The horse reared its head, snorting and shifting restlessly.

She turned and clutched the top of the gate, struggling to form the words as if her lips were numb. Her voice was thick and low.

"I lost my son. He didn't come back from the war."

He moved closer, his soft, worn shirt brushing lightly against her fingertips.

"For a year or so after he died, I could feel him with me. I'd think if I could turn my head just so, I'd be able to see him. Then I'd turn my head. And it was always like I just missed him – I was a little too late."

She drew her hands away from the gate, curling them into fists and holding them against her stomach. "He's in my mind all the time. Sometimes I think I hear him – laughing or singing, or just a little whisper of a word."

He reached across the gate and touched her hair. "Sometimes you forget," he said softly, "and you set a place for him at the supper table."

She jerked her head, lips contorting soundlessly and eyes wide as tears streamed down her face. She backed away from him, stepped up onto the porch, and lowered herself into a rocking chair. Still staring at him, she began to rock.

He stood by the gate a little longer. Then he mounted his horse slowly and took a long, last look at her.

"Good night, Mrs. Fuller."

She didn't reply.

CHAPTER

8

ISABEL WAS SURPRISED WHEN CAROLINE DIDN'T COME THE next morning. She had collected a few dishes for Caroline to play with and put them on the kitchen table, then after deciding the child wasn't coming, stacked them under the bench on the back porch. Free from distractions, she worked steadily into the afternoon before stopping to rest.

She was sitting in the kitchen eating a bowl of cornbread and milk when Piggott appeared, driving Edward's wagon. Mr. Fuller had sent him for more dynamite, he explained, and he wanted to let her know Caroline wasn't feeling well.

"Seemed to be running a fever."

She showed him where the dynamite was stored and helped him load some into the wagon, promising to visit Caroline later in the evening if she could. Piggott said he was sure Caroline would appreciate that. "Seems like she perked up a little after staying with you, ma'am. Leastways before she got sick." Not wanting to keep Mr. Fuller waiting, he tipped his hat and drove away.

The clouds that had started to gather grew heavier as the day went on. The boys were huddled over homework at the kitchen table when Isabel decided she should go see Caroline before it began to rain. She packed food and water in a flour sack and gave the boys instructions for supper in case she wasn't back before Edward came in. Samuel offered to drive her, but she said she would ride instead. "Old Blue and I can both use the exercise."

There weren't as many tents by the river this time, and she found Piggott's tent easily. Tying her horse to one of the stakes, she called to Caroline before pushing the flap aside and stepping inside.

The interior was even more spartan than before, the mattresses on the floor where the babies had slept gone, the two cots separated now, one on each side of the tent. She felt the sadness and loss that hung heavy in the place. And something else she couldn't quite name – perhaps despair or a sense of abandonment.

Caroline lay sleeping on the cot to the left, her mouth open and arms hanging limply over the sides. Isabel knelt beside her. The child's breathing was labored, and she was damp with sweat. The rancid odor of vomit drifted from a bucket on the ground near her head. She pressed her hand gently to Caroline's forehead and then to her chest. The girl stirred.

"Mama?" she whispered hoarsely.

"No, honey. It's Mrs. Fuller. But we're going to get you feeling better real quick."

She picked up the bucket and carried it outside, rinsed it in the river, then filled it with water and carried it back to the tent. She undressed Caroline and began to bathe her with the tepid water.

"Sing, Mama. Sing the special song."

"Mrs. Fuller doesn't know the special song. But I'll sing the ones I remember." In a low, husky voice, she began to sing, bathing Caroline to the rhythm of the lullabies she sang to the boys, humming when she forgot the words. Intermittently, Caroline roused herself and sang a few words. After an hour or so, the fever broke. Drenched with sweat, she opened her eyes.

"The worst is over now," Isabel said. "You'll be fine in the morning."

"I'm thirsty."

Isabel held a jar of water to Caroline's lips. The girl sat up and drank greedily, then looked down and, seeing that she was naked, reached for the blanket.

"Where are your clothes, Caroline?"

Caroline pointed to a small pile on the floor near the end of her cot. Isabel sorted through them, pulled out the cleanest dress she could find, and slipped it over Caroline's head. She took the bedding off the cot, gathered up Caroline's dirty clothes and wrapped them in the sheets, and sat with her another hour until Piggott came.

"She's fine," she said. "Feed her a little supper if she wants it. And boil any water you get from the river before you drink it." She tied the bundle of bedding and dirty clothes to the back of her saddle. "I'll wash these things. You can get them the next time you bring Caroline."

When she had crossed the bridge from Floyd's Landing, she pulled on the reins, looked west along the riverbank, then headed Blue in that direction. After a quarter mile or so, they came to a clearing with a tent sitting at the far edge of it, a small fire smoldering outside. On a log next to the fire sat Reverend Kane, reading a book. She drew her horse to a stop.

He looked up, almost as if he were expecting her. She dismounted and walked her horse across the clearing to the fire, where she stood silently, holding the reins. He studied her.

"Where's the rest of your group, Reverend?"

"They're camped on the other side of the bridge. I like my privacy."

She picked at the peeling leather on the reins. "How did you know that? About me setting a place for Carl at the table sometimes?"

"I know what it's like to lose someone, Mrs. Fuller," he said quietly.

"I thought if I told you about my son you'd recite me some scripture, Reverend. Something about the will of God. And I'd tell you I don't give a damn about His will."

"I understand. I lost two brothers in the war. Folks used to say my mama was the meanest woman alive. They should have seen what it did to her when she lost her boys. She never was the same. None of us was ever the same."

He closed his book. "I'm sure it was hard on everyone in your family. Your husband, your sons."

"Hard doesn't even begin to describe it, Reverend. The little boys idolized their older brother. And Edward – Edward went to the barn and didn't come out for three days. Didn't sleep, didn't eat. The neighbors brought food until it was running out our ears and they couldn't get him to eat a bite."

"That must have been a terrible thing to see."

"I suppose it was. But I had three children to take care of. I didn't think I needed to shoulder the burden of a grown man not sure he could ever live with himself again."

The wind picked up. Dry leaves and dust swirled around her feet, and she smelled the pungent scent of the coming rain.

"People were very kind," she said. "They'd tell me what a comfort it must be to have three other boys. They meant well. I love those boys with a fierce love – a mother's love. But I tell you, Reverend, having three left doesn't make up for the loss of their brother."

He shook his head. "No. It doesn't. When you love someone like that, it leaves a hole that can't ever be filled."

Her next words were interrupted by a low rumble of thunder. Lightning flashed, followed by a loud boom.

"Storm's coming," she said. "I'd better go."

Then the rain began, pelting them immediately and mercilessly with large drops and turning quickly into blinding sheets of water. Kane jumped up and extended his hand. Isabel resisted for a moment, then took his hand, ducked her head, and ran with him. He pushed aside the flaps of the tent and stooped through the opening, pulling her inside. They stood in the center of the tent, drenched and panting.

She looked around, taking in her surroundings. A makeshift bed on one side, a small table and two chairs on the other, the dim light revealing little about the tent's inhabitant. Musty canvas, wet earth, the rain a rapid staccato on the roof.

"It's not much," he said. "But it's dry. At least for now. If this rain keeps up, I don't know."

"It's fine," she said. "Can't expect all the comforts of home when you're a traveling man."

An awkward silence. "Let me see if I can find a towel," he said. He lit a candle sitting on a wooden crate by the bed. The crate was packed with books and beside it sat two more stuffed with clothes and supplies. He squatted, holding the candle with one hand while he rummaged through the supplies with the other.

"You're a reader, Reverend?"

"I am. Anything I can get my hands on. I didn't learn to read until I was almost ten. Too busy causing the schoolmarm misery to actually learn anything. Then we got a new teacher one year and she sat me down and said, 'Micah, I'm teaching you to read if it's the last thing I do.'"

He laughed. "There probably were moments when she did think it would kill her. Then, all of a sudden, it just happened. I read the Sears Roebuck catalogue cover to cover. Havana cigars, toilet paper in rolls, fancy candy, imported olives. Princely shirts for princely men. It was a revelation."

He stood, pulling out a small worn towel. "Here we are. It's even clean." He held the towel out to her. She took it and started to dry her face.

"Wait," he said, moving closer and holding the candle up to her.

"Your face is beautiful when it's wet. Wet with tears. Wet from the rain."

She looked at him across the candlelight and felt his slow, measured breathing as he moved the candle, and his eyes, down.

"You're soaking," he whispered. Her head drooped slightly as he moved the candle to the right, then to the left, then down her belly as he examined her, expecting any second to feel the flame lick out and singe her wet, clinging shirt. Then he stopped. He looked up and their eyes met. A wave of heat shot through her and she shuddered.

"Was there something else you wanted to talk to me about, Mrs. Fuller?"

She swallowed, took a deep breath, and stepped back.

"Yes. I wanted to invite you to supper tomorrow evening."

"Supper." He looked at her solemnly. "Am I still invited?"

She swallowed again. "Yes," she said faintly. "Come around six o'clock." Then she backed out of the tent into the rain.

She ran across the clearing, slipping and almost falling in the mud. Blue was waiting patiently under a cypress tree, sheltering himself from the rain. Grabbing the reins, she jumped on the horse's back, kicked him, and headed east along the riverbank toward New Caney Road.

The rain didn't let up. Blue was skittish at the lightning and thunder, but she rode him at a steady gallop and then let him run when they were almost home. He went straight to the barn without coaxing.

She stopped on the back porch for a moment before going into the house. Hands trembling slightly, she smoothed her wet hair, then took a deep breath and entered the kitchen. Edward and the boys were seated around the table, intent on a checkers game between Ben and Samuel, their supper dishes stacked haphazardly by the sink. They looked up with a chorus of hellos and then resumed their game. She stood uncertainly by the table for a few minutes, shivering, then went to the sink and started to rinse the dirty dishes.

"Isabel." She jumped.

"You'll catch your death. You better get out of those wet clothes," Edward said.

"You're right," she said.

"The boys will wash the dishes. You go on."

She carried a kettle of hot water into Carl's room and filled the basin on the bureau. Returning the kettle to the kitchen, she kissed the boys good night, then went back to Carl's room and closed both doors.

She unbuttoned her shirt and stepped out of her trousers. Stripping naked, she piled the wet clothes near the kitchen door, washed her face at the basin, then dried and wrapped herself in a towel. She lit a stub of candle standing in hardened wax on a saucer, then pressed her face close to the mirror and examined the lines by her eyes, the slight crevices extending from her lips. She unbound her hair, letting it fall in a wet mass across her shoulders and down her back.

Standing on tiptoes and impatient with what she could see, she let the towel drop to the floor, lifted the mirror off the wall and held it out from her in one hand, the candle in the other. She moved the mirror, and the candle, down her body. Breasts still full, but drooping slightly from having nursed four children, waist thickened several inches from having borne them, arms and thighs strong, belly smooth, from years of hard work on the farm.

She felt a tinge of disappointment. It wasn't the face and body that had made every boy for miles around beat a path to her door from the time she was twelve until Edward Fuller put all the rest of them out of her mind. Feeling foolish, she shook her head. She wasn't a girl anymore. She was a woman, and a married one at that. A mother of four, now three, children.

She set the candle on the shelf and hung the mirror on the wall, took her nightgown off the hook, and pulled it over her head. Then, remembering how Kane had looked at her, she reached up under her nightgown, closed her eyes, touched her breasts, and ran her fingertips down her belly, imagining the gentle roughness of his hands on her. She shivered and opened her eyes.

Curtains billowed into the room from the open windows, then slapped back against the screens. The candle sputtered in the wind. The rain had slowed to a steady drumming on the roof, the thunder faint now in the distance. She looked around the room, disoriented for a moment. Then, feeling slightly ashamed, she pulled down her nightgown and blew out the candle.

At breakfast the next morning she told Edward she had invited Reverend Kane to supper and that he should come in early from the fields so they could eat before the Reverend needed to leave for the revival.

"Company on a Tuesday evening?" he said.

"I don't intend to cook anything special." But once Edward and the boys were gone, she sat at the kitchen table drinking a last cup of coffee and planning what she would serve. A Sunday pot roast even though it wasn't Sunday, roasted potatoes and summer squash from the garden, yeast rolls, and a chocolate cake for dessert.

She worked all day preparing supper, bent over her cast iron range, adding wood to the fire box, sweating in the heat and abandoning her other chores. By five o'clock the food was ready. She set the table, taking care that none of the dishes were chipped and polishing the flatware with a soft cloth. After telling the boys to wash their faces and put on clean shirts, she went to dress.

Surveying the meager collection in her closet, she was dismayed to see that most of her dresses were worn and faded, her wardrobe a victim of years of neglect. She decided against her Sunday best and finally chose a pale blue cotton dress with short sleeves and buttons down the front. She unpinned her hair, considered leaving it down then gathered it with a ribbon at the base of her neck.

She was standing at the stove, waiting for Edward and listening to the boys squabble as they played, when Reverend Kane arrived. When she heard his horse, then the sound of his footsteps coming around the side of the house, she stepped quietly to the window over the sink and peeked outside. As if he had sensed her presence, he stopped and looked at her. She met his eyes briefly then ducked quickly away from the window. Face burning, she went to the screen door and eased it open. He stepped inside and stood awkwardly just inside the door, then removed his hat and held out the contents of his left hand to her. Black-eyed Susans and zinnias, bunched together in a wild array of colors. *Wonder whose yard he got those from*, she thought as she took them, found a jelly jar in the cabinet and filled it with water.

"These are pretty," she said, bending over the table to arrange the stems.

He cleared his throat and shifted his hat nervously from one hand to the other. He looked around as if to be certain they were alone. "Mrs. Fuller," he said stiffly. "I have been up all night praying and asking the Lord to forgive my actions of yesterday. Now I'm asking you to forgive me. No man of God should look at a married woman the way I looked at you. It won't happen again."

Heart pounding, Isabel stared at the table, the flowers, plates, and flatware a blur. After a moment, her vision cleared. She saw her faded hair ribbon, the homely dress, the practical shoes, and felt a dull ache in her stomach.

"I haven't given it a second thought," she said. "Have a seat."

Ignoring the pained look on his face, she went to the stove, stirred the gravy until it sloshed over the sides of the skillet, opened the oven door to check on the roast and potatoes, then touched the rolls in the warming closet. She looked out the window to see if Edward was coming then turned back to Kane. He was still standing.

She brushed past him and opened the screen door. "Boys," she shouted, "time for supper." She waited at the door, her back to Kane, until she saw her sons race to the back porch, their shirts already dirty. Samuel leaped onto the porch, with Ben right behind him. James was last and his brothers blocked his way, laughing and shoving him off the porch each time he made it up the steps.

"Quit, now," she said. "Wash up. Reverend Kane's here and sup-per's ready."

"Where's Daddy?" James asked.

"He's not here yet. We'll start without him because the Reverend needs to be on his way."

She closed the screen door, smiled coolly at Kane, and began to put the food on the table.

"Can I help you?" he said.

"No thank you, Reverend." The screen door banged open and Ben pushed James inside. He and Samuel followed, trying to look innocent. James, angry because he had almost fallen into Reverend Kane, turned with his fists clenched, ready for a fight.

"James," Isabel said sharply.

"He pushed me."

"I saw him. Now let it go. I'll deal with him later." She looked sternly at Ben and Samuel and their laughter died. "All of you shake hands with Reverend Kane and introduce yourselves."

The boys did as they were told, shaking hands and telling the Reverend their names and pleased to meet you. He responded in kind, repeating each boy's name and asking what grade he was in at school. They took their places at the table, standing behind their chairs while Isabel showed Kane where to sit.

"Reverend," she said. "Would you bless the food?"

He nodded. They bowed their heads.

"We give thanks for your many blessings, Lord. Grant your grace on this family and the loving woman who sustains it. Amen."

"Amen," the boys said. Isabel looked at her empty plate. "Amen." She raised her head and began to pass the food.

She sat quietly as Kane engaged the boys in conversation. They were impressed with his knowledge of baseball, even more impressed that he was a boxer. He used to box at county fairs, he explained, but gave it up when he answered the call. He could still hit a baseball, though, and he'd be happy to play with them for a while after supper.

"Mama," James said suddenly, looking at her intently.

The conversation stopped.

"What is it, James?"

"You look so pretty."

They all turned to look at her.

"Your mother is a beautiful woman," Kane said in a low voice. "Inside and out."

Suddenly self-conscious, she set her knife and fork on the edges of her plate and smoothed the front of her dress. Their appraisal of her ended with the sound of boots on the back steps and Edward standing in the doorway, surveying the room, taking in the tablecloth and the flowers and the Reverend Kane.

"Edward," she said. "Shut the door, you're letting the mosquitoes in."

Edward stepped toward the table, letting the screen door slam, and held out his hand to Kane.

"Reverend. Sorry I'm late. Thought I'd say hello then wash up for supper."

"Not at all, Mr. Fuller," Kane said, rising to shake his hand. "I know you have work to do. Eating a home-cooked meal with your family is a pleasure. You have some real fine boys."

Edward glanced at his sons. "They're good boys."

"And we were just talking about how pretty Mama is," James said.

Hands on his hips, Edward looked at her. "Were you now?" He gave a brief nod. "Well, you're right. She's a pretty woman." He turned abruptly and went outside.

The boys were finished eating and Isabel excused them, Kane promising to join them outside in a few minutes. "Better practice your pitching," he told them. "I'm gonna hit it to the sycamore tree."

"You can't hit it that far," Ben declared. "Can't nobody hit it that far."

"Wait and see."

The boys went outside, stopping to confer with their father about the possibility of the Reverend hitting the ball all the way to the sycamore tree. Kane pushed back from the table, stretched his legs in front of him, and looked at Isabel. Neither of them spoke. She suddenly felt the oppressive heat of the kitchen. The back of her neck began to sweat. She brushed back a lock of hair that had escaped the ribbon and tucked it behind her ear, shifted in her chair to free the places where her dress clung to her skin, then slipped out of her shoes, her bare feet hidden under the table. She glanced at Kane. Their eyes met, and she was shocked at the current that passed between them in the warm, damp air.

"Isabel," Edward called.

She stood. She moved slowly around Kane's chair, her dress brushing lightly against his outstretched legs, her bare feet soundless on the kitchen floor, Kane's eyes on her back and hips as she stepped to the screen door.

"Yes, Edward."

"I could use a clean shirt."

She turned back to the kitchen and met Kane's eyes again.

"Excuse me a minute, Reverend." She walked across the kitchen, her body fluid in the heat, and down the hall to her bedroom. She pulled one of Edward's shirts from the closet and returned to the kitchen, where Kane still sat, facing the hall doorway as if waiting for her to reappear. She crossed the room and went out the back door.

Edward's trousers were unfastened, his work shirt discarded on the bench. She turned away from the sight of his naked chest and stomach.

"I'll fix your plate," she said. She went back inside, picked up Edward's plate and spooned food onto it, carefully avoiding looking at Kane, knowing that if she did, the jolt from that connection, something she hadn't felt in such a long time, might make her drop her husband's supper. The door opened, and Edward came in behind her. She set the plate in front of him and poured him a glass of water.

"Well now," he said. "Isn't this nice? I have to thank you, Reverend. Not often a man gets a meal like this on Tuesday night."

"Edward's joking," she said before Kane could reply. "He doesn't have much to complain about when it comes to my cooking." She returned to her chair.

Edward put his knife and fork down for a minute, looking across the table at her and then at Kane. He picked up his fork again. "How long you been in the revival business, Reverend?"

Kane said he'd started preaching three years ago, described the revivals he'd held that summer and how attendance at the meetings kept growing. Edward listened intently without interrupting, his knife and fork scraping the plate as he ate, until Kane finally fell silent as if waiting for some response. Edward sopped up the last bit of gravy on his plate with a roll, chewing thoughtfully, then sat back in his chair.

"You're a young man, aren't you Reverend?"

Kane smiled. "Depends on the circumstances, Mr. Fuller. Sometimes I feel too young. Other times I feel awfully old."

"I was just curious about how old a man you really are, Reverend. Thirty? Thirty-one?"

"Thirty-three."

"Never married?"

"Edward!" Isabel said. "That's no business of ours."

Kane laughed. "Never married. Never was as lucky as you, Mr. Fuller."

Edward nodded. He looked at Isabel again, then back at Kane. "Then you must have been in the war."

Isabel drew in a sharp breath and sat up in her chair, every muscle in her neck and back suddenly rigid. Kane leaned forward, his hands clasped, arms resting on the table.

"No, sir. I wasn't in the war. I never was called up."

Edward nodded again. *Don't you say another word,* she thought. *Don't you say another goddamned word about that goddamned war.* She lowered her head into her hands as Edward said, "Some men didn't wait to be called up. Some men served their country without being asked."

Kane shifted in his chair, as if considering his response. She raised her head and put her hand on his arm to stop him.

"Don't pay any attention to what old men have to say about war, Reverend," she said evenly. "They talk brave. But they send boys to do their fighting for them. And their dying."

Edward looked as if she had slapped him. He sat speechless for a few moments as she gazed at him steadily, then raised his hands, fists curled, above his head and slammed them down on the table. The dishes clattered, the flowers in the jelly jar swayed. Kane jerked back slightly, but she didn't flinch. Edward leaped up from his chair, kicking it out of his way, and slammed out the back door into the night.

She breathed deeply, then turned to Kane. He shook his head slowly.

"I am sorry for your loss, Mrs. Fuller. I didn't know you'd lost more than your son."

She put her elbows on the table and rested her head wearily in her hands. "I think you better go, Reverend. I think you better go."

He sat with her a few minutes more, then stood quietly and took his dishes to the sink. Head still in her hands, she heard him collect his coat and hat, the faint creak of the door opening. She thought he turned to her one last time, but she didn't look up.

CHAPTER

9

ISABEL SLEPT IN CARL'S ROOM THAT NIGHT. SHE HAD washed the dishes in a daze, her arms and legs heavy, every movement an effort. The boys came inside shortly after dark, telling her in loud, excited voices that Reverend Kane said he only had time for one pitch, then hit the ball to the sycamore tree just like he said he would. She agreed it was something she'd never seen the likes of before and surely wouldn't have expected from a preacher. She fed them milk and the chocolate cake, which she had forgotten to serve at supper, answering their questions about where their daddy rode off to with the explanation that he went to see about some hired hands to help with the cotton picking in the fall.

Not sure if she was awake or asleep, she heard Edward come in around midnight, walk down the hall to their bedroom then back again, looking for her, standing in the hall doorway, slipping into the room to confirm that she was there. The house was deathly quiet, his breathing as he stood over her at the end of the narrow bed the only sound. She lay motionless on her side until he left, then finally fell into a deep sleep.

She dreamed that it was late at night, and she was alone. Edward and the boys had gone somewhere – she wasn't sure where or why. She was in her nightgown, standing frozen in the middle of the living room. Someone was outside. She heard his breathing, and his quiet footsteps as he moved from window to window, faint metallic rustles as he pressed from screen to screen. The house was dark, but she knew he could see her and, suddenly remembering that the front door was open, the screen door unlocked, she tried to run, but her legs were heavy, and she moved in slow motion. She reached the door as he came up the front steps onto the porch, her fingers numb, struggling with the lock, and managed to latch it just as he began to pull it open. The dark figure grinned and backed away. She stood at the front door to be certain he was gone, then heard the back door open and turned in time to see the man enter the living room from the kitchen, speaking as he came toward her, his words escaping in a rapid stream of gibberish she couldn't understand. She opened her mouth to scream, but all that escaped was a shrill rush of air.

She woke in a sweat, her heart pounding, not sure where she was. Lying on her back, she made out the faint outlines of the bureau and the bathtub, the familiar shapes of Carl's room. *It's daybreak,* she thought. *I need to get up.* She drifted in and out of sleep for a few more minutes, then pushed herself up to sit on the edge of the bed. Neck and back aching, she stood. She retrieved the blue dress she had worn the night before, started to slip off her nightgown then thought better of it. She opened the hall door. The door to the boys' room was closed, the one to her bedroom ajar. She could tell by the stillness in the house that Edward was gone.

She hung the dress in Carl's closet then went to her bedroom, pulled on trousers and an old work shirt, and stepped into her boots. She thought about last night as she pinned up her hair. How could she behave like that with a stranger, give him the impression, no doubt, that there was a possibility that something could happen between them, and shame Edward in his own home? What if the boys had noticed? How could she ever explain herself to them, expect them to forgive her? And Kane himself – she couldn't read him, couldn't summon up any clear understanding of his nature, her perception fogged, perhaps, by lone- liness and desire. She shook her head, resolved not to have any further communication with him, then went to the kitchen to make breakfast. Edward had made coffee, the pot still warming on the stove. She poured herself a cup and turned to see Mary Clara standing by the back door.

"What do you know about this preacher?" Mary Clara said.

"Not a lot. Just what he's told me about himself. Some things I've heard."

"I don't mean talk. What do you see?"

"I don't see anything."

"That should tell you something. He's looking for weakness. And he's finding it."

"You think he's evil?"

"Not necessarily. It comes naturally to some folks – wanting what suits their purpose and nothing more. He may not even know he's doing it. He just sees the world with himself at the center of it."

"Who are you talking to, Mama?" Samuel stood in the doorway from the hall to the kitchen. "Is someone on the porch?"

She set her coffee cup in the sink. Mary Clara had left the moment Samuel appeared.

"No one's out there. I'm just talking to myself."

"Well, stop doing it. If Ben or James heard you, they'd be scared to death."

"There's nothing to be afraid of. It comes from being alone – you start talking to yourself when there's no one else to talk to."

"But you're not alone."

She lifted an egg from a bowl on the counter, cracked it into the cast iron skillet on the stove.

"Sometimes I am."

After the boys left for school, Isabel collected Caroline's clothes and bedding, which still lay in a pile on the back porch. She pumped water, lit a fire, and dumped them in the washtub to soak. She skimmed cream from the milk buckets, carried it to the kitchen, and poured it into the butter churn. She went to the window when she heard a man's voice outside.

Piggott and Caroline were approaching the house, Piggott's arm around his daughter's shoulder, head bent toward her. Caroline dragged behind her father a step or so, Piggott pushing her along as he spoke. Isabel couldn't make out what he was saying, but Caroline was troubled apparently, a reluctant visitor. She stepped outside to greet them.

"Morning, Mrs. Fuller," Piggott said, stopping short of the porch steps.

"Morning. Good morning, Caroline. I'm glad to see you're feeling better."

Caroline eyed her bare feet silently, arms hugging her chest and hair falling in matted strands over her eyes. Piggott poked her with an elbow, but she didn't respond. He grinned up at Isabel.

"She's forgot her manners. I told her it ain't often a girl gets treated so good, but she don't seem to pay no mind to it." He raised his shoulders in an exaggerated shrug.

"It's fine. Come on in, Caroline. I'm washing your clothes and you can help."

Caroline shook her head. Piggott put his hand in the middle of her back and gave her a slight push. "Go on, girl." Caroline swayed but refused to move. Piggott looked up at Isabel and shrugged again.

She walked down the steps and took Caroline's hand. "Come in, Caroline. Everything will be fine." She was surprised to see the girl so listless and pale, and thought maybe she wasn't getting enough to eat. She should have bounced back in a day or two after her illness.

"Bye, Caroline," Piggott said. "Remember what I told you, now."

Caroline didn't answer. Isabel led her up the steps and inside and pulled a chair out from under the kitchen table.

"Sit here a minute. I'll fix you something to eat."

She had wrapped biscuits left over from breakfast in a napkin and saved them for Edward, thinking he might come in after a few hours in the fields. He hadn't. She buttered two of them and put them on a plate with a slice of ham, poured a glass of milk from the pitcher in the icebox, and set the food in front of Caroline. Feet curled around a rung of her chair and arms huddled around the plate, Caroline began to eat.

Isabel sat down next to her and watched quietly. "More?" she said when the food was gone. Caroline shook her head.

"How about vinegar pie?" Caroline looked down at her plate and nodded. Isabel rose, cut a piece of the pie and poured more milk, then sat down again.

"How are you feeling, Caroline?"

Ignoring the fork Isabel had given her, Caroline raised the piece of pie with both hands and took a bite. "I feel fine, ma'am," she mumbled, her mouth full.

"No pain anywhere?"

Caroline swallowed, put the pie back on the plate, and shook her head. "I guess I don't want no more pie."

Isabel pushed back from the table and collected the dishes. "Let's go wash your things."

She showed Caroline how to drain the washtub after the clothes had soaked for a while and how to measure the soap. Together they refilled the tub with water and Isabel picked up the washboard and began to scrub. Her hands and forearms turned red from the hot water and after a few minutes she began to sweat. A dull ache started in the small of her back, but she didn't stop the heavy rhythm of the scrubbing, laying each wet, soapy item on the table and then picking up the next. Caroline watched her silently.

When she had finished scrubbing, she motioned to Caroline. They drained the washtub again, then filled it with water a third time to rinse. They put the clothes and sheets through the wringer, Isabel cautioning Caroline to mind her fingers didn't get caught. Then they hung them on the line to dry, moving down the clothesline in a quiet dance as Isabel draped the worn sheets and the faded little dresses and overalls over the line and Caroline handed her the clothespins.

"I guess we've earned a rest," Isabel said when they had finished. They went inside and she poured two glasses of lemonade and nodded at the cookie jar.

"Get yourself a cookie and we'll go sit under the shade tree."

They lounged on wood benches under the oak trees in front, their feet propped up, waving off the flies and sweat bees that buzzed lazily around the lemonade. Isabel took a handkerchief from her pocket and wiped her forehead, then smoothed back her hair.

"I don't sit out here much during the day," she said.

Caroline didn't reply.

She waited a few minutes. "Washing's hard work," she ventured.

"Seems like a lot of trouble."

"Yes, but it won't get done by itself. I always feel better when I'm wearing fresh clothes."

"It don't matter to me." Caroline sat up and put her lemonade glass on the ground. Crossing her legs under her, she held a cookie to her mouth with both hands, then nibbled side to side like she was playing a harmonica, lips apart and teeth bared, back and forth, taking the tiniest bites she could and collecting the crumbs in her mouth without swallowing, until the cookie was gone, now a wad that she moved from cheek to cheek with her tongue.

"More lemonade?" Isabel said.

Caroline shook her head, gulping quietly.

"The boys like those butter cookies. They tell me to make them big so they don't have to make so many trips to the cookie jar."

Caroline looked at her glumly. Isabel swung her boots off the bench and stood up. "Back to work." She tucked in her shirt and rolled her sleeves up a little more. "You can wash these glasses and the dishes that are in the sink. It won't take long for your clothes to dry in this heat. Then we'll do a little mending and ironing."

While Caroline washed dishes, Isabel collected meat from the smokehouse, and potatoes, onions, and corn from the cellar. She picked carrots and tomatoes from the garden, cut up the meat and vegetables for stew, and when the stew was on, took Caroline outside to gather the clothes from the clothesline. "They're still a little damp, but they'll iron up better that way." They stacked the clean clothes on a chair and set the ironing board by the stove. Isabel put the irons on the stove to heat then turned to Caroline.

The girl was standing in the doorway on the other side of the kitchen, looking into Carl's room. Isabel had left the doors to the room shut when Caroline was there before.

"Whose room is this?"

Isabel felt a catch in her throat. "It was my son's."

"Which son?"

"You never knew him. He was my oldest boy. He died in the war." She turned back to the ironing.

Caroline disappeared into the bedroom. Isabel heard her moving around the room, looking at the books and the bed and the other furnishings, and wondered if there was any trace of Carl left that a stranger might see. Fighting a sudden urge to shout at the girl to get out, she picked up a dress from the pile of clothes and began to iron.

Caroline reappeared in the doorway, head bowed, and spoke so softly that Isabel could barely hear her.

"Can I take a bath?"

Isabel smoothed the front of the dress with her left hand, the iron in her right moving deliberately back and forth across the worn cotton fabric. She set the iron back on the stove, held the dress up in front of her and examined it, laid the dress on the kitchen table and folded it carefully, then looked at Caroline.

"Yes. Help me pump the water and we'll put some on to boil." When the tub was filled a few inches, Isabel said that was enough, fetched a clean towel from the bureau, and showed Caroline the soap.

"Do you want help?"

Caroline shook her head.

"Holler if you need anything." She closed the door to the kitchen behind her as she left the room.

Caroline was in there a long time. Isabel finished the ironing then knocked on the bedroom door.

"Caroline?" There was no answer. She knocked again then opened the door.

Caroline was lying on her side by the tub, huddled into a ball, the towel covering her completely. Isabel stood over her for a minute then gently drew the towel down from her face. The child was sucking her thumb, her eyes closed.

"Caroline." No response. She squatted down and felt Caroline's forehead and chest. No fever.

"Caroline." Caroline opened her eyes, rolling them back in her head for an instant, then sighed and looked blankly at her.

"Can you get up?"

She nodded, then took her thumb out of her mouth, and sat up sluggishly, clutching the towel in front of her. Isabel tucked the towel around her and helped her to her feet.

"Let me get you some clean clothes." Isabel went back to the kitchen and pulled one of the dresses and some bloomers from the small pile of folded clothes.

"Do you want me to help you get dressed?" Caroline shook her head.

"What was his name?" Caroline said.

Her back to Caroline, Isabel answered. "His name was Carl. Carl Edward Fuller. He died on June 11, 1918, at the age of eighteen."

"He's an angel, then, like my mama. Do you think it would be nice to be an angel like Carl Edward and Mama?"

"No." Isabel closed the door so the girl could dress. She collected the sheets from the clothesline and put them with Caroline's clothes in an old flour sack. Caroline finally came out of the bedroom.

"Are you hungry?"

She shook her head. The clothes she had worn that day were tucked under her arm.

"You can leave those dirty clothes here for the next time I do the washing. I don't mind."

Caroline shook her head again, her grip on the bundle tightening. She went to the back door and looked outside, then turned to Isabel.

"My daddy's coming."

Isabel held her gaze for a moment, their eyes locked in wordless communication, and felt a flood of misery coming from the girl. *She has secrets,* Isabel thought, *something she's been warned not to tell. Let it out, Caroline,* she urged silently. *Say it.* The connection between them was so intense that Isabel felt it coming, almost had it, almost knew the answer.

"Evening, Mrs. Fuller," Piggott said, pulling his sweat-stained hat from his head as he came to the door. "Caroline wasn't no trouble to-day I hope."

Caroline's eyes dulled and the connection was lost.

"Not at all. She was a big help." She handed him the sack. "But she's not feeling well. She ought to see Doc Walker."

"Is that right?" He bent down and peered at Caroline. "She's just a little peaked, don't you think?"

"She's more than just a little peaked. If it's the money, you don't need to worry. Doc will take care of her."

"I cain't afford a doctor, that's right. But she don't need one anyway." He straightened and put on his hat. He jerked his head at Caroline and they turned to go. Isabel walked to the corner of the house and watched them until they reached the road.

When she turned to go inside, she caught a glimpse of movement in the milk trough. She stopped, thinking that she must have imagined it, but there it was again. Something splashing in the water. She went to look.

It was a bird. A baby crow by the looks of it, not long out of the nest. The bird was flailing about, its feathers soaked, unable to find a way out of the trough and unable to fly.

"Let's get you out of there little fellow." She reached into the water, cupped her hands around the bird, saying "sshhh" when it flapped its wings. She felt it trembling, its little heart beating. She set it gently on the ground beside the trough. "Where did you come from? I haven't seen any nests around here."

The bird closed its eyes and tucked its head under a wing, exhausted and cold. She sat on the porch and watched it for a while. It made no attempt to fly. She thought finally that it might be dead, but when she moved closer to check she could still see its little breast heaving. She went into the house and when she looked outside after an hour or so, the bird was gone.

It was dark when Edward came in from the fields. She heard the wagon coming, and when she saw a light go on in the barn, she called the boys to help their father. When she heard them at the pump washing up, she took a clean shirt out to Edward. He took it from her and turned his back on her to button it. They didn't speak.

The boys chattered noisily through supper. She sent them to bed when they were finished, then rose to clear the table, picking up Edward's dishes, scraping them, and putting them in the sink. He finally spoke.

"Cleared almost a quarter acre today."

"That's a good day's work."

"Piggott's a pretty good hand."

She lifted the kettle from the stove and poured more hot water into the sink.

"What's he planning to do?" she asked.

"Piggott?"

"Yes."

"I don't know that he's got plans. Why?"

"There's something not right about him."

"He just lost his wife, Isabel. He's got a mess of little children to raise alone. That's enough to make any man not quite right."

"I know that. But there's something else. I don't know what it is. But there's something."

She washed the last dish and lowered it into the rinse water. "I made vinegar pie."

"I'll have a piece."

She cut a slice and gave it to him, then turned back to the sink, lifted the dishes one by one from the rinse water and set them on the drain board, pausing occasionally to gaze absently out the window as she dried them. A hoot owl called, Edward's fork scraped against his plate, moths tapped faintly around the porch lantern. There was no sign of activity at the brush arbor tonight.

Edward pushed back from the table. "I had a visitor today. The good Reverend Kane came all the way to the south forty to see me."

She picked up a bowl and dried it slowly.

"What did he want?"

"Well, now I think back on it, I'm not real sure. He asked if there was something on my mind we should talk about. I said there wasn't anything on my mind."

She opened a cabinet door, her hands trembling slightly as she put the dishes away.

"He'll be gone soon," he said. "He's taking a couple nights off then he'll finish up the revival on Saturday."

She closed the cabinet door, went to the table, and picked up his pie plate.

"He didn't say where he's going next," he said as she bent over the table. "I'll be glad to be done with it. No telling what that fence row looks like by now."

Gripping the edge of the sink with both hands, Isabel stared out the window. Edward was waiting for a response. She dropped her gaze from the empty night to the dishwater in front of her, reached into the water, and found his plate.

"Yes," she said. "It's time for it to be over."

Isabel rose the next morning when she heard Edward stirring beside her. She put the coffee on, went to the outhouse, and when she returned, he was sitting at the kitchen table, pulling on his boots. She poured coffee for him and poured a cup for herself, drinking it while she stood resting lightly against the counter.

"Do you want breakfast?"

"No. I'll take some of that cornbread with me. I want to be in the field by daylight."

"Are you coming in to eat?"

"I don't believe so. We'd waste too much time."

"I'll bring you something. Fried chicken?"

"Sounds good."

The hen squawked and beat its wings furiously, struggling to get away, as Isabel held its legs tightly and laid it on the chopping block. She raised her hatchet, chopped off its head, then let go. Headless and dripping blood, it ran in a short circle, listing to one side and finally dropping to the ground. She watched until it fell, then picked it up and carried it to the back porch. She scalded it in a washtub of hot water, sat in a chair beside the tub and plucked it, then made a short cut with her knife and scooped out the entrails. She rinsed the chicken at the pump, took it inside, cut it up, dipped it in flour and salt, and fried it in a deep skillet of lard.

She put the fried chicken in a pail and bread, tomatoes and two jars of milk in a basket. She found an old blanket and carried it with the pail and basket to the barn and put them in the back of the car. She steered the car out of the barn and turned south at the road.

The southern line of their property was marked by a narrow dirt lane that ran alongside a barbed wire fence from New Caney Road on the west to Little Creek on the east. Isabel turned into the lane and drove slowly past the cotton field to the southeast portion of their property where the land was still rough. She spotted Edward and Piggott working in the brush and tree stumps a few hundred yards up the edge of the creek. She got out of the car, tucked the blanket under her arm and with the pail of chicken in one hand and the basket in the other, walked up the creek to where the men were working. She stopped and watched them.

Edward had wrapped chains around a large stump and hitched the mules to the chains. "Giddup," he yelled, slapping the reins. He and Piggott pushed, their faces red and teeth clenched, as the mules strained forward. The stump barely moved. "Whoa," Edward said. Men and animals relaxed.

"I believe this one'll need dynamite, Mr. Fuller."

"I believe you're right." Edward acknowledged Isabel with a nod. Piggott turned to her and took off his hat.

"I brought food. Fried chicken."

Edward wiped his forehead with his sleeve. "We'll eat down by the creek. We'll blow that stump after we eat." The men washed their hands and faces in the creek while she spread the blanket on the ground and set the containers of food on it. They sat down across from her, and Edward reached into the pail for a piece of chicken. "Help yourself," he said to Piggott.

They ate for a while in silence, tossing the chicken bones in the creek. "I missed seeing Caroline today," Isabel finally said. "Is she not feeling well?"

"She's fine, Mrs. Fuller. Just fine. Didn't want to trouble you having her underfoot every day." Piggott selected a piece of bread, examined it then took a bite.

"Yep," he said, taking another bite of bread. "She's just fine."

She watched Piggott eat, the way he picked at the food with his fingers. How his teeth tore into the chicken meat, the way he curled his lips and sucked the bones. The quivering wattle under his chin, the darkness around his eyes and mouth, and the way he avoided her stare.

She heard a flap and a loud call that sounded almost like a human voice. She turned to see a large crow pecking at a chicken bone that had fallen short of the creek, a purple sheen to its feathers in the sunlight. The crow eyed her suspiciously as it pecked, shaking the bone then dropping it and pecking at it again.

She gazed back at Piggott, his eyes shifting in their sockets just like the crow's. She thought about the drowning baby bird she had found yesterday, and an image suddenly leaped out at her – Piggott pecking greedily, relentlessly at something on a riverbank, then Caroline flailing and struggling silently in the water, trying not to slip under.

Edward wiped his hands on the legs of his trousers and stood. "Time to get after that stump again."

Piggott jumped up quickly. "That was mighty good, Mrs. Fuller. Mighty good."

She looked up at him. "Tell Caroline I said hello."

"I sure will."

She put the empty milk jars in the basket, gathered up the blanket, shook it a few times, then folded it. She watched Edward cut a length of fuse and Piggott set to work with an augur, boring holes in the stump for the powder. She walked down the creek bed and was putting the things in the car when the dynamite went off. Looking back, she saw smoke from the explosion, Piggott walking back from the cover of the creek bed, Edward calming the mules. She shuddered. Shifting from forward to reverse several times, she turned the car around in the narrow lane and drove back to the road. But instead of turning right to go back to the house, she turned left toward Floyd's Landing.

She parked the car in the dirt yard in front of Smitty's, then walked across the road and down the row to Piggott's tent. She called Caroline's name, and when there was no answer, lifted the flap of the tent and peered inside. The girl's cot was unmade, sheets thrown back and hanging off the sides. The clothes they had washed the day before sat in a pile on the floor at the end of the cot. The tent smelled of sweat and dust. Caroline wasn't there.

She dropped the flap, rested her hands lightly on her hips, and looked around. A woman was looking out at her from a tent a few yards to the east but drew her head back inside when Isabel turned to her. Isabel took a couple of steps in her direction.

"Hello," she called. "I'm Isabel Fuller. I'm looking for Caroline Piggott."

There was no response and she stepped closer. After a few minutes, the woman came out, hip jutted to one side and an arm around a baby resting there. She looked to be in her forties but could have been younger. The baby wore only a gray diaper that once was white.

"I know you," the woman said. "I give you sugar water for the babies the day their mama died."

"Yes." Isabel thought back to an earlier conversation with Caroline. "It's Mrs. Jenkins, isn't it?"

The woman's lips formed a twisted smile, only one side of her mouth responding to the attempt. Isabel had noticed the deformity before, the paralysis on one side of the woman's face. There was no other sign that she had been injured. *An illness,* she thought. *Maybe polio.*

"It's Louise," the woman said. "Louise Jenkins. My husband works down at the sawmill. We didn't know the family before coming here."

"You've been a good neighbor."

Mrs. Jenkins straightened a little then leaned her head toward Isabel as if taking her into confidence. "It's a shame what happened, and I wouldn't wish it on nobody. But that woman never should have done that to herself if you want my opinion."

The baby whimpered and kicked. Mrs. Jenkins slapped its legs and told it to hush, then looked back at Isabel.

"She had her reasons, I'm sure," Isabel said.

Looking disappointed, Mrs. Jenkins shifted the baby to the other hip.

"I'm trying to find Caroline," Isabel said.

The woman shrugged. "I ain't seen her today. She's an odd one, I tell you. Don't seem to listen to much of what you tell her."

Isabel nodded absently and looked around again.

"You might look down by the river. I've seen her walking down there before. Sometimes just sitting there doing nothing."

"I'll do that. Thank you for your help." She turned to go, and Mrs. Jenkins called after her.

"I done my best for those children."

She looked back. The baby started to squirm and howl.

"I'm sure you have, Mrs. Jenkins. You take care."

Isabel walked a few hundred yards up the river, then back again. She stayed on the riverbank until she came to the bridge, climbed up the embankment to the road, and crossed the yard where her car was parked next to the saloon. A painted tin sign, "Smitty's Grocery Saloon," was tacked over the doorway, the entrance protected by a screen door listing from broken hinges, screens torn and paint peeling from the wood. It screeched in protest and slammed behind her as she stepped inside. The conversation in the room stopped.

She stood by the door, letting her eyes adjust to the gloom. There was a rough bar in front of her and a few tables and chairs scattered to her left. What passed for the store was to her right, shelves lined with dusty cans and sacks of cornmeal and flour. A beat-up cash register sat on a counter in front of the shelves. The floor hadn't been swept recently and the place smelled of whiskey and urine.

Two men sat at the bar, another stood behind it. The man behind the bar came around it and stopped a few feet from her.

"Lord Almighty, it's Mrs. Fuller," he exclaimed. "What is it, ma'am? What's the trouble?"

"No trouble, Smitty. I'm looking for someone."

"Let's step outside."

Smitty opened the door for her. "Watch that screen now, so you don't get scratched. I keep meaning to fix up around here."

She hadn't seen Smitty in a while. His hair was almost gone, only a few odd tufts of white remaining. He wore dirty black pants held up by suspenders that disappeared under his belly. Large circles of sweat spread under his arms.

"I'm looking for a little girl. Caroline Piggott. She stays in one of the tents across the road."

Smitty scratched one of the bald spots on his head. "I know her daddy. And I seen her once or twice. It's a terrible thing her mama dying that way."

"She's a purty little thing." The slurred voice came from behind them, one of the men from the bar standing at the door.

Isabel glanced sharply at the man, then turned back to Smitty. "Have you seen her today?"

"No ma'am, I sure ain't seen her." Smitty shook his head. "Not today."

She crossed her arms and looked in the direction of Piggott's tent. "I walked up the river a ways. She's not there."

The man behind the screen door spoke up again. "Try the other way. I seen her with that preacher. I hear he's staying somewhere down the river."

Isabel felt a catch in her throat, and a slight flush creeping up her neck. She lowered her head and examined her boots. "Did you see her with him today?"

The man thought for a moment. "Naw, I don't reckon it was today." He sounded unsure. "May have been yesterday. Maybe the day before."

It was getting late. The boys would be home from school soon, and the Reverend's campsite was a quarter mile or more down the river.

"Thank you for your help," she said.

"Anytime, Mrs. Fuller," Smitty said. "Anytime at all."

Smitty and the man inside watched her as she walked across the bridge and stepped carefully down the embankment on the other side. She heard the screen door slam, followed by a laugh and a harsh retort from Smitty. She couldn't make out what was said.

She knew she should stay away from Kane, that even considering a walk to his campsite was breaking her resolve. But she couldn't get the image of Piggott's greasy fingers and greedy lips out of her mind, the way he picked at the food and sucked on the bones. The darkness around his eyes and mouth and how he wouldn't look her in the face. Pecking and pecking. Caroline struggling and flailing about in the water.

Cypress and willow trees along the riverbank broke the glare of the midday sun. Her boots crunched on fallen sticks and leaves. Dragonflies buzzed over the water. She stopped to pick a handful of blackberries growing wild beside the river, savoring the pulp with her tongue while the sweet juice ran down her throat. She knelt and splashed water on her face, held her hands in the current, then shook them dry as she continued on her way. The stickiness was gone, but the berries had stained her fingers and palms purple.

After a while she thought she must be getting close to the Reverend's campsite. There was no sign of Caroline. She stopped and brushed back her hair, considering whether to go on or head back, then saw something move. She went a little further then stopped again. Kane stepped out from behind the bushes and turned in her direction. She stood motionless as he walked slowly toward her.

He must have been swimming in the river. He wore only a pair of trousers and held a small towel loosely at his side. His body was tanned, his shoulders broad, hair wet, the skin on his chest and arms still damp. *He moves like a dancer,* she thought. *Or a fighter.* He stopped a few feet from her. She lowered her eyes.

"Mrs. Fuller?"

"I'm looking for someone."

He took another step toward her, and she suddenly felt lightheaded. Dust and insects danced in the afternoon sunlight piercing through the trees; the smell of moss and mud hung in the air. She saw a flicker of movement out of the corner of her eye and heard a slight splash in the river. *Water moccasin,* she thought. *Big one.* She closed her eyes and rubbed her forehead, then opened them again. He was watching her.

"Caroline Piggott," she said. "I want to make sure she's all right."

He didn't answer. He took another step toward her and let the towel fall from his hand, then reached out slowly and took her left hand in his right, pulling her slightly toward him and examining her fingers.

"Blackberries," she said awkwardly.

He nodded. Then he shifted his grasp to her wrist and pressed her hand to his side. She caught her breath and began to tremble as she moved her hand gently up his side, his skin soft and warm, rising and falling with each breath. He slid his left hand around her waist to the small of her back, pressing his fingers down her spine to her tailbone. She moved her hips instinctively, and he slipped both hands across her buttocks and pushed harder to bring her closer. A low guttural sound escaped her lips, and she closed her eyes as he bent his head and kissed her briefly. He licked her lips slowly, then took her lower lip between his teeth and kissed her again.

"Blackberries," he whispered.

One taste, she thought. *One taste of that sweet fruit will never be enough.* Fear and longing gripped her, and she opened her eyes. He smiled at her. She pushed him away.

She rubbed her mouth with the back of her hand and turned from him toward the river. He reached for her arm, but she brushed him back, went to the edge of the river, squatted on her haunches and splashed water on her face, dipping her hands again and again. Then she bowed her head and rested her elbows on her knees, arms open and stretched wide in front of her as if in supplication. Kane came up behind her, his trousers rustling as he sat beside her.

"I'll be leaving in a few days."

Elbows still on her knees, Isabel lifted her hands to her face. Kane picked up a handful of small rocks. She raised her head at the sound of the first one hitting the water then watched as he tossed them in the river one by one. When the last one had disappeared, he sighed and brushed his hands.

"I used to think sometimes I'd be dead before my thirtieth birthday from all the drinking and fighting and carrying on. And I didn't give a damn, because my life wasn't worth living. All that changed late one night three years ago when I heard God talking to me just as clear as I'm talking to you. I gave myself up to Him that night and I've never looked back."

"But something comes over me when I see you," he said. "It's like a spell." He groaned and beat one fist on the ground. "Truth is, it's not just when I see you." He looked at her. "I should be about the Lord's work. But I'm thinking about you. How you look, how you smell. It's not supposed to be like this. Not since I answered the call."

She held up her hand. "We all have our demons, Reverend. I don't plan on being yours. And if you think otherwise, you're mistaken." She stood.

"We let you onto our land for your revival. It wasn't meant to be an invitation for you to meddle in our lives." She turned to go.

"Wait," he said. "Caroline's here. She's in my tent."

Her eyes narrowed. "What's she doing in your tent?"

"She's asleep. She wanders up here every once in a while. She didn't look good, so I gave her a little food and she crawled in my tent and went to sleep. I planned on taking her to her daddy after I washed up."

She thought for a moment. "Is your wagon here?"

"Yes."

"Then you can take us back to Smitty's. I'll go see how she is while you get dressed."

"There's a path up there," he said. "Just past the bush with my shirt hanging on it."

She took the path up the embankment to the campsite, crossed the clearing and went inside the tent. Caroline was lying on the bed on her side, her back to the center of the tent. Isabel leaned over her and saw that the child wasn't asleep.

"How are you doing today, Caroline?"

There was no answer.

"I was surprised when you didn't come see me, so I came looking for you."

Caroline didn't respond. The tent flap opened.

"How is she?" Kane said.

Isabel straightened. He had put on a shirt and combed his hair. "If you'll just hitch up the wagon, Reverend, we'll be on our way." She helped Caroline to her feet.

"Reverend Kane's going to take us back to Floyd's Landing. Then I'm going to take you for a ride in my car. Have you ever been for a ride in a car?"

Caroline shook her head. Isabel led her outside. Kane hitched up the wagon then lifted Caroline onto the seat. He held out his hand to Isabel, but she ignored it and hoisted herself up beside Caroline.

A rough trail ran at the edge of the fields alongside the river. Old man Coggin owned most of the land they passed on their way to Floyd's Landing, but it lay fallow. Edward talked to Coggin regularly about buying some or all of it, but in Edward's opinion the price was too high. "It's good land," Coggin would insist. "There's still a fair price for good land," Edward would say. Isabel tired of hearing about their negotiations. "Why don't you just quit talking to him about it," she'd said. "Because it's good land," Edward said.

The wagon bounced and lurched along the trail. Kane held the reins and glanced at Isabel from time to time as she and Caroline held on. When they got to New Caney Road he eased the horses and wagon onto the road, across the bridge, and into the yard at Smitty's.

"I expect this is your automobile?"

"It is."

He jumped down and tied the horses to a fence post. Isabel carried Caroline to the car, settling her into the passenger seat. Kane turned the crank, then moved to the driver's side of the car and stood with his hand on the door handle, blocking Isabel's way.

"Thank you for the ride, Reverend."

He opened the door for her, closed it after she crawled in, and leaned in the window.

"Are you taking Caroline to your place?"

"No. I think Doc Walker should have a look at her."

"Will you let me know how she is?"

She started the engine and shifted the car into reverse. "I'll send word." She eased her foot off the clutch and backed slowly away.

Isabel looked at Caroline every so often as she drove. Caroline stared mutely out the window. When they got to the Fuller place, Isabel saw her sons playing on the swing in the front yard, James and Ben perched on the sawdust-filled gunnysack hanging from a rope in one of the trees, Samuel pushing them higher and higher. She slowed the car, turned into the lane, and the boys came running.

"This will just take a minute," she said to Caroline.

She got out of the car and was greeted by shouts of "where have you been, Mama" and "what's Caroline doing in the car with you?"

"Caroline's not feeling well. I'm taking her to see Doc Walker. How was your day, James? Better?"

"Better," James said. "Cordie Overman didn't come to school today, so Miss Moxley wasn't so crazy."

"Cordie's cousin says Cordie quit school," Ben said. "Never coming back."

"That's so foolish," she said. "But he's an Overman and I've never known an Overman that had a lick of sense. Is everyone's homework finished?"

"Mine is," James piped. "I told them they better do their homework, or they'd get in trouble. Then I saw you coming down the road, and I said Mama's coming, you're in trouble."

"Shut up," Samuel said.

"Samuel, I'm tired of the way you speak to your brother," she said. "Being oldest doesn't give you leave to be the meanest."

Samuel looked wounded, then angry. He opened his mouth to speak, then closed it again.

"What?" she said.

He shook his head. "Nothing."

She turned to Ben and James. "What about chores?"

Ben gave James a shove. "He ain't done his chores. So who's in trouble now, mister?"

"Say hasn't, not ain't," she said. "Finish your homework and chores. I'll be back in time for supper." She got back in the car. "Go on," she called. The boys made their way reluctantly toward the house.

Caroline had perked up a bit at the sight of the boys and craned her neck to watch them until they were out of sight.

"They're funny," she said.

Isabel was relieved to see some response from the girl. "They are funny." When they were almost to town, she asked Caroline if she remembered Doc Walker. "He came to see your mama before she died."

Caroline buried her chin in the front of her overalls. "Mama was hurt. Couldn't nobody help her."

Isabel slowed the car as they entered town. The old men sitting in front of Lambert's store, straw hats nearly identical and hands resting on canes propped between their knees, peered at her curiously as she passed. She waved and they waved back in unison. She turned onto Third Street and stopped in front of Doc's house, then got out and went around to open the passenger door. Caroline clutched the sides of her seat with both hands.

"What's he going to do?" she asked anxiously.

"He'll just look you over and see if there's anything we can do to get you feeling better," Isabel assured her. "He was my doctor when I was a little girl. Still is."

Caroline didn't budge. Shep, lying in his usual spot in the shade, roused himself from his nap and lumbered to his feet. He came to Isabel, drooping head and lolling tongue witness to the effort, and she scratched his ears. Shep pulled away from her, raised his front legs onto the running board and rested his head in Caroline's lap. He rolled his eyes to look at her, then rolled them shut. Caroline let go of the seat and patted him gingerly.

"That dog's shameless," Isabel said. "I think he likes you."

Shep yawned and stepped down from the running board, ambled across the yard and onto the front porch, scratching the screen door and whining until Doc appeared in the doorway. "I thought I heard visitors," he said.

Isabel held out her hand to Caroline, who took it and got out of the car.

"I've brought Caroline Piggott to see you, Doc."

"Have you now."

She told him that Caroline had been sick and didn't seem to be bouncing back like she should.

"Come on in and let's have a look," he said, holding the screen door open for them.

"My examining room is in the back," he said to Caroline. "Would you like Mrs. Fuller to be in the room with you?"

Caroline shook her head.

"Isabel, why don't you sit in the hall, and we'll leave the door open a little. Then if Caroline decides she wants you to come in, we'll tell you."

Doc led Caroline into the examining room, closing the door most of the way. Isabel sat in one of two chairs in the hall, sinking into the worn upholstery. She studied the wallpaper, remembering the first time she'd seen it, the day she and Edward and Carl arrived from the hills. She'd looked at the fine paper and the wood moldings and told herself she'd have that someday. The paper was worn now like the chairs, peeling in a few places, water-stained in others where the roof had leaked in a hard rain. *I should tell Doc to get that paper fixed,* she thought. *He tends not to notice such things.*

She leaned her head against the back of the chair and closed her eyes, listening to Doc wash his hands and examine Caroline, his voice soothing as he explained everything he did, her replies to his questions low and inaudible. She heard Doc wash his hands again when they were finished. The door creaked open, and the two of them stood in the doorway.

"Caroline, why don't you go outside and play with that old dog," Doc said. "I'll talk to Mrs. Fuller for a minute and then we'll let her take you home."

When Caroline was outside, he lowered himself into the chair beside Isabel.

"Did you find anything?"

"Yes." Doc sighed and rubbed his face wearily. "There's no sickness I can see. But there's something bad wrong." He leaned forward and rested his elbows on his knees. "A man's been at her. More than once."

She uttered a low groan. Sudden rage shot through her, and the thought crossed her mind that if any man other than Doc were sitting next to her, she might hit him.

"You didn't ask her who."

"No. I want to think on what's the best way. I may want you to talk to her."

They fell silent for a while. Then she spoke.

"It's the father."

"Most likely."

"No. There's no doubt."

He looked at her. "I'll take your judgment on that. We need to get her away from him until we figure out what to do with her."

"I'll take her to our place. She can stay there a few days. I'll talk to Edward."

Doc agreed. "I'll go see Sheriff after you leave. We'll be down to see Edward late this evening."

She stood, and Doc pushed himself to his feet. They went to the door and stepped out onto the porch, near where Caroline was sitting in the dirt with Shep. She had made a garland of grass and clover and set it on the dog's head. Shep raised his head at the sight of Doc and Isabel, careful not to upset his crown. She kissed Doc goodbye and went to Caroline, who lifted her arms, and Isabel thought of the baby bird, exhausted but still flapping its wings, trying to fly. She picked Caroline up. The child wrapped her arms around Isabel's neck and her legs around her waist. Isabel held her tight for a moment, felt her trembling, her little chest heaving, her little heart beating. Then she carried her to the car and took her home.

CHAPTER
10

T HE BOYS WERE OUTSIDE AGAIN, PLAYING PADDLE AND wheel. Isabel parked the car in the barn, then she and Caroline walked to the front yard together.

"Play with Caroline while I fix supper."

Ben and James looked dubiously at Caroline.

"What do you reckon she likes to play?" Ben said.

"Why don't you ask her."

Samuel decided he would interpret the will of Caroline and impose it on the two younger boys and Isabel left them arguing whether Caroline would prefer hide and seek or ante over. She went to the kitchen, and it wasn't long before she heard the four of them shouting and laughing. She was frying baloney for sandwiches when she saw Edward at the barn. She waited until he had crossed into the backyard to call the boys and Caroline for supper. They raced to the back, Caroline slowing when she saw Edward, the boys pushing and shoving to rinse their hands at the pump. Edward slapped at them playfully, then stopped, surprised, when he saw the girl.

"I don't believe your daddy knows you're here, Caroline."

Isabel stepped outside as Caroline backed slowly toward the corner of the house.

"Caroline's having supper with us. She may even spend the night."

Edward drew up at the tone of her voice.

"Is that right?" He went to the porch and took the towel she held out to him. "Well, we're mighty pleased to have you, Caroline. Go wash up." He followed Isabel into the house.

"Her daddy went on back to Floyd's Landing," he said. "We didn't know she was here." He pulled a chair out from under the table and sat down.

"He'll likely come looking for her," she said. She went to the stove. Stabbing baloney slices with a fork, she lifted them out of the frying pan and put them on a plate, then cut diagonal slices in the edges of four more pieces and dropped them into the pan. Pushing the baloney around as it fried, she told about the trip to Doc's, then turned to look at him.

"Her daddy's been at her. Using her as his wife."

Edward was pulling off his boots. He stopped in midair, the boot he was holding suspended for a few seconds, his expression one of sick disbelief, then dropped the boot on the floor. She winced and turned back to the frying pan.

"Lord God Almighty. Are you sure it's him?"

"She hasn't said. But I'm sure."

He pulled off his other boot.

"He's a good hand," he said. "We don't want to be too quick thinking it's him."

"When was I ever too quick about such things? Who else could it be?"

He raised his hand. "All right, all right."

"Doc and Sheriff will be by later."

He stood. "Let's get the children to bed." He went to the back door and called the boys and Caroline through the screen. They ate a quick supper of sandwiches and milk, then Isabel took Caroline to Carl's room to put her to bed. "Do you think this will do?" Caroline nodded. "I'll find you something to sleep in." She went to the boys' room and found one of Samuel's undershirts, took it to Caroline, then left the room so the girl could undress. She waited a few minutes and when she went back into the room Caroline was standing by the bed, the undershirt hanging almost to her knees.

"Hop in bed." Isabel blew out the lantern, then sat beside her. After a while, Caroline spoke.

"Am I staying here all night?"

"Yes. I think you'll stay here with us for a while."

The girl was quiet for a moment. "Does my daddy know?"

"Not yet. We'll let him know."

Isabel waited, but Caroline didn't say anything more. Even though the room was dark, she could see her eyes wide open, arms across her chest and hands pulling at the covers as if she were offering up some twisted, silent prayer.

"You'll be safe here." She sat patiently until she saw Caroline's eyes flutter, then close, then fly open again at the sound of an argument in the boys' room and Edward threatening them all with a whipping if they didn't hush. Isabel smiled slightly.

"He almost never whips those boys," she said in a low voice. "Last time I remember him even trying was when he caught Samuel swimming in the creek when he'd told him not to. Edward cut a switch, but Samuel saw him coming and took off running. Edward chased him clear across the field but only got in a lick or two. He never said anything more about it. I think he hated to admit Samuel outran him."

Caroline's eyes closed again. Isabel waited a while, then slowly got to her feet and stood for a few minutes listening to her sleep. She crept across the room to the hall, leaving the door open behind her so if there was any breeze in the night it would blow through the house. She went to the boys' room. They were lying in bed whispering, quieter than usual.

"Mama's gonna whip you two," Samuel said, "because it takes a woman to do it."

"Keep up that smart talk," she said, "and I'll get my broomstick after you."

That tickled Ben and James. She kissed them and told them to go to sleep. She left their door open, too, but closed the door from the hall to the kitchen, not wanting the boys to hear their conversation.

Edward sat at the table, waiting for the coffee he had put on to perk. She went to the sink. "I didn't bake today. There's canned peaches in the cellar."

"I'll get some in a minute."

She bent over the sink, hands in the hot, soapy water, and raised her head to look out the window while she washed dishes. She saw a flash – flames leaping from the brush arbor, an image of someone running toward it in panic, and she was filled with dread. Something terrible would happen there, she was certain. Her knees began to buckle and she grabbed the edge of the sink. She closed her eyes, took a deep breath, and looked up again. The fields were dark, silent. There was no revival tonight.

She gathered up the wet dishtowels, took them outside, and was draping them over the clothesline when Doc's car pulled into the lane. The sheriff had ridden with him. She greeted them and the three of them went inside. They accepted her offer of coffee and peaches, exchanging observations about the weather with Edward while she served them, Doc spooning the last of the juice from his bowl when he was finished and Sheriff agreeing they tasted mighty fine. Then they got down to business.

"I hear we got some trouble," Sheriff said.

"You could call it that," she said.

"Sheriff and I talked about it," Doc said. "We could send her to stay with Sister for a while. Piggott wouldn't have to know where she is."

Mae Walker, a year older than Doc, was "Sister" not only to her brother Doc but to everyone who knew her. Sister had married Hasty Walker, no relation, ten years ago and moved to Memphis. She always said she liked being Mae Walker and it took her a while to find a man where she could go on being Mae Walker. Hasty was a successful cotton merchant and a widower who, after a few trips to New Caney, was smitten by Sister's charms.

"It's a thought," Edward said.

"It can't be more than a visit," Sheriff said. "We can't take her away from her daddy for long."

"Then what happens to her?" Isabel said.

"Hard to say. Not much we can do."

"He's got the other young'uns living with kinfolk," Edward said. "We can tell him to go on back to the hills. Tell him to bring some of his people down here who can speak for him and take care of the girl. Then we let her go with the family."

The men looked at Isabel. She stared for a moment into the lantern on the table, then rose and began collecting the dishes.

"It's the best we can do for now," she said. They all turned to the sound of footsteps on the back stairs and a knock at the screen door.

"Evening," Piggott said. "I've come looking for Caroline."

Edward rose and went to the door, and Doc and Sheriff Dennis pushed back their chairs. When Piggott saw the sheriff, he laughed nervously.

"I didn't know you had company, Mr. Fuller. I'll be on my way – no need to disturb you."

"We'll walk you to the road," Edward said. Doc and Sheriff followed.

Isabel went through the living room, out the front door, and sat in a rocking chair. The men were standing at the gate talking.

"I'm her daddy," Piggott said.

"We know who you are," Edward said.

"I take good care of that girl."

"No, you don't. Whether it was you or not, you're not taking care of her. Act like a man and find somebody to take care of your daughter."

Piggott laughed harshly. "You ain't the one to talk about being a man, Mr. Fuller."

Edward took a step toward him. "What do you mean by that?" he said softly. Piggott backed away.

Sheriff Dennis stepped between them. "You go on back where you come from," he said to Piggott. "Then you bring your people here to talk to us like we said."

Piggott shook his head and looked around, unable to meet anyone's eyes. "You got no right to keep my girl."

"Go on now," Sheriff said. "Don't come back until you've done what we told you."

Piggott shuffled to the road and set off in the direction of Floyd's Landing. A minute or two had passed when they heard him shout. "You got no right to keep my girl!" A few minutes later, when he was almost out of earshot, they heard him again. "You ain't a man, Fuller!"

Edward, Doc, and Sheriff turned back to the house. The sheriff was embarrassed when he saw Isabel sitting on the porch. He was a big man, with wide shoulders and huge hands, but soft-spoken and polite. "Piggott's been drinking," he said.

"I could see that," she said.

Sheriff reached into his back pocket for a handkerchief, took off his hat, and wiped his forehead. He started to put his hat back on, but, glancing at Isabel, apparently thought better of it.

"I'll get word to Sister that she's coming," Doc said. "The question is who takes her to Memphis."

Edward looked at Isabel. "I'll take her," he said. "There's a sale up near there. Man died, I read it in the paper. Starting Saturday, they're selling everything – horses, livestock, the farm. I'll take Caroline over on the train, then have a look at that sale."

"I appreciate that, Edward," Sheriff said. "I'll look in on Piggott tomorrow. Make sure he's leaving." He turned to Doc. "It's late, Doc."

"It is," Doc said. "Miss Hazel will be wondering where you are."

Sheriff cleared his throat and examined his hat carefully. His wife had died last year, and word was getting around that he was keeping company with Hazel Matthews.

Doc and the sheriff said goodbye to Isabel. Edward walked them to their car, then stood in the lane and watched until they were out of sight. He looked up at the night sky, went slowly to the porch, and stopped at the bottom of the steps, hands in his pockets.

"Not a cloud in the sky," he said. "We used to go walking sometimes on nights like this."

Isabel rocked. "That was a long time ago."

"It was." He came up the steps.

"I'll take Caroline on the Friday afternoon train," he said.

"Take the boys with you."

"The boys? All three of them?"

"They haven't seen Sister in a while, and they need new clothes. I'll send Sister a list. She'll be happy to shop for them."

"I reckon they'd be good company for Caroline."

"The only time I hear her laugh is when she's with them."

"Still. We might manage better without all of them going."

"They should go to the city more. So they don't think this is all there is in the world."

He crossed his arms and rocked back and forth on his heels, then reached for the screen door. "I'm going to bed." He went inside but stopped on the other side of the door. "This is a good place."

"I didn't say it isn't." She heard him walk through the house and get ready for bed. She sat on the porch until she heard the sounds of his snoring coming through the open windows of their bedroom.

When Isabel told the boys about the trip the next morning at breakfast, Ben and James jumped up from their chairs. "We're going to Memphis, we're going to Memphis," they chanted. Samuel shook his head in disgust, but she could tell he was excited, too.

"Shush," she said. "You'll wake Caroline." Caroline hadn't even moved when Isabel checked on her earlier in the morning.

"Are you going, Mama?" Samuel asked.

"No, you boys and Daddy are taking Caroline to stay with Sister for a while. But you can't tell anyone about it, especially about her staying with Sister."

"We better not go to school then," James said. "We might tell someone if we go to school today."

She looked at him sharply. "If you're not big enough to keep a secret, then you're not big enough to go on a trip to Memphis with your daddy."

Ben made faces at him and Samuel mouthed the word baby until James turned red. "It won't be a secret when we get on the train," James said in his defense.

"That train goes for hundreds of miles," she said. "If anyone asks, you're going to Walnut Ridge to look at some horses for sale. That's not a fib, because you are – even if it might not be at Walnut Ridge. Now finish your breakfast."

"What about Caroline's daddy?" Samuel asked. "Does he know where she's going?"

"No." She lowered her voice, the boys listening intently. "He's got some trouble he needs to work out right now. He's leaving town and I don't think he'll come near you. But if he does, you don't say anything to him and just walk away. You understand?"

The boys looked at each other and nodded soberly, not really under-standing at all but feeling important to be included in this information.

"Samuel, you tell Miss Moxley the three of you won't be in school for a few days and if she wants a note from me, I'll send it when you get back."

When they had finished breakfast, she shooed them away from the table and out the door, then went to pack for their trip. She pulled Edward's old leather suitcase out from under the bed, wiped the dust off with a rag, then set it on the bed and opened it. She knew Sister would march them all to church on Sunday morning, never mind their opinion on the matter, so she packed Edward a change of clothes and his Sunday suit. The suitcase would hold a few more things but they would need a second bag for the rest of the boys' clothes and to carry back their purchases. She went to Carl's room to find his duffle bag, opening the door quietly. Caroline was still in bed, but she was awake.

"Good morning." She went to the windows and opened the curtains. "How are you this morning?"

"Fine," Caroline said. She sat up.

"Do you want some breakfast?"

She nodded.

"Do you need to go outside first?"

She nodded again.

"Go on then."

Isabel made the bed, smoothing the sheets and adjusting the covers until there was not a wrinkle or lump to be seen, then looked in the closet for Carl's duffle bag and found it at the back of one of the shelves. Edward had bought the duffle bag for Carl before he left for the war. When the army sent it back with Carl's clothes and a few possessions, she had propped it at the end of his bed, where it stood for several days. Then one day after Edward and the boys were gone, she had opened it.

She had taken out the shirts and trousers, and the heavy coat she insisted he take because she didn't want him to be cold. She hung the coat in the closet and took the clothes outside to wash, scrubbing until the last stain was gone, then hanging the clothes up to dry, and when they were dry, ironing them over and over again. Then she folded the clothes carefully and put them in the bureau drawers and emptied the remaining items from the duffle bag. It wasn't until she pulled Carl's shoes from the bag that she began to shake. She leaned her back against the wall and slid down it until she was huddled on the floor, the shoes wrapped in her arms. She heard a strange noise and realized it was her, wails escaping in sobs so violent that she began to retch. Edward had found her there when he came home, the house dark and no supper on. He bent down to her, but she wailed and kicked at him, and he let her do it until her rage at him was spent. Then he carried her to bed.

She shook the duffle bag and laid it flat on the bed. The screen door slammed, and Caroline reappeared.

"Am I staying here?"

"Yes. We'll talk about it while you eat."

Isabel spooned oatmeal into a bowl and poured a glass of milk, then sat beside Caroline while she ate. She explained that Caroline would be going to stay with Doc's sister until her family could come get her, and that things weren't quite right with her daddy so other people would take care of her for a while. Caroline put down her spoon. A few drops of oatmeal had spilled on the front of Samuel's undershirt, and she rubbed them anxiously.

"Don't worry," Isabel said. "It'll wash out. Did you get enough to eat?"

She nodded. Isabel stood.

"Let's wash the dishes. Then we'll go to town and see if we can find a dress for your trip."

They were drying the dishes when Caroline spoke.

"Daddy's sad because Mama died."

Isabel's stomach turned. "Sometimes when people are sad, they do things that hurt other people. Have you ever been hurt by someone like that?"

Caroline was quiet. Then she shook her head.

Isabel waited a few minutes, but the girl didn't say anything. "I'll get the car out of the barn while you dress and we'll go to town."

When she pulled the car up to the house, Caroline came running, wearing the overalls she had worn the day before. She was barefoot. Isabel couldn't recall ever having seen her wear shoes – not that it was unusual, because in the summer her own boys wore shoes only to church.

"Do you have any shoes?" she asked as they drove.

"I had a pair. But they may have wore out."

She parked the car in front of Lambert's store. "If we can't find a store-bought dress to our liking, I'll make you one this afternoon."

As she had suspected, there were only two dresses in Caroline's size and the prices were too much to pay – $1.18 for a plaid percale and $1.98 for a prettier blue gingham. She told Caroline she could make a gingham dress for thirty cents, saving enough to buy her a pair of shoes, and they settled on a pair of brown leather Oxfords, socks, and two pairs of bloomers. Isabel found a pattern for a dress and Caroline chose blue gingham fabric like the dress in the store. They set their purchases on the counter by the iron cash register.

"Who's this young lady with you, Isabel?" asked Wally Lambert, the store's proprietor.

"This is Caroline Piggott. Her daddy's done some work for Edward. Her mama died a little while ago, and we're making Caroline a new dress."

Wally rang each item up on the cash register, wrote the total on a tablet, and Isabel signed for it. "Come show me your new dress when it's made," he said as they were leaving. "There's nothing prettier than a girl in a blue gingham dress."

Isabel put a pot of ham and beans on for supper, then spread the fabric for the dress on the kitchen table, held the pattern up to Caroline, and pinned it on the fabric. She cut the pieces for the dress and took them to the living room to sew. Caroline followed and sat on the floor, watching her pump the foot pedals of the sewing machine as the dress took shape.

It took her most of the afternoon to make the dress. She did a final fitting on Caroline, pinning the hem and the sleeves to finish by hand. The boys came home from school, and she told them what to pack because she hadn't gotten around to it. They called her to inspect the duffle bag when they were finished. She took a few items out and added a few more.

The boys taught Caroline to play cards while they waited for their father, bickering over which brother was cheating at any given time. When Edward came in from the fields they ate together, the boys telling Caroline about Memphis even though it was three years since they'd been there, and Isabel occasionally correcting bits of serious misinformation about the city. After supper she sent the children to bed then sat at the kitchen table to hem the dress, moving the lantern to her end of the table for more light. Edward leaned back in his chair at the other end of the table, his face in the shadows.

"She say anything about her daddy today?"

She shook her head. "Just that he's sad since her mama died."

"Sorry's more like it," he mused.

They were quiet for a while, Isabel drawing the needle and thread in and out of the fabric, Edward leaning forward to sip his coffee, then back again.

"I need to figure out how much money to take," he said.

They added it up out loud – $5 one-way for each railroad ticket, at least $20 for clothes for the boys, money to leave with Sister for Caroline, and some extra. Isabel would pack food for the train and Sister would insist on cooking for them, but Isabel wanted the boys to eat in a restaurant while they were there. "Tell Sister you're taking her out Saturday night. Some place nice. She'll know where to go."

"Be hard to get much better cooking than Sister's."

"That's true. But eating at Sister's every meal doesn't get the boys out."

He went to the bedroom and she heard him slide the bureau away from the wall; he came back carrying a small metal box, which he set on the table in front of his chair. He sat down and opened the box, counted out the amount of money they had talked about, then closed the box and looked at the stack of bills on the table. "Sure seems like a lot."

"It is. But there's plenty left in that box. And in the other boxes."

Edward didn't trust banks. He kept an account at the bank in town to keep down any talk that he might have money hidden somewhere in his house, but he kept most of his money and all of his important papers in metal boxes that only he and Isabel knew about. One was in the house, in a space under the floorboards beneath the bureau in the bedroom. The others were hidden in different places around the property.

He pulled a worn leather wallet from his back pocket. Usually, he carried only a dollar in it, more than enough for a piece of pie and a cup of coffee at Etta's Café if he happened to be in town. He tapped the stack of bills on the table, then carefully put the money in his wallet and returned it to his pocket. He got up and went to the screen door and stood looking out into the yard, dimly lit by the porch lantern.

"Why don't you go with us," he said, his back to her.

She held the dress up to examine the hem. She was almost finished.

"Somebody's got to look after the place."

"Samuel could do it. We could leave him here."

"And come back to cows not milked and chickens not fed. Besides, he'd be awfully disappointed not to go."

He picked up the metal box.

"That's a pretty dress. You should make yourself a new dress."

She put the last stitches in the hem, then got up and reached for the ironing board.

"I don't know where I'd wear a new dress. But maybe I will."

Isabel let the boys sleep in a little the next morning. After they'd eaten breakfast and done their chores, she told them to clean themselves up and get dressed. She washed Caroline's hair over the tub, picked up a brush and pulled it gently through the tangles.

"Ouch!"

"I'm sorry. When was the last time you washed your hair?"

Caroline thought a moment. "With soap?"

"Yes."

"I can't remember."

"I'm not surprised."

She worked on Caroline's hair until the brush went through it smoothly, then braided it in a long ponytail.

"Now let's see how that new dress looks."

Caroline pulled the dress over her head and Isabel buttoned it up the back. It fell a few inches below the knees.

"Turn around."

Caroline held her arms out and spun around quickly, slipping and almost falling in her sock feet.

"Slowly, so I can look at the hem. And put your arms down."

She looked at the dress with a critical eye as Caroline turned.

"It looks fine. And you look very pretty."

Caroline grinned and sat on the floor to put on her shoes, then jumped up and opened the door to the kitchen. The boys had come inside, and they whistled loudly when they saw her. Caroline blushed.

"That's enough," Isabel said.

Edward came in the back door, drying his face and neck with a towel. "Caroline," he said. "That's a pretty dress on a pretty girl."

She smiled shyly and looked down at her new dress and shoes.

Isabel and the boys loaded the bags into the car while Edward changed clothes. When Edward was ready, they drove to the station on the east side of town and Isabel got out with them to wait for the train. Sheriff Dennis appeared a few minutes before the train's scheduled arrival. He took Edward and Isabel aside while Caroline and the boys sat on the platform, looking down the tracks.

"Piggott's gone. I went down to Floyd's Landing to check on him. They said he packed up yesterday and left early this morning."

"Good," Edward said. Sheriff Dennis looked at Caroline.

"I wouldn't even have recognized the girl. She looks like Isabel Fuller got aholt of her."

They heard the whistle of the approaching train.

"Isabel," Sheriff said. "You let me know if there's anything you need while Edward's gone."

"Thank you, Sheriff. I will."

Edward and the sheriff shook hands, then Isabel walked with Edward to where the children were waiting, the boys elbowing each other and shuffling their feet impatiently. The train pulled into the station, puffing steam, iron shrieking against the rails. Ben and James fought over who would carry the suitcase until Ben promised that James could carry it coming home. Samuel hoisted the duffel bag over his shoulder, bent and kissed his mother goodbye, gave a little salute, and disappeared into the train.

Isabel felt a sudden catch in her throat, remembering another day when a boy as big as a man had left her standing on the station plat-form. She blinked back tears. Ben and James came to kiss her goodbye, apparently thinking it was all right because Samuel had done it, then followed him onto the train. Caroline hung back, sitting on a bench with her feet dangling in her new shoes and looking uncertain about what she should do.

"You'll like Sister," Isabel said. "And you'll have a good time in the city." She walked with Caroline to the train, where Edward was waiting to board.

"Be sure to let Sheriff know if you need anything," he said.

"I'll be fine."

"Can I bring you something from Memphis?"

"I don't need anything."

He took a step toward her. She turned her head, and he kissed her on the cheek.

"We'll see you Monday."

"Have a good trip."

She watched as the train pulled slowly out of the station, the boys and Caroline waving to her from the windows, and she waved back until the train disappeared. The station was deserted. No one else had gotten on or off the train.

On her way home through town, she stopped at the store, waved at Wally, who was behind the counter waiting on a customer, made her way to the dry goods section, and was thumbing through dress patterns when Wally came up behind her.

"That's a smart one, Isabel. Just in from St. Louis – the latest fashion."

The dress had a tight-fitting, embroidered bodice, with a square neck and long sleeves. A sash tied to the left, low across the hips, with a flowing skirt that fell just above the ankles. Isabel knew instantly that if she wore that dress, she could make a man's head spin.

"Let me show you the material I got for it." Wally rummaged in the piles of fabric underneath the sewing counter, pulled out a roll and unwound it. The fabric swept across the counter, waves of silk the color Isabel had always imagined to be the color of the sea, green or blue depending on the light and the angle you looked at it. She moved down the counter slowly, touching the fabric lightly with her fingertips.

"Edward will be the envy of every man in the county with you in that dress at the harvest dance."

She drew her hand back. "We haven't been to the dance in years."

"High time you went," Wally said. "High time you went."

"How much?"

"Just $2.59 a yard." Seeing her reaction, he added quickly, "It's a little expensive, I know, but this is special, very special, you don't see material like this every day."

"I'll think about it."

Wally was disappointed. Every year saw a few more families in the county who could afford a luxury once in a while. The Fullers, he knew, were one of them – not that he'd been able to talk Edward or Isabel into any yet. Then he brightened.

"Got something else to show you." He led her to a shelf lined with soap and toothpaste and other toiletries and took two small bottles from the shelf.

"Just got these in, too. Bath salts and shampoo." He looked at her conspiratorially and spoke in a hushed voice. "French."

She took the bottles from him, examined the labels, and laughed. "Maybe French made in Chicago."

Wally looked hurt. "All right," she said. "I'll take these."

He smiled and took the bottles to the cash register, and while he wrapped them in paper, she inquired about his wife. She hadn't seen Mrs. Lambert around the store lately, and Wally confirmed that she was down in her back again. He tied the package with string and handed it to her.

"I do thank you." He called after her one more time as she opened the door to leave. "You think about that dress, now."

CHAPTER
11

ISABEL PARKED THE CAR IN THE BARN AND TOOK HER PACK-
age into the house, then went outside. She hoed the garden, fed the
livestock and milked the cows, and threw some feed into the chicken
yard. It was almost sundown when she finished, her shirt soaked
with sweat, her hair damp and itchy against her scalp. She went into
the kitchen and pulled a butcher knife from the drawer, then went back
outside and cut a watermelon off the vine for supper.

She carried the watermelon to the back porch, set it down and sat
beside it, her feet resting on the steps. She split it open with the knife,
set one half of it in her lap, and began to eat, avoiding the seeds and
cutting chunks out of the heart. She ate it in gulps, not caring how she
looked since she was alone, the cool, sweet juice running down her chin
and arms and the front of her shirt. While she ate, she gazed across
the field at the brush arbor where people were starting to arrive for the
revival and wondered if the Reverend was already there. She set the rind
on the porch and started on the other half.

When she had finished eating, she lay on the porch, stomach bulg-
ing, eyes closed, and thought she could sleep there all night under the
stars. A memory of her father crossed her mind, one of the few that
came to her unbidden on occasion like a welcome, long-lost guest. She
remembered that he would take her outside on summer nights and

they would lie side by side on their backs in the grass, looking at the sky, while he pointed out the Big Dipper and the Little Dipper and the North Star, and other than the Big Dipper she wasn't sure what he was pointing to. She always asked what you would find if you flew past the stars, but her daddy couldn't say. Sometimes they caught lightning bugs in a jar. Her daddy would put her up on his shoulders and they'd walk in the dark, holding the jar out in front of them to let the lightning bugs light their path, until Mother called her in for bed.

She roused herself and rubbed her face. She got up and collected the watermelon rinds and the knife, then cut the rinds and fed them to the hogs. She walked back to the house, knife by her side, sweaty and dirty and sticky. She set the knife on the kitchen table, then went to pump water for a bath.

When the tub was full, she checked the front door to see that it was locked. She latched the back screen door, carried the package she'd bought at the store into the bedroom, stripped off her dirty clothes, and threw them in a pile in the corner. She added bath salts to the water, the smell of lilac hanging in the damp air above the tub, then eased herself into the tub and bathed, the lilac scent in the room even heavier as she shampooed her hair. After she had bathed, she wrapped a towel around her head then slipped into a nightgown, took off the towel, and brushed her hair.

She padded to the kitchen in bare feet, wet hair falling down her back, made herself a cup of tea, and carried it to the living room. She took a book off the shelf, then settled with pillows on the sofa to read. She was asleep in a few minutes.

She wasn't sure what woke her. Something she sensed, or a sound, among all the night sounds, that wasn't quite right. Her eyes flew open, and she lay tensed on the couch, feeling herself break out in a cold sweat. The curtains moved with a slight breeze. She sat up slowly, blowing out the lantern on the table by the sofa. The living room went dark, still lit slightly by the light from the kitchen. She listened intently.

She heard it again – the sound that had awakened her. A soft foot-fall, just outside the window. She stood and walked soundlessly across the room to the hall and to the front bedroom. She reached Edward's bureau, where she slid the top drawer open and searched under a stack of handkerchiefs to find his pistol. It was gone. He must have taken it with him.

She heard footsteps on the front porch, then heard them cross to the bedroom window, just outside where she stood. She dropped to a crouch in front of the bureau. Then he spoke.

"I know you're in there, Mrs. Fuller." It was Piggott. He pushed his face up against the window screen. "Or maybe I'll call you Isabel."

She opened her mouth and breathed silently, not moving a muscle. After a few minutes Piggott shuffled away from the window. She could tell by his walk that he'd been drinking but was still sober enough to know what he was doing. She slipped into the hall again, walked to the kitchen, and blew out the lantern on the table just as she heard his footsteps on the back stairs. She picked up the butcher knife she had used on the watermelon and, holding it by her side, backed out of the kitchen and hid behind the doorway to the living room. The screen door was latched. It wouldn't take much to force it open.

Piggott stood outside the screen door. "Come on out, miss high and mighty. I got a lesson for you. One your husband ain't man enough to teach you."

He kicked at the back door. "Come out, Isabel," he yelled, his voice harsh and rising angrily the longer he waited. "I don't mess with little girls. It was the Reverend got after my girl, not me."

He kicked again. "You found her down at his tent. Why don't you ask him why he wouldn't leave my girl alone?"

She tensed, knife ready. Then a soft voice called from the yard.

"I think you've lost your way, Mr. Piggott. This is the Fuller place. Seems there's no one home."

Piggott turned.

"Well, if it ain't the Reverend Kane. She's in there, Reverend. All by herself. Her men folk stole my girl."

Kane walked halfway up the steps.

"I don't know anything about that," he said. "But I know you don't belong here, so you'd best be going."

Piggott stepped across the porch and glared down at the Reverend. Kane backed down the steps and Piggott followed him, taking it as a sign of weakness, but at the bottom of the steps, he stopped short at something in the Reverend's manner one wouldn't anticipate from a man of the cloth.

"They got no business taking my girl."

"I don't know anything about that," he said again. "You go on now, you hear?"

Piggott slunk around the corner of the house, made his way haltingly to the road, then yelled. "I'll be back, Isabel. Ask him what he done to my girl."

Kane waited until Piggott was gone, then stepped up onto the porch and knocked on the screen door.

"Mrs. Fuller?" He waited. "It's Reverend Kane, Mrs. Fuller. He's gone."

Isabel stepped out of the doorway between the living room and the kitchen. She went to the back door, butcher knife still in her hand.

"What time is it?" she said.

"It's after midnight."

She stood in the dark kitchen, just inside the screen door. She could see Kane clearly in the porch light.

"What are you doing here?"

"I'm sorry. I didn't mean to meddle. But I was on my way home from the revival meeting and I heard a ruckus when I passed by your house."

"A ruckus. I guess you could call it that." She started to tremble. Still clutching the knife, she wiped her forehead with the back of her hand.

"Are you all right?" he said.

"I'm fine."

"Then I guess I'll be going." He walked across the porch and started down the steps.

"Wait," she said. "Come inside. I'll fix some tea."

She unlatched the screen door and let him in. He hung his hat on a peg and she lit the lantern on the table. She went to the stove and put the kettle on, motioned for him to sit down. She poured two cups of tea when it was ready and took them to the table with a plate of cookies. She took her seat at the end, still dressed only in her nightgown. Kane picked up the plate and offered it to her. She shook her head.

"What happened to Caroline?" he asked.

She set her cup in her saucer, crossed her arms, and looked steadily across the table at him.

"She's gone away for a while. To get her away from the man who's had relations with her." She saw the shock register on his face and wondered what shocked him – the idea, or the fact that she'd said it. She watched as the shock turned to sadness.

"Good Lord," he said, his voice low. "The violence we do to our children."

She was surprised by the intensity with which he spoke. Her eyes filled unexpectedly with tears. "Yes," she said. "How can they ever forgive us?" She looked down at her lap, swallowed, and cleared her throat.

"I heard Piggott yelling," he said. "Now I understand what he was saying."

"He says you did it."

"I did not." He looked her in the eye and appeared even more shocked by the accusation. "I am as unworthy before the Lord as any man, but I would not do that."

She believed him. She told him about Edward and the boys going to Memphis, and then asked what his plans were. Looking a little embarrassed, he told her he would be going to Memphis himself, settling down in a church outside town that needed a pastor. It would give him time to do what he'd been thinking about for a while, he explained, which was go to college. He loved preaching, he said, but thought the Lord would be better served if he wasn't such an unlearned man.

"You think I'm as crazy as I am ignorant? A man my age going to school?"

She shook her head. "You're not crazy. And you're not ignorant. Ignorant people are happy knowing only what they think they already know. My son Carl was going to college. Edward would say he didn't know how we could afford it. I told him we'd sell a hog or a heifer whenever tuition came due."

She picked up her cup and swirled it gently, disturbing the tea leaves settled on the bottom.

"I still have the letter they sent him. 'We are pleased to inform you.' I keep it in the box with the other one. 'It is with deepest regret that we inform you –'"

Her voice broke. She looked at him, stricken, then leaned her elbows on the table, buried her face in her hands, and wept. Tears streamed through her hands, and she shook from sobs she couldn't control.

She heard Kane's chair scrape as he pushed back from the table, his soft footsteps on the wood floor. He stood next to her, and then he touched her, his fingers gentle on her hair and then moving up and down her spine in a slow caress.

"I'm sorry, Isabel. I'm so sorry."

She cried until there was nothing left, and her sobs slowed to intermittent gasps.

"It's so hard. There are days when I don't know if I can get out of bed."

"I understand."

She felt his hand on her back, his warm breath on her neck, and raised her head. His face was next to hers. She looked at him for a moment, then stood.

"It's the middle of the night. I need to get some sleep."

"I'll stay if you want. In case Piggott's still out there."

"I don't think he'll come back. But it's a long way to your place this time of night. You can sleep in the boys' room."

She showed him where to sleep, then went to her bedroom and closed the door. It was almost dawn before she fell asleep. She woke to sunlight streaming through the curtains and the smell of bacon and coffee. She dressed hurriedly and went to the kitchen to find Kane standing at the stove, shirt sleeves rolled up, lifting bacon out of the frying pan with a fork.

"Just in time for fried eggs," he said.

"I'll do that."

"No, no. Breakfast is one thing I can cook. You sit down."

He had set two places at the table. She told him she'd be right back, then went to the outhouse, and washed her face and hands at the pump. He was putting the food on the table when she returned. They sat down. Fork and knife poised over his plate, he turned to her.

"Shall I say grace?"

She shook her head.

"Then let's eat."

They ate without talking, Isabel stealing an occasional glance at Kane when he wasn't looking, until he caught her at it. He put down his fork and grinned.

"Do I amuse you, Mrs. Fuller?"

"A little. You obviously enjoy your own cooking."

"It's not so much my cooking." He tore a piece of bread and sopped up the last bit of egg yolk on his plate. "It's the company I'm enjoying."

She dabbed her lips slowly with her napkin, pushed back from the table, and carried her dishes to the sink. He rose and followed her. Her back to him, she moved to one side, thinking he was bringing his dishes to wash, but he moved with her, trapping her against the sink, his hands resting on the counter on either side of her. He pressed gently against her, his mouth close to her ear.

"I have to go before someone comes looking for me," he said. She fought the urge to lean into him.

"You'll tell me if I'm meddling too much, won't you?"

She nodded.

"Shall I come back tonight?"

The clock on the wall ticked persistently against the still heat of the kitchen. A horsefly droned angrily at the window screen. The fork slid off her plate and clattered into the sink. She closed her eyes.

"Yes," she whispered. "Come back tonight."

CHAPTER

12

I SABEL CARRIED A CHAIR FROM THE KITCHEN TO THE HALL closet and stood on it to reach to the back of the top shelf, where she found two wood boxes. She carried the boxes to the kitchen, set them on the table, and opened one.

It was full of papers and other mementos. She took the stack out of the box and went through it as she had hundreds of times before, knowing the contents by heart. There were the letters she had told Kane about last night. She read them again, folded them, and set them aside. There were the birth certificate, the death certificate, the certificate of baptism and confirmation. Faded blue and red ribbons won at spelling bees and races, testimonials of childhood victories, chronicles of dreams lost forever. Poems and stories he had written in thick pencil, with careful handwriting escaping the lines on the paper to his frustration.

She opened the letters he had sent her on his trip to France – descriptions of the trip to St. Louis, and on to New Jersey, the small towns they passed through, and the cold, wet, miserable nights in the detention camp while they waited for their ship. A night on the town in New York City, the Statue of Liberty, Red Cross sandwiches and coffee before they went up the gangplank of the ship that carried them across the Atlantic. Seasickness, and fog, and packed like hogs going to market. Billeted in a barn on a farm outside a small village in

France, bathing in a pond with some of the boys in his outfit, and the old women of the village coming to stand on the bank to watch while they got out and dressed. The other boys trying to cover themselves, but Carl standing up and giving the old women a good look at what they came to see. Isabel had covered her mouth and shook her head when she first read it, saying she hadn't raised her boys like that. The drills, the hikes, the gas masks, the dead.

She carefully put it all back in the box, then closed the lid and set it aside. She opened the other box, the one she hadn't looked in for a while. It held the war medals, Carl's baseball, his prized arrowhead, his watch, the silver dollar Doc gave him for memorizing the first chapter of Luke one Christmas, and the black sock that held what she was looking for.

She set the sock and its contents on the table, put the boxes back in the closet, then returned to the kitchen. She reached into the sock and pulled out Carl's pistol, a Smith & Wesson .38 that Edward had given him on his sixteenth birthday. It was heavy, well-balanced, its walnut grip burnished to a soft gleam. She reached into the sock again and found a box of bullets.

The gun hadn't been fired in years. She tied a piece of string around a small rag, dabbed the rag with oil, then drew the string and cloth through the barrel, cleaning it methodically. She wiped the pistol free of dust, then loaded it. When she looked up from her task, Mary Clara was sitting in the chair in the corner.

"When's the last time you fired a gun?" Mary Clara said.

"About five years ago, I think."

"You remember how?"

"It'll come back to me. You taught me well, Mother. And what was it you told me? About the two main things I needed to know to get along in life?"

Mary Clara cackled. "The first was that you're smarter than any man likely to come along. The second was how to shoot a man if you needed to. You weren't but a little thing the first time you heard that."

"Six years old," Isabel said. "Not long after Daddy died. The day those two drifters came through, looking for food and money. When they left you dragged me out of the house and gave me my first lesson on how to fire a gun."

"I was afraid," Mary Clara said. "Afraid for you and your brothers."

"You sure never showed it."

Mary Clara pursed her lips. "I'm afraid for you now."

Isabel hefted the pistol from one hand to the other. "No need to worry about me, Mother."

Mary Clara shook her head. "That's not what I'm afraid of."

"What is it, then?"

But Mary Clara was gone.

Isabel went outside to practice. She set a block of wood on top of a fence post, figuring that would be about chest high on an average man. She stepped back twenty feet, grasped the pistol with both hands, looked down the barrel, and fired. The block jumped off the fence post to the ground. A clean shot to the heart by her reckoning.

"There you go, Mary Clara. You'd be proud," she said with satisfaction. She emptied the gun with practice shots, then went back inside, reloaded, set the gun on the kitchen counter within easy reach. She latched the screen door even though it was the middle of the day.

She felt somewhat at a loss about what to do with the rest of her Saturday. She'd just been to town the day before, and there wasn't any reason to cook. She stood at the sink looking out the window, feeling Kane at her back, his voice and breath hot against her ear. She paced restlessly around the kitchen, then through the house, and finally to her closet, where she pulled out the blue dress she had worn the night the Reverend came to supper. She would go visiting, she decided, then to the revival.

She collected two jars of peaches from the cellar, put them in a basket, and set the pistol next to them under a napkin. Reaching inside a kitchen cabinet, she found a key to the house, seldom used, and locked the front and back doors before leaving for town.

She considered a visit with Lois Lambert, since Lois was down in her back again, then remembered the last time she'd been to see the woman: the sour smell of cabbage and illness assaulting her as she walked in the door, Lois's dog nipping at her heels and looking more like a rat than a dog, Lois's face drawn and taking on somewhat the same appearance. Isabel couldn't imagine keeping a dog in the house, but she knew Lois did it to keep her company while Wally was away for long hours at the store. The Lamberts were childless, a fact repeated in hushed tones among the residents of the town as if it were significant, although it was unlikely anyone could say exactly what the significance was. She decided to stop by Hazel Matthews' house instead.

Hazel lived alone on a farm north of town. She had two grown sons who farmed the place and a daughter who'd married and moved to Indiana. In her early fifties, she was a handsome, lively woman who'd kept her figure well, so it was no surprise that the sheriff was attracted to her. His car was parked in front of Hazel's house when Isabel drove up.

Hazel was delighted to see her. Sheriff Dennis sat on the sofa in the front room and rose when she entered. She said hello as if it were the most natural thing in the world to see him there, and he relaxed.

"I'm fixing supper," Hazel said. "Come eat with us."

Hazel wouldn't take no for an answer, and the three of them talked and laughed more than Isabel could remember having laughed in a long time. After supper they invited her to stay and play cards, but she declined.

"I should get home. I may stop over at the revival since it's the last night."

"I reckon Edward will be glad to get that over with," Sheriff said. "They've been there what – three weeks?"

She shrugged. "It's been fine. They haven't bothered us at all."

"I get all kinds of reports on the Reverend Kane," he said. "Been keeping an eye on him."

"What kind of reports?" Isabel asked cautiously.

"Nothing serious. People seeing him places at odd hours. Him claiming to be a seventh son. You know how that gets folks agitated, thinking he's got powers." He chuckled. "I'm sure the Reverend's happy with that kind of talk, as long as it turns into more contributions."

"Is he a seventh son?" Hazel asked.

"Lord. Who knows?" he said. "It's hard to get that kind of information. He comes from a big family, at least. A lot of them didn't turn out too well from what I hear."

Isabel rose. "Let me help with the dishes."

Hazel wouldn't hear of it, insisting that she take advantage of not having any men around. The sheriff walked her to her car, glancing back at the house to be sure Hazel had gone to the kitchen.

"You haven't seen any more of that Piggott fellow, have you?" he asked, opening the car door. She settled herself behind the wheel and looked up at him.

"No. Haven't seen him."

"Let me know if you do. I can send a man down to watch your place until Edward and the boys get back."

It was almost dark. She started the car and turned on the headlights.

"I don't think that will be necessary," she said.

There was a large crowd at the revival, long lines of cars and wagons stretched along the roadside, and Isabel decided not to stop, thinking she would walk from home. She drove on to the house, the place pitch dark on a moonless night. She parked the car in the lane, picked up the basket from the seat, got out and slammed the car door. Basket in one hand, she grasped the porch railing with the other, moving slowly up the steps in the dark. She patted the shelf beside Edward's wash basin to find the matches he kept there. She touched his soap and shaving brush, toothpaste, hair tonic and the extra comb for the boys. Her fingers fumbled the entire length of the shelf. The matches were gone.

She bent over and felt along the bench, thinking maybe she had set the matches there yesterday evening after lighting the lantern. They weren't there either. She straightened. Then she froze. The hair on the back of her neck began to prickle. The night was still, the music from the revival faint in the distance. She turned slowly to face the backyard. She couldn't see anything, but she was sure someone was there.

Her heart jumped at the sudden sound of a match striking a box. The match flared a few feet from the porch.

"Looking for something, Isabel?"

It was Piggott. He tossed the match toward the porch. The flame died as the match arced and struck the porch in front of her. He lit another one.

"Reverend Kane's busy tonight," he said. "Or is he coming by later to stay like he did last night?"

He tossed the match in her direction.

"I come back last night, Isabel. I hid out by the barn 'til morning, when I seen Kane come out to the privy."

He lit another match. She didn't say a word.

"I reckon Mr. Fuller would be mighty interested in what the good Reverend was doing here all night, now wouldn't he?" He threw the match again.

Isabel finally spoke.

"Mr. Fuller knows all about a good man chasing off a coward. He's done it himself."

She could see the anger in Piggott's face as he lit the fourth match. He shook his head.

"Folks act like you own this county," he said. "Like you're something special. But you ain't nothing but a couple of dumb hillbillies got lucky. And old Edward Fuller's forgot who wears the pants in the family."

The match he held had burned down to his fingers and he dropped it to the ground. Instead of lighting another one, he started slowly toward the porch steps. "Let's you and me agree on something," he said. "You get my girl back for me." He stepped heavily onto the bottom step. "And I won't tell Mr. Fuller how you went chasing other men while he was gone." He took two more steps up. "Maybe I won't even tell him how you come chasing after me tonight."

As he took the last step up onto the porch, Isabel raised her arm in his direction. He stopped when she cocked the pistol.

"How about we make a different agreement," she said. "You agree to get off my property. And I agree not to kill you."

She could hear him breathing, smell his sweat and his fear. He swallowed and gave a short laugh.

"You ever shoot a man, Mrs. Fuller?"

"No," she said evenly. "But this is a short shot compared to target practice this morning. I don't think I'll miss. Even in the dark."

Piggott stood where he was.

"Sheriff's sending a man down here to watch for you until Mr. Fuller gets back," she said. "But if you set foot on my property again, I'll kill you myself. Now get out."

He laughed uncertainly, then backed slowly down the steps.

"Piggott." He stopped. "Leave my matches here."

He wavered. Then he tossed the box of matches onto the porch and stumbled backwards to the side of the house. She held the pistol in his direction as he disappeared around the corner, listening as he walked to the road. When she heard his tread on the gravel, she rounded the house, pistol still pointed ahead of her. When she couldn't hear his footsteps anymore, she dropped the pistol to her side. She went to the front porch and sat down in a rocking chair. Then she began to shake.

She sat on the porch for a long time, holding the pistol in her lap, the shaking gradually subsiding to an occasional tremor. She lost track of time, dozing and floating back to consciousness every now and then at the sound of voices or a car starting as people drifted back to their wagons and automobiles from the revival. When the noise of the departures had subsided, she fell asleep. She woke with a start at the sound of the front gate creaking open.

Heart pounding, she fixed her eyes in the direction of the gate. She saw a dark form, heard quiet steps on the walk. She raised the pistol and drew back the hammer. The footsteps stopped.

"Mrs. Fuller," Kane said.

She blew out the breath she was holding, then released the hammer and set the gun down on the porch beside her chair.

He stepped closer to the porch. "I should have announced myself sooner. I thought you might be asleep since the house is dark, and I didn't want to disturb you."

"It's all right, Reverend. I'm a little jumpy."

"I thought you might come to the meeting."

"I planned on it. But I had a visitor again tonight."

He came up on the porch and sat down beside her. She told him what Piggott had said and done, and how she had chased him off.

"I told him if he comes back, I'll kill him. I will, too."

He studied her solemnly. "I believe you will."

"You think that makes me a hard woman?"

He shook his head. "You're hard-headed and tough, in ways I've never seen in a man. But you're gentle and kind." He paused. "More woman than most men will ever know."

She reached for the pistol and stood up. She took the key out of her pocket and opened the front door.

He looked up at her. "Should I go?"

"No. Come inside."

He followed her through the dark living room into the kitchen. She set the pistol on the counter, then lit the lantern on the kitchen table and drew the curtains across the windows. She opened the door to Carl's room, leaving it open so the light from the kitchen filtered into the room, then went to stand by the bed. He stopped at the doorway, watching her. She unpinned her hair and shook her head, letting it escape down her back. Then she unbuttoned her dress and, shrugging her shoulders, let it fall. She turned to him, trembling with lust and shame and a sense of danger, terrified that what she was about to do would change her life forever, but unable to stop herself.

He came to her slowly, unbuttoning his shirt and taking her in with his eyes. He stopped a few inches from her and threw his shirt on the floor, then reached out and unbuttoned her camisole, drawing it back, and bent his head to her breast. He licked her nipple then drew it between his teeth. She gasped. He slid his tongue up to the base of her neck and then, both hands in her hair, drew her mouth to his lips. He kissed her, the kiss long and slow, moved his hands to her breasts and down her sides. He slipped his hands inside her underwear, then cupped his left hand on her buttocks and buried his right hand between her legs, stroking her until she was wet, still kissing her lips and neck. Then he stepped back.

He unbuckled his belt and stripped in front of her. She watched him, thinking about how she had never been with any man but Edward, and how this was different, the feel of Kane's skin so smooth against hers, but so many things about a man the same. When he was naked, he pulled her underwear down and pushed her back on the bed, then knelt by the bed and she forgot everything but his tongue on her and his fingers inside her and she arched her back and grabbed his hair until she shuddered in release. He got up from the floor and lay beside her on the bed, kissing her while her breathing slowed, then turned over onto his back and pulled her on top of him. She got up on her knees, straddling him, and lowered herself onto him. They moved in time together, eyes locked, his hands on her hips, gently at first and then harder as he pushed inside her as deep as he could. She drew her fingers through her hair, her elbows in the air and breasts jutted toward him. He sat up and pulled her legs around his waist and they clutched each other and rocked hard against each other until they were finished and fell back panting on the bed.

They lay side by side, quiet for a while, their legs entwined and Kane stroking her back. "That was wonderful," he said in a hushed tone.

"Yes. It was."

He pushed himself up on his elbow, craning his neck to look around the room and then back at her.

"Was this your son's room?"

She turned over onto her back. "Yes."

"Tell me about him."

"What do you want to know?"

"Who he was. What he was like."

She folded her arms across her chest, gazing up at the ceiling. "That's like trying to tell what life is. How can you ever say enough?"

He drew his fingers lightly up and down her belly. "Try."

She drew in a deep breath. She started to talk, slowly at first, then the words and the stories were coming in a rush as if she couldn't get them out fast enough. How Carl had worked hard and loved a good joke and got to where the schoolteachers couldn't keep up with him. How he'd drive his little brothers to distraction not paying enough attention to them, then wake them in the middle of the night to help him push the outhouse over, conspirators in the crime. How he'd borrowed Doc's car and driven his father all the way to Little Rock when he was just fourteen, with Edward off on business and the two of them deciding they would see the sights between here and there. Carl knew where all the stills in the county were, although he never touched a drop of liquor so far as his mother knew. He'd save his money and the next thing she knew she'd hear he'd given it to a sharecropper family out of work and hungry. "Every girl around had her eye on him. That's not just his mama talking either. Plenty of families wanted one of their daughters to marry Carl Fuller."

He smiled. "If he was anything like his mother, I'm sure they would."

"He was so smart, so insightful," she said. "One time he – he –." She stopped, looked at Kane in a panic.

"What is it?"

"I can't remember," she whispered. "The story I was going to tell. Oh God, I can't remember." She began to cry.

He pulled her close, moved his hand down her belly then between her legs. He kissed her, muffling her sobs, touching her until her sobs turned to moans. He rolled on top of her, and she raised her hips and pulled him inside her. They moved together again until he collapsed on her. They lay there sleepily for a while until he raised his head.

"You won't be able to remember everything about him, Isabel. As time goes by, there will be some things you forget."

She pushed him and he rolled off her.

"I have to remember. If I don't remember, who will?"

She stood.

"Where are you going?"

"Down the hall to sleep. This bed's too small for the two of us."

He grabbed her hand. "I don't want you to leave."

She pulled away from him.

"Good night, Isabel."

"Good night."

CHAPTER

13

ISABEL SLEPT SOUNDLY AND WOKE LATE. SHE DIDN'T HEAR Kane up, so she crept down the hall and looked in on him. He was still asleep, snoring softly. She closed both doors to Carl's room, then went outside to clean up and brush her teeth. She came back inside, still in her nightgown, put the coffee on and opened the curtains, then sat down, drumming her fingers on the table.

The door to Carl's room opened. Dressed only in his trousers, Kane smiled at her from the doorway. She flushed, then started to get up.

"No, wait," he said. "Sit back down."

She did, looking at him uncertainly.

"Stay there. I'll be right back."

He went outside. The door to the outhouse slammed, then he stepped up onto the porch and back inside and came to her. He stood behind her for a moment, then bent down, his lips soft on her shoulder, then on her neck and up to her ear.

"This is what I wanted to do Friday night when we were sitting here together," he whispered. He wrapped his arms around her and touched her breasts, then moved his hand down to her belly. She sighed and bent back to him, raising her arms behind her to grasp his shoulders. He pulled her up out of the chair so she was standing with her back to him and pushed hard against her from behind. His left arm around her waist, he moved his right hand slowly up and down the insides of her thighs. She shuddered and her breath came faster. He drew her nightgown up over her hips and bent her slightly forward over the table. She braced herself against the table with her hands as he pushed her legs and buttocks apart, then worked on her until liquid fire shot from her belly into her thighs and her knees buckled under her. He held her up, not letting her fall, and turned her around and laid her back on the table, then pulled her nightgown over her head and threw it to the floor. Lying naked on the table, she watched as he unbuckled his trousers and stepped out of them. Still standing, he pulled her hips to the edge of the table and pushed inside her. Arms over her head, she grasped the sides of the table and wrapped her legs around his waist. They strained against each other until she cried out and he fell on top of her, groaning as he pumped himself into her and broke into a sweat.

They lay there trembling. Finally, he pushed himself up on his elbows.

"My God," she murmured.

He sighed. He stood and drew her up off the table, held her close, and kissed her.

"I can't get enough of you," he said.

"We should get dressed. In case someone comes."

She retrieved her nightgown from the floor, slipped it over her head, and went to her bedroom. He was pulling on his trousers when she returned.

"You look ready to work," he said.

"The livestock is wondering where I am. I've been late the past two days."

"I'll help."

"You don't need to."

"I want to. Some outside work will do me good."

"Don't you have to go to church this morning?"

"No. People in New Caney have been very supportive of the revival, and I figure it's good public relations not to give their pastors any competition on Sunday morning. Everitt invited me to speak down at Floyd's Landing, but I told him I had plans to minister to the shut-ins."

"Was this what you were thinking about?"

He laughed. "It might have crossed my mind," he admitted.

They worked for several hours, Kane finishing one task and Isabel pointing him to the next. She sent him to the barn to groom the horses while she took the hoe to the garden. She had almost finished hoeing when Doc's car pulled into the lane and stopped near the front of the house. She put down her hoe and went to greet him as he ambled toward the garden.

"Working on Sunday," he said. "I stopped by to see if you're all right when I didn't see you in church this morning."

"Everything's fine, Doc."

He looked over her shoulder. She turned and saw Kane coming out of the barn and heading their way. Doc looked at her and then back at Kane.

"Doc," she said. "Have you met the Reverend Kane?"

Kane held out his hand.

"Don't believe I have," Doc said. "Israel Walker."

"Micah Kane. Pleased to meet you."

"Reverend Kane stopped by to thank us for letting him hold the revival here," she said. "When he found out Edward and the boys were gone, he offered to help me with the chores."

"Is that right."

"Yes," Kane said. "It's hard for me to know how to express my gratitude to Mrs. Fuller."

Doc studied him thoughtfully.

"I'll go make some lemonade," Isabel said.

"Thank you, Mrs. Fuller, but none for me," Kane said. "Is there anything else I can help you with?"

"No, you've done more than enough, Reverend."

"Then I'll be on my way." He shook Doc's hand. "Pleasure to meet you, Dr. Walker." He turned to Isabel and bowed slightly. "Thank you again, ma'am."

They watched his progress on the road for a while, then went inside. Isabel made lemonade and they went to sit on the front porch. Doc took off his hat and fanned himself as he rocked.

"Sheriff got word last night that Piggott didn't leave town," he said.

Isabel took a sip of lemonade.

"He was drinking down at Smitty's. By the time Sheriff got there he was gone."

She set her glass down on the porch.

"That bunch down at Smitty's said he was saying things about you and the Reverend Kane."

She felt a sudden urge to run, a stab of panic that she would be the subject of the town's gossip for years to come. That her boys would reject her in disgust and that she would regret what she had done for the rest of her days.

"I wouldn't worry too much about what someone like Piggott says," she said.

"No. Sheriff told those boys if he saw Piggott, he'd lock him up. And if he heard any more talk like that from them, he'd lock them up, too."

She picked up their glasses, went inside to pour more lemonade then returned to the porch.

"Edward and the boys coming back tomorrow?" Doc asked.

"They were planning on it, so I'll be at the station."

They sat a while longer, Doc getting sleepy in the afternoon heat and Isabel tense, unable to stop herself from thinking about the implications of the talk going around at Smitty's and equally unable to stop herself from thinking of Kane. Doc finally roused himself and said he had to go. She walked him to his car.

"Things all right with you and Edward?" he said.

"Things are fine," she responded automatically. Then she folded her arms and gave a little shake of her head. "No. Things haven't been all right between Edward and me for a long time." She attempted a smile, but it turned into a grimace.

"You have some mighty fine boys to raise, Isabel."

She swallowed her sudden anger. "You think I don't know that? You think I don't know that what I want or need isn't important, that the only important thing is those boys?"

"What do you want, Isabel? What is it you need?"

"I want Carl back. I want my mother back."

"They're not coming back, Isabel. Those are the two things you can't have."

"I know." She shook her head. "And other than that, I have no idea."

Doc reached out his hand and she took it. "You let me know if there's anything I can do."

She squeezed his hand and patted it. "I will." She backed away from the car and took shelter from the afternoon sun under the shade trees, waving to him as he drove away.

She went inside after Doc left, planning to bake bread and cookies for the boys. She got out the flour and sugar and her mixing bowls, but after surveying the supplies laid out on the counter, sat down wearily. It was too late in the day to bake, she decided. The heat in the kitchen would be unbearable and, after all, it was Sunday, and she should rest a little. She latched the screen doors and took the pistol with her to Carl's room, set the pistol on the nightstand, then took off her boots and lay down.

Sunlight filtered through the curtains. The elm tree at the corner of the house gave some relief from the heat, although Carl used to say that its limbs scraping the roof on a windy night sounded like the boogerman coming to get him. "Ain't no boogerman," the little boys would say, and Carl would grin at them fiendishly. "You'll think no boogerman when you wake up some morning and find me gone for good," he'd say. Isabel would tell him to shush and stop scaring his brothers. On more than one occasion after Carl had left for the war, James, just five then, asked anxiously if it was the boogerman that took Carl away.

She closed her eyes. A dog barked somewhere in the distance. The barnyard was quiet, the animals dozing in any shade they could find. The sheets on the bed felt damp, the smell of Kane's shaving lotion on the pillow, the seductive scents of their night together on the sheets. She would have to wash the bedding in the morning. She fell asleep, restless in the heat at first, then losing all consciousness.

The sun was setting when she woke. She closed her eyes in the early evening gloom, almost drifting off to sleep again before she forced herself to sit up. She was groggy, her mouth sour with the stale taste of lemonade. She swung her legs over the side of the bed, picked up the pistol and carried it with her to her bedroom. She took a gingham house dress from the closet and changed clothes, then put the pistol in her pocket and went to the kitchen.

She made a bowl of oatmeal and took a jar of milk from the icebox, then sat down at the table to eat, her mind wandering to Kane, wondering what he was doing and whether he was thinking of her, not sure when he was leaving town or whether he was coming back tonight. She rested her head on the back of the chair, eyes fixed unseeing on the ceiling, and thought about what she and Kane had done, feeling him on her and in her, and wanting him again.

"I told you to take care, Isabel."

She blinked and dropped her gaze from the ceiling to Mary Clara sitting across from her at the table.

"I thought you were talking about Piggott."

"You think I'd worry about you handling that ignoramus?"

"I should have known. You never had any trouble sending his kind packing over the years. But you could have been more specific."

Mary Clara took a deep breath and blew it out slowly. "I can't spell it all out for you. What's worrisome is that you didn't see this coming."

Isabel shrugged. "Maybe I didn't. Why does it even matter?"

"Because it's like lopping off a part of you. You want a man who does that to you?"

Isabel sat up straight in her chair, leaned closer to her mother.

"I'll get back on schedule tomorrow. I'll bake. I'll be washing clothes for days after Edward and the boys come home, and the garden's full of vegetables that need canning. Summer's almost over. There will be so much work to do this fall, I won't have time to think."

"You won't have time to think?" Mary Clara shook her head. "I'll be back. You can let me know how that goes."

Isabel did the evening chores and then washed herself and wet her hair, telling herself that she wasn't doing anything special on the chance that Kane would come. She put on a yellow summer dress she hadn't worn in a long time, having let it hang unused in the closet because she'd decided it was a little girlish for a woman her age. She took extra care with her hair, looking in the mirror and crimping its natural curls with her fingers as it dried in the evening heat until she was satisfied with what she saw. Then she felt foolish. She was all dressed up on a Sunday night. And she was alone.

Taking the pistol with her, she went outside to sit on the front porch. It was a beautiful night in spite of the heat, the oak trees in the front yard silhouetted against a starry sky, two pairs of eyes shining at her from a low branch. The raccoons stared at her a while longer, then slipped away. Occasionally a wagon or a car passed by on the road, filled with people on their way home from Sunday evening services or a visit in town, their tired voices drifting in fragments on the evening air. She sat for a long time, wide awake after her long nap, then finally rose and went inside, angry at Kane that he hadn't come, and determined that if he did come at this late hour, he wouldn't find her sitting on the front porch as if she'd been waiting for him.

She latched the screen but left the front door open, then lit the lamps in the living room, brewed a cup of tea and went to the bookshelf. She'd collected an odd assortment of books over the years – some Doc had given her, some she'd bought from drummers and estate sales for a few pennies each, all of them worn and dog-eared when she got them. She opened a book of poems, sat down to read, and stared uncomprehendingly at the page. It was after ten. She took a drink of tea and stared at the page again, then closed the book when she heard a sound. Horse hooves trotting on the road from the south, the horse slowing as it approached then turning into the lane. She picked up the book again and didn't rise from her chair until she heard a knock.

"Isabel," Kane said.

She stood inside the screen door. "I didn't think you were coming."

"I tried not to," he said in a hushed voice, leaning towards her, his arms pressing on the door frame. "I prayed for the strength to stay away from you. Then I thought I'd go crazy if I couldn't touch you again."

"Come around to the back. I'll light the porch lantern and you can put your horse in the barn."

She blew out the lamps in the living room and went through the kitchen to the back porch. She handed the lantern to Kane, watched its bobbing light as he led his horse to the barn and came back again. She took the lantern from him and hung it up, then took his hand and led him inside, through the dark house and down the hall to her bedroom. He pulled her to him and kissed her.

"Let me undress you," he whispered. He stepped back a little. "Turn around."

She did. He unbuttoned her dress, then turned her around again and slowly, deliberately, stripped her clothes off until she stood naked in front of him, only inches away, his breath warm on her. She shivered and lowered her eyes. She wanted him to touch her, but he just looked at her for what seemed like a long time.

"Look at me, Isabel." She looked up at him and he smiled. She reached out, fingers trembling, and unbuttoned his shirt. Then she undressed him, the way he had undressed her, and he finally put his arms around her and pulled her tight against him. They fell to the bed together, straining to get closer, to feel every inch of each other. At last, he collapsed on his back, pulling her on top of him where she lay sweating and exhausted, her eyes closed. She dozed for a while, then rolled off and curled up by his side.

"I shouldn't stay here tonight," he said sleepily.

"No, you can't," she mumbled. "It's Monday, folks will be up and out early."

He groaned and sat up, then stood and began to dress. She lay on her back, one arm behind her head, the other resting on her stomach, watching him. He put on his shirt and trousers, then sat on the bed to put on his shoes.

"When will I see you again?" he asked.

"Edward and the boys are coming home tomorrow. When are you leaving for Memphis?"

"Wednesday. I'm having supper with some folks the next two nights. Meeting with a prayer group Tuesday morning." He bent over her, palms resting on the bed on either side of her.

"Stop by sometime before you leave," she said.

He kissed her. "We should talk about how we can be together again. You coming to Memphis, or me meeting you somewhere."

She turned away. "No. We don't need to talk about that. It's best we not even think about that."

He looked at her silently, then sighed. She got up, pulled her dress over her head, and followed him to the back porch. He carried the lantern to the barn, came back leading his horse, and handed her the lantern.

"Tell me how I do that, Isabel. Tell me how I stop thinking about being with you again."

She didn't reply. She blew out the lantern and hung it on the hook, went inside and leaned against the door frame, staring out at him. He waited a moment. Then he got on his horse and rode away.

Isabel slept only a few hours, rising before dawn. She stripped the sheets off the beds and took them out to the wash table. Working by the light of the porch lantern, she filled the washtub with water, then gathered a load of firewood and started a fire under it. She added lye soap and when the water was hot put the sheets in, poking them under the water with a paddle, and left them to soak just as the rooster started to crow. She milked the cows, collected eggs, fed the livestock, then went back to the washtub. She scrubbed the sheets against the washboard, refilled the washtub with rinse water, and put more wood on the fire. After a quick breakfast, she hung the sheets on the clothesline, then baked and dusted while they dried, made the beds, and changed clothes when it was time to meet the 4:30 train. She hid the pistol in the bureau in Carl's room, left the doors to the house unlocked as they would usually be, then pulled the Ford out of the barn and drove to the station.

It was deserted, the ticket booth locked and dark. Trains came through no more than once or twice a day this time of year. The station master, Otis Ivey, would wander over every once in a while to see if anyone was there to buy a ticket. Most of the time folks just stopped by his house, which was not far, to tell him they needed a ticket, and Otis would gladly escort them to the station and sell them one. When the crops started coming in, Otis would get busy again.

Isabel stretched out on a bench on the shaded platform, crossed her legs at the ankles, and closed her eyes. She would be glad to see the boys. It was funny how little she had thought about them while they were gone, but she knew she would begin to miss them if they didn't return soon. Her mind wandered to Kane – his smile, the look on his face when he touched her – and she was surprised at the sudden, hollow ache, like someone had hit her right between the chest and the stomach. She was lonely to the core. She sat up and rested her elbows on her knees, buried her face in her hands, and rubbed her eyes. The train whistle blew in the distance. She looked around.

"What am I doing here?" she whispered. The whistle blew again. She stood.

Ben and James waved to her from the window as the train pulled into the station, and she smiled and waved back. When the door opened, James stepped down with the duffel bag, Ben following closely with the suitcase. She walked quickly to them, and they dropped the bags and hugged her tight.

"You both look like you've grown a foot." She looked up. The door had closed and the train was starting to pull away.

"Where's Samuel and your daddy?"

Ben and James looked at each other importantly. "We rode the train by ourselves," James said.

"You did!"

"Daddy bought two horses and a wagon," Ben said excitedly.

"He didn't want the wagon," James said. "But he bought some tools and equipment, too, and he had to have some way to get it home."

"Daddy and Samuel are coming home with the wagon," Ben said. "Daddy said to tell you they should be here by Wednesday evening."

"Isn't that something? You two sure are big to ride the train by yourselves."

She offered to help carry the bags to the car, but in their new grown-up status they wouldn't hear of it. They struggled to lift the bags into the car, then jumped into the back seat, telling her all about their trip on the way home. Sister said to tell her hello and come visit soon, and Caroline was doing fine. Sister's husband had a great-niece who lived not far from them, and she came to play with Caroline today. There's another girl Caroline's age, too, who lives down the street. They had supper at a fancy restaurant Saturday night, had to get dressed up to go.

"It wasn't that fancy," Ben said.

"Was too," James said. "It had tablecloths on all the tables."

She smiled. It was good to have them home. She stopped the car near the back porch. The boys unloaded the bags then ran to get their baseball equipment while she drove the car to the barn. They were playing catch when she returned, having lost interest in carrying the bags any further. She picked up Edward's suitcase with one hand and dragged the duffel bag with the other, setting both bags in the corner of the kitchen. She put supper on the table and called the boys in.

They were hungry. Sister had packed them a snack for the train, they said, but they'd eaten most of that before they left the station in Memphis. Their new clothes were in the bag. Sister had made sure they'd gotten everything on the list, even talked Daddy into buying a new shirt and tie for his Sunday suit.

"And," James said, "we got you a surprise, Mama. But Daddy's bringing it."

"You weren't supposed to tell," hissed Ben.

James reddened. "I didn't tell her what it is."

"That don't matter. Now she knows she's getting a present and it isn't a surprise."

She told James not to worry, that she wouldn't even think about it until Daddy and Samuel got home, so by the time she got the present it would be a surprise all over again. She asked about the horses. Two fine mares, the boys explained. Daddy said he planned on breeding them and maybe they would foal next summer.

After supper she pulled the bags to the table and went through them. Sister had obviously helped with the packing, because the clean clothes were separate from the dirty ones. She was pleased with the new clothes. Good quality (but not expensive) trousers and shirts, a sweater for each of the boys, and a new coat for Samuel who was too broad-shouldered to wear his daddy's hand-me-downs anymore. Just getting Edward to buy a new shirt and tie was worth the trip. She would write Sister a note tomorrow to thank her.

She put the new clothes away and piled the dirty ones on the back porch, slid Edward's suitcase under the bed and put the duffel bag back in Carl's closet. She called Ben and James in and sat with them for a while as they lay awake after prayers. They were tired and insisted they shouldn't have to go to school tomorrow, but she told them they had to go because they'd missed two days already. School would be out soon enough for the harvest.

"What did you do while we were gone, Mama?" Ben asked sleepily.

"I did chores, which is a big job with no boys around to help. I went visiting. I read some books."

"Did you miss us?" James asked.

She bent and kissed them both. "I missed you something awful."

The boys were tired the next morning. James said he thought Isabel should drive them to school in the car, and Ben told him he was crazy. She sent them off walking with their books and lunch pails and went to the living room to write Sister a note. Not wanting to waste any paper, she sat for a while thinking about what she would say. Then she wrote:

> *Dear Sister,*
>
> *Thank you for your kind hospitality to Caroline Piggott. I am sure Edward has explained her circumstances to you. If you find you need more money for her support before we can come to get her, please let me know.*
>
> *I appreciate the shopping you did for Edward and the boys. I unpacked the clothes, and they are what I would have chosen.*
>
> *There's not much to say about life here. Things haven't changed since you've been gone. I hope to get to Memphis again one of these days.*
>
> *Yours fondly,*
>
> *Isabel Fuller*

She folded the letter and put it in an envelope, set it on the kitchen table, and thought of all the things she should be doing. Then she picked up the envelope, went to the barn and saddled Blue, and headed towards the post office. She hadn't gone far when she decided it was silly to ride all the way to town just to mail a letter. She pulled Blue up, turned him back in the direction of home, then went on towards Floyd's Landing. She cut to the west across old man Coggin's land, then south to the river, approaching Kane's campsite from the opposite direction of Floyd's Landing.

There was no sign of him. She tied her horse to a tree, then peeked inside his tent. He had begun to pack, but he wasn't there. She made her way down to the riverbank. She didn't see him anywhere, but not wanting to go home, sat down in the shade. She hadn't been there long when she heard him call her name from the top of the embankment above her.

She turned. He was silhouetted in the mid-morning sun.

"I saw your horse," he said.

"I came down here to fish."

He stumbled down the embankment. "Where's your pole?"

"I'll cut a pole in a minute."

He sat down beside her. "What are you fishing for?"

"Catfish. What else would I be fishing for in this river?"

"Nothing I can think of. Nothing at all."

They sat beside each other, Kane glancing at her occasionally, and Isabel staring, unmoving, at the water. Finally, he got up and went to the edge of the river, knelt, dipped his hands in the water, raised his hands, then opened his fingers and let the water run down his forearms.

"Were you baptized, Isabel?"

"Of course."

"How old were you?"

"Eleven."

"Did you feel your sins washed away?"

"I don't think I'd done much sinning by then." She crossed her legs Indian style, picked up a rock, and tossed it in the river. "But I remember the way the elders looked at me when I came up out of the water with my white robe sticking to my skin. Like there was something sinful in a girl about to turn into a woman." She tossed another rock into the river. "Whose sinning do you reckon that was about?"

He stood, took off his shoes and stepped into the river. He walked into the water until it was up to his waist, then turned around and held out his hand to her. She hesitated, then stood up and kicked off her boots, following him into the river, stopping a few feet from him. He took her hand and led her farther into the river, then put his hands on her shoulders, and pushed her gently down into the water. She resisted at first, then ducked underwater and rose with her clothes soaked and clinging. She put her hands on his shoulders and pushed him down; he went willingly, then came up and rubbed the water from his face.

He put his hands on her waist and pulled her to him. Buoyant in the water, she wrapped her legs around his waist and felt him hard against her. They held each other for a while and then they kissed, long and sweet, and she thought she would remember that kiss for the rest of her life. Still carrying her, and moving her gently against him, he stepped slowly to the bank and then out of the water. She slid her legs down and stood, her arms still around him, face buried in his chest. He looked around, then led her to a weeping willow several yards down the river-bank, pushed the branches aside and drew her in under the shelter of the tree and pulled her to the ground. Lying on her back, she watched as he undressed her. Then she forgot everything but his mouth and his hands, gentle on her, then rough, as he lay on top of her and drew his fingers through her hair and looked in her eyes.

Finally, he spoke. "Sometimes I think you've given yourself up to me completely, then I realize there's part of you I can't even touch. I don't know what it is. Maybe it's the circumstances. Maybe it's Carl."

He was on his side, leaning on his elbow, searching her face intently. She turned away.

"It eats me up inside," she said.

"Carl?"

"Yes."

"That he's gone?"

"That. But maybe even more, the thought of him dying. I wonder how long it took him to die. Whether he called my name and wondered why I didn't come."

She sat up and drew her knees to her chest. She rested her chin on her knees and, huddled with arms around her legs, began to weep silently, tears streaming down her face and her legs. She drew a deep, gasping breath.

"I wonder if there was anything to give him comfort. Did an angel hold him close like I would have? And whisper in his ear he didn't have to be afraid?" She looked back at Kane. "What do you think?"

"Maybe so."

She shook her head. "I've watched people die. Not a one ever said anything about an angel." She reached for her shirt and pulled it on.

"It was hard when my mother died. I laid her out and washed her. I dressed her in her best dress and fixed her hair, then I sat up with her all night and buried her the next day."

"It was hard," she said again. "But there was something about being with her, touching death, that helped me let her go."

She stood up and pulled on her trousers. "I used to imagine Carl's funeral. See him lying in his uniform, like my mother in her best dress." She wiped her face with her shirt sleeve. "You know how they buried those boys, Reverend?"

He nodded slowly.

"They dug pits," she said. "They dug pits in the morning and dumped the bodies in at the end of the day. I read all about it, all the information I could find, because I wanted to be sure that was right. Then when I'd get to imagining how Carl looked when he was buried, I'd have my mind right about it."

She wiped her face again. "I got my mind right about those pits. The bodies stacked in there, stinking and rotting in no time at all." She sat down and pulled on her boots.

He reached out and held her arm. "Don't go."

"I have to. I have a lot to do before the boys get home from school."

He rolled over onto his back. "I didn't think I'd be with you like this again," he said. "I thought yesterday, saying goodbye to you, was the saddest day of my life, but I knew that day had to come. Now it's the saddest day all over again."

She got up on her knees and buckled her belt, then bent over him and kissed him again, a lingering kiss that had him reaching for her until she stood and backed away.

"Will you stop by the house before you leave?" she asked.

He turned his head. "No. We'll pay a price for this sin, Isabel. A high price."

She crossed her arms and shivered, chilled by her wet clothes and the shaded riverbank, wanting more than anything to lie down beside him again and never get up. She gazed around her at the shadows and the water and the sunlight dancing in random points of light through the trees.

"I don't know who I am anymore," she heard herself say. The words weren't directed at him. They escaped involuntarily, giving voice and shape for the first time to something that had been buried so deep inside for so long that she had no idea it was coming. She looked down at him in dismay. "Goodbye," she whispered. Then she slipped through the willow branches and hurried away.

CHAPTER

14

ISABEL SPENT THE NEXT TWO DAYS CLEANING AND COOK-
ing, pulling weeds in the garden, killing the cutworms that were
after her tomatoes, getting the boys into bed and off to school, and
moving through life automatically without noticing what she was
doing. Every so often she found herself thinking about her childhood.
Who was Isabel Johnson, she wondered; what happened to the girl she
was? She could hardly remember. At night when the boys were asleep,
she sat in the dark, willing her mind blank until thoughts of Kane
overtook her, her body aching for him until she pounded her fists on
her thighs and cursed him for ever touching her.

On Wednesday, Edward and Samuel came home. It was almost
noon when she heard the sound of horses pulling a wagon into the lane
and went outside. Samuel leaped to the ground and ran to her, picking
her up off the ground and kissing her. She hugged him and asked where
his daddy was.

"He stopped in town."

"What for?"

Samuel shrugged. "He said he wanted to talk to Sheriff for a while.
Maybe stop at the bank. He said he'd get a ride or walk home."

She thought that was strange but didn't ask anything more.

"Show me what you bought. Ben and James told me about the horses."

"Two fine judges of horseflesh," he said dryly.

She smiled. "Well, they were right." She examined the mares and rubbed their faces and necks, then they went through the contents of the wagon together. They'd bought a feed grinder, a disc sharpener, a pitchfork, a shovel, and an adze. Boxes of bolts and rivets, a length of heavy chain, a wheel of barbed wire, two buckets of axle grease, five bags of feed and a shotgun. She saw, tucked in a corner of the wagon, two boxes wrapped in brown paper. She assumed they were her presents from Memphis and didn't mention them.

"Good prices, I hope."

"Real good," he assured her. "They were selling everything on the farm, even all the furniture and dishes in the house. Daddy said you might like some of the things in the house, but he wasn't sure."

She nodded absently and told him to take the wagon to the barn and unload it.

"Feed the horses and brush them," she said. "They're tired after that trip."

She worked in the kitchen while Samuel was in the barn, making chicken and dumplings for supper and a coconut cake to celebrate everyone's return. When Samuel came inside, she asked him about the trip. He said he liked the city, and he'd talked to Daddy on the way back about maybe getting a job there in a couple of years. Sister had an extra bedroom and she told Samuel to come stay and work for a while whenever he wanted.

"What did your daddy say about that?"

"He said he wasn't sure. He'd have to talk to you."

She beat the cake batter over and over with a spoon until it was smooth. "I don't see anything wrong with it," she said. "I imagine all you could get would be a factory job, though, and you can't do that for long."

"Why not?"

"Because you're going to college."

"I don't need to go to college. Daddy never went."

She set the mixing bowl on the counter. "You will go to college. We're not working this hard so our sons can get factory jobs."

She hugged him to her and, for no reason she could explain, started to cry. He squeezed her and rested his chin on her head. "I won't go to

Memphis, Mama. I won't ever leave you." Arms around each other, they rocked gently back and forth.

"You should leave me," she said after a few moments. "It's only natural that you should leave. But leave for the right things and the right reasons."

"Like what?"

"College. Traveling. Seeing the world."

He pulled away from her. "That's why I was thinking about going to Memphis. I could work for a while, save my money and then travel."

"Where would you go?"

A shy, sweet smile crept across his face.

"I bought a map in Memphis," he said. "A map of the world. Do you want to see it?"

"Yes, of course."

He went to the back porch and returned with a long tube. He unrolled a large map on the kitchen table, and they bent over it, Samuel pointing to the places he wanted to go. San Francisco, New York, London, Paris. Rome, Cairo, Athens.

"I want to go everywhere," he said. "See everything."

"You should, Samuel."

They studied the map in silence, tracing with their fingers the distances between oceans and continents, mountain ranges and deserts, lost in the wonder of it.

Before Samuel was born, while she was carrying him, Isabel had seen him often in her dreams, hiking in lush evergreen forests the likes of which she'd never known, scaling treacherous cliffs, gazing down at valleys from dizzying heights. She saw him paddling a canoe down a wide river, buying silk in a crowded Asian market. In one dream, he was walking barefoot by the ocean, waves crashing against the shore, a brown-skinned girl by his side. The dreams were colorful and wild and left her breathless in her sleep. She would wake to Samuel turning and kicking inside her as if he'd seen what she'd seen and couldn't wait to get out and find it. Looking at him now, she knew that before long he would leave her for Memphis and then for parts unknown. She felt a sharp stab of regret – for the years that couldn't have been easy for him, the times she hadn't paid enough attention, how she would miss him, and that as much as she might want, she couldn't go with him.

"If you went to Paris," she said finally, "would you travel up to where Carl died?"

"I've thought about that. I'd want to see where he was."

"It would only be right. If you were in that part of the world."

They fell silent again for a while.

"Do you think about Carl?" she asked. "Do you remember him?"

He hesitated. "I don't think about him so much anymore," he admitted. "But I remember him. Mostly I remember all the good times we had when he was here. Picnics by the river. Firecrackers on the Fourth of July, family trips to the state fair. The jam cake you made specially for him at Christmas and decorating the tree. Things like that."

"We still have picnics sometimes," she said. "We still decorate a tree at Christmas."

"I know," he said. "But for you and Daddy, there's always something missing."

He rolled up the map.

"He wasn't perfect, you know," he said.

"Carl?"

"He could be mean. Like any older brother."

"Samuel. How can you say that? I won't have you talking that way."

"It's true, though. You don't talk about him much but sometimes when you do it's like he wasn't real. Like he was Jesus in the stories we get in Sunday school. I hear you talk like that and I think, I can't be Jesus. And I'll never be Carl."

Her eyes welled again with tears.

"I cannot abide anyone saying anything bad about him," she said. "I cannot abide it."

"I understand, Mama. But it's not talking bad when you're talking about how he actually was. The oldest brother is supposed to pick on the young'ns. I don't hold it against him."

She touched his cheek. "I know Carl wasn't perfect. And I don't want you to be him. I'm sorry, Samuel. I'm sorry I haven't been a better mother to you."

He pushed the map into the tube, then kissed her on the cheek.

"What are you talking about, Mama? That's crazy talk. You're the best mother anyone could have."

Edward didn't come home until almost suppertime. Isabel heard a car stop in front of their place and a door slam, and went to the front porch to see who it was. Edward had gotten out of the sheriff's car and was bent toward the window talking. He stepped back and the sheriff drove away, then he turned to the house and saw her. Their eyes met. She knew instantly that something was terribly wrong.

He walked slowly to the house, stopping at the steps, and looked up at her.

"How was your trip?" she asked.

"The trip was fine."

"Did you have business in town?"

"I had a few things to take care of."

She waited, but he didn't say anything more.

"I guess I'll go take a look at the livestock," he said.

"Supper's almost ready."

She went back inside, watching him from the kitchen window, the boys calling to him when they saw him and trailing after him to the barn.

Edward was quiet at supper, his forearms resting on the edge of the table and head bowed toward his plate. Everyone had second helpings of the chicken and dumplings, then Samuel cut the cake, making sure his piece was the biggest and taunting his brothers about it.

James jumped up and whispered excitedly in Edward's ear. Edward whispered back, and James raced out the back door, reappearing a few minutes later with the packages Isabel had seen in the wagon. He set them on the table in front of her and was delighted when she acted surprised.

"She's not surprised," Ben said. "James told her as soon as we got home that we bought her a present in Memphis."

"I didn't tell her what it was," James protested.

"I forgot all about it," she said. It was true. It had been the farthest thing from her mind the past two days.

"Open them, Mama," Ben said.

The boys looked at her expectantly. She smiled and picked up the first package and unwrapped it carefully. "We'll save that string and paper," she said. She opened the box and pulled out a dove gray dress made of fine wool, the collar and cuffs a matching satin.

"This is beautiful." She stood up and held it against her.

"Open the other one," James said.

It was a hat to match the dress, the latest style cloche with the brim turned up on one side. She put it on, tucking her hair up under the hat.

"Try on the dress, Mama," Samuel said.

She told them she didn't want to get the dress dirty so she'd wait until after she'd had a bath to try it on, but she was sure it would fit, and that it was the prettiest dress she'd ever seen. The boys beamed. She took the dress to her room and hung it in the closet. Then she took off the hat and set it on the shelf. She went back to the kitchen and put the paper and string in a drawer and sent the boys to bed. Edward was still sitting at the table when she bent over the sink, her back to him.

"Was Caroline all right staying with Sister?" she asked.

"Seemed to be."

"Sheriff have any word on Piggott?"

"No. Other than he didn't leave town right away." He leaned back in his chair. "And that he was saying things about you and the Reverend Kane."

Her heart leaped to her throat.

"There wasn't any need for Sheriff to tell you that," she said quietly.

"He figured I'd hear it anyway, so best it came from him."

"I'm sorry to hear that kind of talk."

"Piggott's trash. Nobody believes it." He got up from the table and brought his coffee cup to the sink.

"Nope. Nobody believes it." He set his cup on the counter. "Nobody but me."

Isabel felt herself go numb. She thought she should look Edward in the eye, say something. She couldn't do it.

He walked out of the kitchen and went down the hall. She heard the door to the bedroom close behind him. She stood quietly at the sink for a while, staring unseeing out the window into the night, then put the dishes away, swept the floor, and stood the broom in the corner. She went into Carl's room, closed the doors, sat down on the bed, pulled off her boots and unbuttoned her shirt, then stood up again to take off her trousers. She crossed the room to the bureau, discarding her shirt along the way, and poured water slowly from the pitcher to the basin.

The numbness had left her. She felt oddly alert, her senses acute, the sound of the trickling water loud as it hit the basin. She turned to the mirror. It was dark, her reflection lost in the shadows of the room. She lit the candle, then bent closer, contorted her face and drew her lips back in a hideous grin, looking evil, unrecognizably ghoulish, in the distorted surface. Then she relaxed, her face soft in the candlelight, looked at herself a while longer, searching for familiar features. She blew out the candle and went to bed.

Over the next few weeks Isabel and Edward spoke to each other only when necessary. In mid-September school recessed for two months so the children could help with the harvest. The boys were happy about school being out until they remembered how hard Edward worked them from dawn until dark. Isabel spent most of her time canning food from the garden and planting radishes and squash. The heat finally broke a little, and once in a while there was a breeze at night.

It seemed to her that Edward was waiting for a denial or an explanation. She couldn't think of one to give him. She did her work mechanically during the day, and at night she rocked on the porch or lay in bed thinking of Kane, and of Carl.

The last week in September it began to rain. Isabel was canning the last of the tomatoes when the wind shifted to the east and the sky went dark. She hurried outside, pulled shirts off the clothesline as rain started to plop in huge drops, slowly at first and then picking up speed. She ran, arms full of clothes, and made it onto the porch just as the sky opened up and the drops turned to sheets of water. She piled the clothes on a chair in the kitchen, heard shouts outside and went to the back door to watch the boys race from the field to the barn, and then from the barn to the house, Ben slipping and falling in the mud and Samuel and James laughing at him. They jumped onto the porch, muddy and soaked to the skin, and James reached for the door.

"Don't come inside with wet clothes," she said. "I'll get you some towels."

She brought towels to the door and handed them out, instructing the boys to strip off their clothes and leave them on the porch. Then she went back to her canning, listening to the whooping and hollering that went with three boys stripping naked outside. The screen door soon slammed and the three of them were inside, towels wrapped around their waists and shivering from the rain and the wind. The commotion moved from the kitchen to their room and then back again as soon as they were dressed.

"Where's your daddy?" she asked.

"He wasn't far behind us," Samuel said. "I saw him go in the barn while we were waiting for you to bring us towels."

The rain kept coming, water pooling between the rows in the fields and forming little streams and gullies in the yard and in the lane. Isabel closed some of the windows where the rain was blowing into the house, stopping at the windows in Carl's room to look out at the barn, dark and silent in the rain. There was no sign of Edward. She supposed he had plenty of work to do inside while waiting out the storm.

The rain finally let up a little at sundown. She stood on the front porch for a while, leaning against a post, drinking in the scents of wet dirt, rain, grass, and cotton, the clouds still heavy and the yard and fields taking on an orange and yellow glow as the sun went down. She went inside when she heard Edward coming in the back door and the boys calling to him from their card game in the living room. Over supper the boys told him about their run from the field in the rain.

"You should have seen Ben wallering in the mud, Daddy," James said. "It was so funny."

The boys looked at Edward, bent over his plate.

"Sounds like it," he said. He didn't look up.

They turned to Isabel, and she tried to smile. James started the story over again, thinking maybe he had forgotten something in the first telling. Samuel told him to shut up, and the boys fell quiet as they did more and more these days in response to the silence between Edward and Isabel, finishing their supper hurriedly and resuming their card game in the living room. Edward scraped the last bit of food from his plate, then left it sitting on the table when he went to join the boys.

The card game came to an end when James threw the cards at Samuel, accusing him of cheating. Samuel stood up and would have thrown a punch, but Edward got between them.

"You're big enough to hurt him, son. No fighting." He turned to James. "You. Don't start something you can't finish."

"Time for bed," Isabel said.

"I'm not sleeping in the room with those two anymore," Samuel said. "I'm moving to Carl's room."

Edward looked at Isabel.

"Well," she said. "We'll talk about it."

"What's there to talk about? You said I could have it and I want it. I'm too old to be sleeping with the babies."

James turned red and clenched his fists. "I am not a baby!"

"Enough," she said. "It's just not the right time, Samuel." She followed the boys to their room, telling James and Samuel twice to stop their arguing and then telling them she wasn't going to tell them again. She kissed James, then bent to kiss Samuel, but he pulled his pillow over his head and turned to the wall. She sighed and went to Ben.

Lightning flashed and lit the room. Thunder followed close behind, first a crack, and then a deep boom that rattled the windows and shook the house.

"Mama," Ben whispered.

"It's okay, Benny," she whispered. "I'll sit with you a while."

She sat on the side of the bed, one hand holding his and the other gently smoothing his hair. Ben had always been afraid of thunder. The other boys, even his younger brother James, never seemed to pay much attention to the storms that swept through. Isabel loved them, loved to sit outside watching the lightning and the rain, wondering sometimes how wild a storm would have to get before she'd be afraid. Wild enough to kill her, she supposed. She wondered if one would kill her some day before she had time to be afraid.

Ben's eyes were closed and his hand had gone slack, but she didn't think he was asleep. Thunder shook the house again. His eyes flew open and he grasped her hand tightly.

"Mama."

"Do you want me to lie down beside you?"

"Yes," he whispered. She stretched out beside him and drew him close. She heard Edward go to bed, the other boys snoring, and Ben's breathing slow to a gentle slumber. She drifted in and out of sleep, then finally dozed off lying beside him, cramped in his little bed.

The thunder woke her around midnight. She sat up groggily on the side of the bed and pushed herself up. The next blast of thunder knocked her to the floor. She gasped and grabbed the side of the bed, struggling to pull herself to her feet. Lightning flashed around her and the house rocked with the force of the storm. She went down again.

"Mama!" The wail turned to a scream. She looked up. It was Carl, lying on the bed, his uniform soaked with blood and his eyes filled with terror but not seeing her.

"Mama!"

She reached for him, but the thunder threw her to the ground again. "Carl!" she screamed. "I'm here!"

She pulled herself to her knees and crawled to the bed. She pressed her hands to Carl's chest, then to his stomach, blood oozing between her fingers, blood everywhere. She bent close to his face, but he didn't see her. "My God," she sobbed, "my God." She wrapped her arms around her son and lifted him to her lap, rocking him gently, wiping the blood and tears from his face until he closed his eyes.

"Go to sleep, baby," she whispered. "Mama's here."

She rocked him for a long time, crooning "Rock a bye, baby" in a husky voice, the same song over and over again with her eyes closed. When she opened her eyes, Ben was fast asleep. She laid him gently on the bed and tucked him under the covers. Wiping her face with her sleeve, she shuddered and fought back nausea, staggering out of the boys' room, through the kitchen, and out the back door. She stepped to the edge of the porch and vomited until her stomach was empty, the rain blowing in on her, bent in pain as her stomach heaved over and over until the spasms stopped. Mouth sour and hair and shirt wet from the rain, she dropped to her knees, then lay on the porch on her side, the left side of her face pressed to the floorboards. The wind gusted and rain drenched her again. She marked familiar things in the yard with each lightning bolt – the pump, the wash tub, the clothesline, the milk trough – until darkness covered them again.

And there, at the corner of the porch, stood Mary Clara. Isabel blinked and the lightning flashed, but Mary Clara was still there, arms folded calmly, head cocked slightly, looking sadly at her.

"Mother?" she whispered.

Mary Clara didn't say anything, just looked at her.

"He was calling for me, Mother. He couldn't understand why I wouldn't come." She retched again, then again. She wiped her mouth with the back of her hand.

"I was telling – someone – telling someone – about him the other day. There was a story I wanted to tell that showed how smart and insightful he was. But I couldn't remember what it was. How could I not remember?"

"He was only three years old," Mary Clara said. "He asked you, 'Where did I come from?' And you told him that he started out as a seed and grew inside you until he was a baby ready to be born."

"That's it. Now I remember. He looked at me and said, 'But where was I before that?' And I said, 'None of us knows for sure. But I think you were with God.' Three years old. How could a three-year-old ask that question?"

"Did you believe what you told him? That he was with God before you ever knew him?"

"I did then. Because then I was looking into the face of a miracle." She groaned. "Such a loss. Such a terrible loss."

"Do you still believe it?"

"I don't think so." She drew up her knees, huddled into a ball. "Help me, Mother," she whispered. "Help me."

Mary Clara shook her head. "I can't help you, Isabel. You're wallowing in your misery and doing things that only make it worse."

"That's harsh, Mother."

"It is. But it's true."

"I'm not as strong as you were."

Mary Clara snorted. "You're every bit of it. I lost your daddy, but I never lost a child. You'll carry that grief the rest of your life. But it won't kill you. What will kill you is losing everything else that makes you get up in the morning." She unfolded her arms and pressed her hands to her chest. "A child calling for its mama. It's the hardest thing, Isabel. The hardest thing. It tears your heart right out." Then she disappeared.

Exhausted and cold, Isabel finally sat up. She pushed herself to her feet and stripped off her wet clothes, then stepped to the edge of the porch, naked, and let the rain wash over her again. Drenched and shivering, she went inside and dried herself with a towel. She stumbled into Carl's room and fell into bed.

It was still raining and dark when she got up the next morning. She heard Edward go outside then come back in, and she dressed and went to the kitchen to find him standing at the stove, starting a pot of coffee.

"I'll do that," she said. She took the pot from him. "Do you want breakfast?"

He shook his head. "Not yet."

"Might as well let the boys sleep."

He nodded. "We won't be doing much in this rain." He walked to the screen door and looked out, watching the rain against the light of the porch lantern.

"What are your clothes doing on the back porch?" he asked.

She measured flour and butter for biscuits into a bowl. "I was sick last night. I went out on the porch and my clothes got wet."

He leaned against the door frame, still looking out at the rain.

"I picked them up to see what they were. It'll be hard to get those stains out." He turned to her. "Almost looks like blood."

She pushed the mixing bowl aside and gripped the edge of the counter. A bitter, metallic taste filled her mouth and for a moment she thought she might vomit again. She drew a deep breath and reached for a cup, pouring one for him and then one for herself.

"It's not blood," she said.

He went to the table and sat down. She took her coffee to the table and sat at the other end.

"Are you all right now?"

"I'm fine."

They drank their coffee while the sun came up behind the clouds, the sky still dark and the rain steady. Edward put on his hat and went to the barn to milk the cows. When he came back the boys still weren't up, and she knew he was inclined to wake them.

"Dark and cool like this," she said, "they'll sleep a long time. They need the rest."

He paced restlessly around the kitchen.

"I think I'll go to town," he said. "Take one of the new mares to the blacksmith and have her shod."

"That's a good idea. Do you want breakfast before you go?"

"Naw, I'll stop at Etta's."

"Pick up the mail while you're there."

She was relieved when he'd gone. She went to the hall closet and retrieved a stack of mending and her sewing kit, then sat on the front porch sewing until the boys got up.

It rained the whole day, and the next. Edward made several trips to town, staying away as much as possible and leaving her the task of keeping the boys occupied. She knew he was worried that if the rain didn't stop, he wouldn't get the cotton crop out of the field, and she was glad he was off somewhere else to do his fretting. But she was at wits' end with the boys. She'd had them clean the barn and the chicken coop and wipe down the car. They had hung all the quilts on the clothesline to wash in the rain, where they still hung, their sodden weight straining the lines, waiting for the sun to come out and dry them. She tried to interest them in reading, but that didn't last long. Finally, at the end of the fourth day, the rain slowed to a drizzle. The boys were in the living room bickering over a game of checkers and she told them to saddle up two of the horses and go fishing.

"Come back by dark. We'll fry what you catch for supper."

They jumped up, whooping with delight.

"And don't get in the river," she said. "It'll be too high and fast after all the rain."

She watched them from the front porch as they rode off, with Ben and James on one horse and Samuel on the other holding the fishing poles in his right hand, the reins in his left. The rain had almost stopped. She went inside. The house smelled musty, and felt wet and cramped, so she stepped back outside and sat in a rocking chair, glad to be outside and even more glad to be alone. Dark, heavy clouds moved slowly across the setting sun, rays of fiery orange red sunlight piercing through as a slight southern breeze finally began to push the storm to the north.

The sun had almost set when she saw the horses coming at a gallop on the road from the south. The boys must have caught a mess of fish in a hurry, or maybe killed a water moccasin. She stood as they turned into the lane and drew the horses up short in front of the house. She didn't see any fish or a snake, not even a snapping turtle. They leaped down from the horses and came running, breathless with excitement. She stepped down from the porch and they gathered around her.

"Where's our supper?" she said.

"You'll never guess what happened," James said.

"Shush." Ben pushed him. "Let Samuel tell." Ben turned to his older brother. "You tell, Samuel."

She looked at Samuel. He drew a deep breath.

"We didn't go fishing," he said. "We rode down to Floyd's Landing, thinking we'd fish off the bridge. Daddy and Sheriff and Doc were there." He stopped. She waited.

"Go on," Ben said. "Tell."

Samuel gulped. "They found a dead man," he said in a hushed voice. "Caught up on a log down by where Reverend Kane was camped."

James leaned toward her, eyes wide. "A body in the river," he whispered.

Isabel felt her heart stop for a moment, then begin to thump wildly. Her throat tightened, and she struggled for breath. "Who is it?" she said, the words forced through clenched teeth.

"They can't tell," Samuel said. "They figure he's been dead a while. Sheriff says he may have been buried somewhere on the riverbank, then washed up with the rain."

"We asked Daddy if we could see the body," James said. "But he wouldn't let us."

"Good," she said. "You don't need to look at a man dead that long."

"Murder," Ben broke in. "They think it's murder."

"They don't know," Samuel said with a withering glance at Ben. "They were talking all kinds of things."

"Daddy says likely it was a migrant worker fell in the river drunk and drowned," James said.

Samuel turned to her. "The sheriff will be investigating."

"We offered to help," Ben added. "But Daddy told us to come home."

She pressed her hands to her forehead, then wiped her sweaty palms on her pants legs. "Well," she said faintly. "This is an awful thing."

"Haven't seen the likes of it around here in a long time," Samuel said. "Leastways not since Sheriff Dennis started wearing the badge."

She looked at him wearily. She could almost hear the men talking, their voices low and weighty with unrevealed inside information, the mystery of law enforcement guarded from the ordinary onlooker.

"Let's get some supper," she said. "There's a pot of beans on the stove. I had my mouth set on catfish, but beans will do."

She fed the boys and sent them to bed, then sat in the living room waiting for Edward. He didn't come home until after ten o'clock. She ladled beans into a bowl and set it on the table with a plate of cornbread when she heard him ride in.

"Have you eaten?" she said.

"No. This looks good."

She stood by the stove and watched him eat. She asked him about the dead man, and he told her, recounting not much more than she had learned from the boys. "Doc'll do an autopsy. Sheriff's checking on reports of anyone missing. Reckon we'll know more in a day or two." He stood up and brought his dishes to the sink. She took them and lowered them into the water.

"They don't have any idea who it is?" she asked.

He poured himself a cup of coffee and sat back down. "Who do you think it is? Or maybe the question is, who are you worried about?"

She washed his dishes in silence, rinsed them, and set them on a towel on the counter to dry. Then she turned to face him. "The day you came home from Memphis. Where did you go after Samuel dropped you off in town?"

He stirred his coffee, then sipped it without looking at her. "I had business."

"What business kept you in town all afternoon?"

He set his cup on the table and stared down into it. "I don't recall," he said softly. He looked up at her. "I don't recall."

They stared at each other for a moment. He took another drink of coffee, then pushed back from the table and stood up. "I'm going to bed." He left his cup sitting on the table and she picked it up after he left the room, wanting to throw it against the wall, hear it shatter into tiny pieces and see the coffee run, staining the wall. She clenched her hands around the cup, took it to the sink and washed it. She blew out the lanterns and went to bed in Carl's room.

She couldn't sleep. She lay on her back, staring at the ceiling in the darkness. The dead man couldn't be Kane, she thought. She'd been by his campsite on her horse once after he'd left, and his tent and wagon were gone. She'd heard that his followers left before he did, going back to their homes. But surely, if he was missing, someone would have come looking for him. She thought about their first night together: how his skin felt on hers, how his face looked when she was on top of him. Being with him had seemed like the most natural thing she'd done in a long time. She groaned and turned over on her side, facing the wall. Then she heard the bedsprings creak as Edward got out of bed.

She listened as he walked quietly in her direction, closing the door to the boys' room as he passed. The footsteps stopped in the hall, and he stood in the doorway. She didn't look up. She didn't move.

"Isabel."

She didn't answer.

"I know you're awake."

He stood a while longer, then crossed the room and sat down on the edge of the bed, put his hand on her shoulder and rolled her over onto her back. "I want us to be together again," he said. "Like a man and wife are supposed to be."

He lay down on his side, his head on the pillow next to hers, stroking her hair and his breath heavy on her neck. She lay still. He moved his hand down to her breasts, touching her through her nightgown. She couldn't bear it. She pushed his hand away. He hesitated, then rolled on top of her, pinning her underneath him. He was bare-chested, wearing only his underwear. She put her palms on his chest and tried to push him away.

"I don't want this," she said.

"Think about what I want for once." He slid his left arm under her back and around her waist, pulling her tight against him. With his right hand, he pulled her nightgown up over her hips and pushed her legs apart. She resisted, but he pushed with his hand and his hips until he was between her legs.

"I don't want this," she repeated. He didn't say anything. He pushed himself inside her, then wrapped his right arm around her waist along with his left, pulling her to him as he pumped against her, slowly at first and then faster, breaking out in a sweat. She lay motionless, her eyes open but unfocused, tears rolling down her temples into her ears and onto the pillow, until he was finished. He groaned, then fell away from her onto his back, lying with his side pressed against her in the narrow bed.

She pulled her nightgown down and got up. She took the bar of soap from the bathtub and went to the bureau, pouring water from the pitcher into the wash basin, then dipping a cloth into the water and rubbing the soap onto the cloth until it was covered with lather. She reached up under her nightgown with the cloth and washed herself, rinsed the cloth and washed herself again, rinsing the cloth four more times and wiping herself until the soap was gone. She dropped the cloth back into the basin, then opened one of the bureau drawers and felt for a towel. Her fingers touched cloth, then cold metal. Carl's pistol, where she had left it last summer. Fingers trembling, she pulled the gun from the drawer, metal scraping against wood as she drew it out from under the towels. She held the gun in front of her, looking at it in the moonlight, and heard her own breathing, harsh and uneven.

"Who do you want to kill, Isabel?" Edward said quietly from across the room. "Me or you?"

She turned to him. He was lying on his back, arms crossed under his head, staring at her. The rage she'd felt earlier was gone. Now she felt nothing but utter despair – emptiness like she had never known before. She turned back to the bureau, put the pistol in the drawer, and pulled out a clean towel.

"There's nothing left to kill, Edward. We're already dead."

CHAPTER
15

I SABEL SLEPT IN THE LIVING ROOM THAT NIGHT. SHE stripped off the nightgown she was wearing and put on a clean one, found an extra blanket in the hall closet, wrapped it around her and lay on the sofa. It was a cool, clear night in late September, a breeze blowing through the open windows, the curtains in the living room slapping gently back and forth, ghostlike in the light of the moon. She shivered for a while, her muscles jerking in protest, until the heat of her body wrapped in the blanket finally warmed her. Huddled underneath, she stared out the front windows, watching the dark shape of the oak branches moving in the wind until she fell asleep.

She woke the next morning with the sunrise. The sky was clear, birds calling as the sun came up. She covered her ears and tried without success to sleep through the chorus. Eyelids heavy, she watched the light slowly enter the room. She smelled coffee, heard Edward in the kitchen and the boys murmuring sleepily in their beds. She knew there were days past when the sounds and smells of a morning like this had made her happy. She tried to remember one, but none came to mind.

She got up, the blanket still around her, and went to her bedroom to dress. She folded the blanket, took it back to the hall closet, then peeked in the boys' room. They were up, but not moving very fast. She went to Carl's room and stripped the sheets off the bed, then sat on the edge of the bed and waited. When she heard the boys go to the kitchen for breakfast, she joined them.

Edward had gone outside, and the boys sat around the table, yawning and rubbing their eyes. She cut thick slices of bread and fried them with butter, which the boys ate with honey while she scrambled eggs. She was scooping eggs onto their plates when Edward came in. She took the skillet back to the stove and cut more bread to fry, not looking at him. When the bread was ready, she put it on a plate and set it on the table in front of Edward, then turned to the boys.

"Who wants more bread?"

"Me," they all said. She went back to the stove.

"What are we going to do today, Daddy?" Samuel asked.

"Cotton's ready to pick as soon as the fields dry. We'll get ready to pick it."

The yard and garden were still too muddy for Isabel to work outside. She opened all the windows in the house and drew back the curtains to let the sunshine in, carrying a bucket of water and a rag with her and wiping the windows and windowsills as she went, her hands working in a steady rhythm while she thought about Kane.

She didn't know how to contact him. He had wanted to give her that information, but she had refused, thinking it needed to be over, knowing in the back of her mind that she could probably find him if she wanted to. But she couldn't just up and go to Memphis to look for him. She finished the last window, carried the bucket of dirty water to the back porch and emptied it into the yard, watching Edward and the boys move in and out of the barn. She set the bucket on the porch, then headed to the barn to saddle Blue. If she couldn't talk to Kane, she'd do the next best thing. She'd go talk to Doc about the dead man.

"Hey, Mama," Ben called as he saw her approach. He and James were carrying cotton sacks from the barn to hang over the fence to dry. They'd gotten wet from a leak in the roof, James explained. Edward and Samuel were repairing a wheel on one of the wagons. She went into the barn, fitted the harness over Blue's head, and threw a saddle blanket on his back.

"Where are you going?" Edward stood outside the stall.

"To town."

"What for?"

"Because I haven't been out of the house for four days, that's what for." She picked up the saddle and lifted it onto her horse. "And there's mites in the flour," she said, tightening the straps. "And the curtains are about worn out and I need some material to make new ones." She slapped Blue on the belly and tightened the saddle again. "And there's a hundred other reasons I need to go to town, but I guess I don't have to explain them all to you."

She led Blue past him and out of the barn. "There's stew on the stove if you and the boys get hungry. I'll be back by suppertime."

She pulled herself into the saddle and waved goodbye to Ben and James. She urged Blue into a gallop when she got to the road, his heels kicking up mud behind them. When she was past their property line, she felt the freedom of being away from the house and she relaxed for the first time in days.

She rode through town to Doc's house, pulled up by the gate and hopped down, then tied the reins to the fence. Shep rose to greet her, his tongue wagging, moving a little faster, but not much, now that the summer heat was over. She bent and pressed her face to his, rubbed his head and patted him, then stepped onto the porch and knocked at the screen door.

"Coming," Doc called from inside.

"Isabel!" He opened the door, drew her inside and hugged her.

"It's been a while," she said.

"Too long. Come in and sit."

He led her to the sofa, and they talked about the rain and the crops and what the boys had been doing.

"I guess you heard about the body they found down in the river," he said at last.

"Yes. The boys never saw so much excitement."

"Something tells me that's why you're here."

"It's one reason. Do you know any more?"

He shook his head. "There wasn't much of him left. I hate autopsies."

She patted his hand.

"We know a few things about him. One leg was a little shorter than the other, but not so much that folks would notice. He broke his left arm a few years back. And he was shot. One bullet to the temple that killed him."

She drew in a sharp breath. "How tall was he?"

"Average height. Not as tall as the sheriff. Not as tall, say, as that preacher who came through last summer."

She closed her eyes in relief.

"So the question is, who is he?" he said. "And who killed him? You reckon the Reverend Kane would know anything about that?"

"What makes you ask that?"

He shrugged. "They found him down around where Kane was staying. Course, there's no telling where on the river he started out. I'm sure Sheriff will be thinking about all the possibilities."

She stood. "I'm sure he will." She took his hand and helped him up and he saw her to the door.

"Reckon it's almost picking time," he said.

"Yes. Edward's getting ready. Soon as the fields are dry enough, he'll start."

"He have all the hired help he needs?"

"I suppose. We haven't talked about it. But I better find out how many he's got since I'll be cooking for them."

She kissed him goodbye.

"Don't be such a stranger," he said.

On her way out of town, she stopped at the store and bought a newspaper and a sack of flour. She looked at fabric for curtains but didn't see anything she liked for a price she wanted to pay. Wally assured her he could order anything she wanted, just let him know.

"Sounds like a project for this winter," he said.

Isabel blanched. She didn't want to think about the winter months ahead and the long hours they'd all be cooped up in the house together.

Edward and the boys were sitting down to supper when she got home. She asked Edward when the picking would start and how many men he would have.

"Day after tomorrow if the weather holds. Should be twenty or so hired hands if they all show up."

"Ben and James can stay with me," she said. "They can help with chores then help me bring the food."

Ben and James were unhappy about that. "Daddy's paying Samuel to pick cotton," James said. "We want to get paid, too."

"You do the chores," Edward said. "Then you can come pick cotton 'til you get tired, which I reckon will take about half an hour, and then you can help your mama with the food."

"Will you pay us?" Ben asked.

"You eat. That's pay enough," Edward said. "But," he added, "I'd be willing to pay a little. Depends on how much cotton I see in your sacks."

Ben and James were satisfied with that. She knew Edward was right. They'd get out in the fields with high ambition, and after a few minutes they'd be tired and wanting to go back to the house. She rose from the table and sent the boys to bed. "It'll be long, hard days once the picking starts."

Edward took the newspaper she had bought to the living room. She was sweeping the kitchen floor when he appeared at the doorway.

"Where did you go today besides the store?"

She swept harder. "To see Doc."

"Find out anything about the dead man?"

She stooped and swept the little pile of dirt she had collected into the dustpan. "No. He asked if I knew about it and I said I did. That was all." She finished sweeping, took the dustpan outside and poured its contents into the yard, then put the broom and dustpan away and went down the hall to her bedroom.

Edward was lying in bed with his arms crossed behind his head. She went to the bureau and, opening the drawers one by one, took out her underclothes and nightgowns. While he watched, she moved to the closet, taking as many dresses, shirts and trousers as she could carry. Her arms full, she turned to Edward, who stared wordlessly at the clothes she held. She crossed the room, shifting the bundle slightly when a shirt threatened to fall off the pile, took her things to Carl's room, and put them away.

She lay on the narrow bed, feeling the weariness in her muscles, feeling it right down to her bones. She sighed, her eyes closed, already half asleep. She tensed, awake again, when she heard the bedsprings creak as Edward rolled over. She listened until she heard him snore. Then she finally relaxed and fell asleep.

By the first of October it was dry enough to pick cotton. It would hurry them to get the crop in before winter, and there were thirty acres of wheat to thresh after the cotton was in. Edward and Samuel and the hired hands worked every day without stopping, even on Sundays. Isabel spent the mornings cooking for the men then worked until dark every day to keep up with the chores and the washing and ironing. Edward and the boys fell into bed exhausted every night. She was relieved that she and Edward had little opportunity to speak to each other.

She stayed up for a while each night after her family was asleep. Sometimes she sat in the living room and read by the light of a lantern, the rest of the house quiet and dark. Other times she sat on the front porch listening to the night sounds, occasionally seeing a falling star out of the corner of her eye and catching a glimpse of it the second before it was gone. She stayed awake as long as she could, her only hope for sleep to tire herself out until she could hardly walk to bed. Even then, her mind would often wake up the minute her head hit the pillow, recalling Kane's lips and hands and the way they moved, questioning, to make her body answer. She grieved the loss of him, not like she still grieved Carl, but feeling the loss of the only thing in years that had brought her comfort and made her forget her sorrow for a little while. The longer Kane was gone, the more sorrow, her familiar companion, returned.

Toward the end of October, Doc and Sheriff came to visit. Edward almost had the crop in, the wagons with their high rails having left for the cotton gin in a steady stream over the past weeks, returning for their next load empty except for stray tufts of cotton stuck here and there. It was a Tuesday night. Isabel was setting the table when the sheriff's car pulled into the lane, and he and Doc got out. She hadn't been to town in days and was glad to see someone besides Edward, the boys, and the hired hands. She led them to the living room and told them to sit, that they had to stay and eat. They said they would.

Twilight turned to dark that settled in on the house along with the evening chill as they waited for Edward and the boys. They finally heard the wagon and saw the swaying light of the lantern as it approached, the sound of voices carrying on the night air. She went to the back porch and told them they had company. After supper the men pushed back their chairs and Isabel sat at the table with them.

"We know who it was we found in the river," Sheriff said.

Edward sat up straighter.

"Appears to be Piggott. His kin haven't seen him since he left the hills last spring, and the shorter leg and broken arm match what they tell us about him."

The kitchen was suddenly quiet, as Isabel and Edward and their guests drank coffee and avoided looking at each other.

"Are you sure it's him?" Edward said.

"Pretty sure," Sheriff said.

"Any idea who killed him?" Isabel said.

Sheriff shook his head. "All kinds of people might want him dead. But no one comes to mind." He looked at Edward, then at her. "The way I figure it, we let it go. What's done is done. Everybody should go on about their business."

"What happens to Caroline now?" she asked. "And his other children?"

"The other children are still living with their kinfolk. Piggott's mother is coming to get Caroline. Said they'd be here before winter to fetch her."

"Did you tell them where the girl is?" Edward asked.

"No. No need to drag Sister into it any more than she already is. Doc says he'll go get Caroline and she can stay with Hazel until her family gets here."

Isabel rose and began collecting the dishes. "No need for that," she said. "I'll go. And Caroline can stay here like she did before."

Edward looked at her sharply. "There's a lot of work to be done around here."

Doc and the sheriff shot uncomfortable glances at each other.

"The cotton's almost in," she said. "I'll get Everitt's wife to come while I'm gone. I may stay in Memphis a few days, but we'll have Caroline back in plenty of time."

Doc stood. "This old man needs his rest. We'd best be going, Sheriff."

"Doc, maybe you want to go along with Isabel," Edward said. "Be a good excuse for a visit with Sister."

Doc looked at Isabel. "I told Sister the last time I was in Memphis not to expect me back soon," he said. "It's too crowded. I told her if she got to wanting to see me, the train runs both ways."

Isabel and Edward walked them to the sheriff's car. "Come see me before you leave," Doc said.

"I will."

"Doc could have gone after her," Edward said as they walked back into the house.

"The trip would be hard on him. And Caroline will feel more comfortable coming home with me." She went to the sink to finish the dishes.

"How long you reckon you'll stay?"

She scraped chicken bones from a plate into the scrap bucket, put the plate in the water, and picked up another one.

"Probably not long. But it's hard to say."

Isabel told Everitt Wilson the next morning that his wife should come on Thursday and plan on helping out around the house for a week or more. She knew they needed the money and Everitt said she'd be glad to come. Thursday morning Ruth Wilson knocked on the back door shortly after Edward and the boys had left for the fields.

She had hired Ruth on occasion before. Her cooking and cleaning weren't up to Isabel's standards, but she would do an adequate job. Isabel sat at the kitchen table with her and made a list of what to cook and when she should do the washing and ironing and cleaning. She didn't think Ruth could read, although she pretended to, but Ruth would take the list home to Everitt and he would go over it with her each morning before she came.

Isabel left Ruth cleaning the kitchen and went to see Doc. A buggy was parked in front of his house when she got there, so she waited on the front porch. Before long, he came to the door with Laverne Emerson, a widow slightly younger than him who lived in the next town. Isabel spoke to her briefly, then Doc escorted Laverne to her buggy. Laverne was reluctant to leave, but Doc said goodbye and walked back to the house. Accepting momentary defeat, Laverne waved at Isabel, then drove away. Doc let out a sigh as he sat down next to her.

"I can guess what's ailing Laverne," she said.

"I'm charging a fee next time she comes. Even though there's nothing wrong with her."

"I imagine she'll find it a small price to pay for you listening to her heart."

He pretended to be shocked. She laughed and patted his leg.

"Are you leaving for Memphis tomorrow?" he asked.

"You're changing the subject. But yes. I came to see if you have anything to send to Sister."

He did. They went inside and he gave her an envelope that she knew had money in it. Doc had given Sister money for years, always worried about her, even though she protested and tried not to take it. He would have done the same for Isabel but was afraid of hurting Edward's feelings. She slipped the envelope into her pocket.

"I'll bring you something from Memphis. What do you want?"

He waved his hand in dismissal. "I don't need a thing." They walked outside to the porch. The wind picked up, catching the leaves on the trees in a shimmer of fall color. She shivered and Doc looked up at the trees.

"Come back soon, Isabel."

She tried to smile. "Don't you worry." She kissed him goodbye and patted Shep on her way to the car, then waved to him again as she drove away. She drove through town toward home, but on New Caney Road she stopped and turned the car around, drove back to town, and pulled up to the jail.

She opened the door and stepped inside to a tiny reception area. The sheriff's office was to the left, and in the back were two cells, unoccupied at the moment. Sheriff Dennis stepped out of his office.

"Isabel." He motioned for her to sit down, and she took the chair behind the reception desk. Sheriff leaned his huge bulk against the wall near the door, looking alternately at his feet and out the window. "You're not a visitor here very often."

"No. It's Edward's job to get the hired hands out of jail."

He nodded thoughtfully.

"I suppose he comes every once in a while just to pay you a visit."

He cleared his throat. "He does."

She leaned forward and rested her forearms on the desk. "I understand he came here the day he got home from Memphis. To report on taking Caroline to stay with Sister."

The sheriff examined his fingernails, rubbed his chin, then shifted and crossed his hands behind his back. "He did come here."

"It was early afternoon when Samuel dropped him off," she said. "But it was suppertime when you brought him home. You must have had a lot to talk about."

He shuffled his feet slightly. "As I recall, Edward wasn't here all afternoon. He borrowed one of my horses – said he had some people to see. He was gone a few hours. When he came back, I took him home."

She examined the surface of the desk, scarred from years of stray ink marks and knife scratches and indentations from boot heels. "Who do you suppose he went to see?"

He sighed heavily and rubbed his face. "I don't know, Isabel. And I don't intend to find out."

Her stomach roiled. She pushed back from the desk, the chair scraping on the cement floor. The sheriff straightened so he was no longer leaning against the wall and put his hands on his hips.

"Edward's a good man," he said. "One of the most respected men in this community. You won't find a better man than Edward Fuller."

He held out his hand and she shook it. "Thank you, Sheriff." She opened the door and closed it carefully behind her as she left.

Edward and the boys were quiet at the breakfast table Friday morning. Ruth had come early and helped put the food on the table, moving awkwardly around the kitchen and almost dropping a skillet of eggs. Isabel knew Ruth would relax once she was gone. Samuel, watching Ruth with a bemused expression, finally spoke.

"Why do you have to go to Memphis, Mama?"

"Someone has to fetch Caroline. Why wouldn't I go?"

"Because she's not family. We hardly know her."

"She needs our support. Our charity." She thought Edward might contribute to the conversation, but he didn't.

"You've already bought her clothes and made her a dress," Samuel said. "Kept her and fed her and we took her to Memphis. Seems to me that's enough."

She stood. "It isn't. There's still more to do." She left Ruth to wash the dishes and went to Carl's room to pack. She was folding the last few items into the suitcase when she heard Edward's step in the hall.

"I'll take you to the train station," he said.

She bent over the suitcase. "You could send Samuel."

"No. I'll take you. I'll be in around twelve."

He walked through the kitchen and out the back door. She watched from the window as he collected the boys and they climbed into the wagon, the boys pushing to claim the seat beside their father. He drove the wagon toward the lane, and she went to the back porch to wave goodbye.

"Bring us something from Memphis," Ben called.

"You were just in Memphis yourself," she called back.

"Please, Mama," James said, bouncing in the back of the wagon.

"We'll see." She went back inside, where Ruth had finished cleaning the kitchen and was making the beds. She closed the doors to Carl's room to dress.

She put on the gray dress Edward had bought her in Memphis, then went to the mirror to pin up her hair. Bending closer to examine her face, she saw that she was gaunt and pale, with faint circles under her eyes, and realized for the first time that she had lost weight. The dress that had fit her at the end of the summer hung loosely from her hips. She looked colorless in gray, like a woman in mourning. She took off the dress and packed it in the suitcase, put on a navy-blue skirt and a white blouse, then opened the bedroom door and went to the hall closet.

She rummaged behind the sheets and towels until she found a worn satin bag wrapped with a frayed ribbon. She took the bag back to Carl's room, stood in front of the mirror again while she opened it, and pulled out a small jar of rouge. The rosy cream inside was cracked and dry. She went to the wash basin and sprinkled a few drops of water inside the jar, then rubbed until she saw color on her fingers, went back to the mirror and dabbed her cheeks. The lipstick was in the same dried condition, but she added water and rubbed until there was enough red to put on her lips, then opened a jar of powder and brushed it across her face.

She put the jars and the lipstick back into the satin bag, stuffed the bag into the bottom of the suitcase, and snapped it shut. She carried the mirror to the window so she could see herself in the full light of the sun. She hung it back on its nail, then wet a towel in the wash basin and scrubbed her face, the rouge and powder staining the towel. She picked up the suitcase and carried it and the towel to the back porch, dropped the towel on the laundry pile and set the suitcase down, then went back into the house to check on Ruth one more time while she waited for Edward.

He came at twelve and she went out to meet him. He stood at the bottom of the steps and looked up at her, then reached for the suitcase and loaded it into the wagon. She sat beside him, and they drove to the train station in silence.

Otis Ivey happened to be at the station when they arrived, sitting on a bench by the tracks, and jumped up to man the ticket office when he saw them coming. Isabel climbed down from the wagon, feeling Otis's eyes on her as he peered out the window of the office. Edward tied the team to a post, lifted the suitcase from the back of the wagon, and they walked side by side to the ticket office. He set the suitcase down.

"Afternoon Edward, Isabel," Otis said.

"Afternoon," they said.

"Looks like somebody's going somewhere."

"I am," she said. "I need a ticket to Memphis, please."

"Round trip?"

"One way for now."

"That'll be one dollar to Jonesboro and four dollars for the transfer from Jonesboro to Memphis," Otis said.

She opened her purse and pushed the dollar bills for the tickets through the window. Otis slid the tickets toward her, and she put them in her purse.

"Train's running a little late today," he said.

Edward picked up the suitcase and carried it to the bench. Isabel followed him and they sat down. She checked the contents of her purse, snapped it shut again, looked down the empty tracks, and adjusted the cuffs on her sleeves. He leaned forward to look down the tracks, took off his hat and rested his forearms on his thighs. He fiddled with the brim of his hat, turning it over slowly and then back again.

"When you reckon you're coming back?"

"I'm not sure."

He turned his hat a few more times. "What are you planning to do in Memphis besides fetch Caroline?"

She folded her hands over her purse. "I don't have any plans." She looked at the clock. They sat quietly a while longer, then he cleared his throat.

"I don't know how it got like this between us," he said, his voice strained and low. "It hasn't been the same since Carl died." He looked up at her. "I don't know what to say to you anymore."

She stared at the clasp on her purse. The gold finish was scratched, and the clasp didn't fasten all the way anymore. He sat up.

"Don't you have anything to say to me?"

Anger shot through her in a wave, her hands tightening on her purse, her neck reddening, wanting to stand up and hit him and scream until there was nothing left to scream.

"What do you want me to say, Edward? You get what you want from me. Even when I've got nothing left to give, you take what you want."

He leaned forward on his elbows again and rubbed his face in his hands. "I didn't mean it to be like that. I just want you to come back to me, Isabel. I want it to be like it was."

She groaned and shook her head. "Don't you see it won't ever be like it was? How it was, I had your babies and raised them right. I worked harder than any man and I was a woman to you in ways men dream about. How it is now, you cut the life out of me. You sent my boy to die." Her voice broke.

He dropped his head. "I didn't send him, Isabel. I said it was the right thing for him to go. But he was going on his own. He was a man making his own choice."

"He was a boy. And he was scared, Edward. He was so scared. The night before he left, I couldn't sleep. I rocked on the porch, and I prayed to God to take me, not my boy. Then I went in to kiss him good night and he was still awake, worrying about leaving like he always worried about things. I lay down beside him like I did when he was little."

She gasped quietly and struggled to breathe. "He cried, Edward. He laid his head on my shoulder and cried and I rocked him and told him he was my baby, he'd always be my baby, until he finally fell asleep. And I knew I was lying there with my boy for the last time."

She looked at him. His head was bowed, tears streaming down his face, and she watched them drop silently, one by one, onto the platform by his feet. The train whistled in the distance. She stood.

"I loved him as much as you, Isabel." His voice was so low she could hardly hear him.

The train pulled into the station.

"You promised me, Edward. You promised me a long time ago that you'd look out for him. And you could have stopped him. He was looking to you to tell him what a man would do. No one else around here volunteered. If he hadn't gone, he'd be living life as a man instead of dying a cold, scared boy a long way from home."

"It might not have made a difference that he volunteered, Isabel. He might have gotten called up anyway, and he would have had to go."

"We'll never know that, will we? Look at our life now. And tell me it didn't make a difference."

She picked up the suitcase. He stood and reached for it, but she turned away. "I'll let you know when I'll be back," she said. She walked to the train and stepped aboard, stowed her suitcase, then settled herself into a seat by the window. She looked out at Edward, sitting on the bench again, head in his hands. He didn't look up as the train pulled away.

CHAPTER
16

THE ROWS OF COTTON STRETCHING AWAY FROM THE
tracks beat a silent rhythm to mark Isabel's passing, most of
them brown and forlorn as the picking season drew to a close,
but some still lined with stalks bearing their white fruit like
an invitation. Occasionally a child looked up and waved over the straw
hats of parents bent over their labor in the fields, unmoved by the sound
of the train. More passengers got on at each stop as they drew closer to
Memphis, Isabel a witness behind the window glass to their partings.
At one stop she saw young lovers embrace, the boy leaning back in the
shadows against the wall of the station, the girl pressed up against him,
his hand sliding down the back of her dress. They moved apart, and she
saw that the boy was instead a man, a drummer by the looks of him,
and twice the girl's age. The girl wore red lipstick, smeared now above
her lips and on her chin. The man slapped her lightly on the buttocks,
carried his bag onto the train, and stopped beside Isabel. She looked
him squarely in the face, then set her purse on the seat beside her. He
tipped his hat and moved on.

Night fell, and she dozed. She woke as the train passed over the
Frisco Bridge to Memphis, the lights of the city near. Suspended over
darkness, she looked down at the inky black of the Mississippi River,
imagining the train turning abruptly off the bridge and plunging in a

long arc into the water, the connections between the cars shattering apart as the nose of the locomotive hit the river bottom, and the loud sighs of metal as the train sank slowly into the depths. She rubbed her eyes as they cleared the bridge and pulled into Union Station, collected her purse and suitcase, and stepped down from the train. She heard someone calling her name and turned to see Sister hurrying toward her and Caroline lagging several steps behind. She dropped her bag and surrendered to Sister's embrace.

"Let's have a look at you," Sister said, pushing back, her hands on Isabel's shoulders. Isabel was glad to see her but brushed her skirt and smoothed her hair to avoid Sister's observant eye.

"I'd hate to see what I look like after that train ride." She gently freed herself from Sister's grasp and waved to Caroline, who was watching shyly.

"Caroline," Sister said. "Come say hello to Mrs. Fuller."

Caroline came toward them hesitantly and tucked herself under Sister's outstretched arm.

"It's nice to see you again," Isabel said. "You look well."

"Of course she does," Sister said when Caroline didn't answer. "Hasty's done his best to spoil her, but like he says, you can't spoil a fine girl like Caroline. Now let's get home. Hasty's waiting in the car."

Isabel picked up her suitcase and followed Sister's bustling retreat. Hasty jumped from the car when he saw them coming and stored her suitcase in the trunk. Isabel sat in the back seat with Caroline, half listening to Sister's chatter and murmuring an occasional response when Sister pointed out landmarks barely visible in the darkness. She felt Caroline watching her, but when she turned to look, Caroline jerked her head away. She wondered if the child knew her father was dead, and whether she would think her prospects with his kin were any better than her life before.

The Walkers lived in a two-story house on a quiet street in Annesdale Park. Although she had been there several times, Isabel couldn't stop herself from gawking at the proudly lit, well-kept homes they passed. When they arrived at the Walker home, Sister ordered Hasty to show her to the guest room, then come help in the kitchen. Hasty seemed to take Sister's bossiness in good-natured stride, waving off Isabel's insistence that she knew where the room was and could manage the suitcase herself. She followed him up the stairs, waiting just inside the door while he sat the suitcase on a chair in the corner. Sister's handiwork was everywhere, with crochet on the bureau and a quilt and handmade pillows on the bed.

"Hope you have enough room in here," Hasty said. "Mae's filled it up with gewgaws and furniture so you can hardly move." He stepped around her to the door. "Bathroom's down the hall, as you probably remember."

She set her purse on the bureau and hung her jacket in the closet, then went to the bathroom. She used the toilet then stood in front of the sink, running her hands across the cool white porcelain and sniffing the new bar of Ivory soap before washing her hands. She held her hands under the faucet, letting the warm water run down her forearms, then washed her face. She dried her hands and stepped out of the bathroom, hoping her manner didn't reveal what a luxury the past few minutes had been.

Sister and Hasty were waiting in the kitchen, a place set for her at the table. They had sent Caroline to bed. Sister fed her fried chicken and apple pie until she insisted she couldn't eat any more. Hasty washed the dishes, then Sister sent him to bed as well. "I'll sit and visit with Isabel for just a minute, then I'll be right behind you," she said.

"I've never seen Mae visit for just a minute," he said. "Don't let her keep you up all night."

Sister led her to the sofa in the living room, then moved a chair slightly so she could see her better, Isabel thinking to herself that Hasty was right about Sister's visiting habits as she watched her settle in.

"Caroline looks good," she said.

Sister nodded. "We'll miss her when she's gone. What do you know about these kinfolk of hers?"

"Not much. The grandmother says she can raise Caroline. I hope she's a better human being than that son of hers was."

"Lord, yes. I'm not saying killing's right. But some people just need killing and it sounds like Caroline's daddy was one of them. And if you ever say I said that I'll swear you were mistaken."

"You and I generally see eye to eye on human nature. Does Caroline know he's dead?"

"Yes, we told her. I haven't seen her shed a tear over him yet. But sometimes she runs off and hides, and it takes us forever to find her."

"She had a lot to hide from. Still, she's likely sad. She had feelings for her daddy, even as mean as he was."

Sister asked how things were at the Fuller household and Isabel told her they were fine. The boys were growing, and it looked like they'd make a good crop this year even with all the rain. Not much to report, she said. Then she yawned. Sister took the hint. They carried their cups to the kitchen and Isabel stood at the back door, parting the lace curtains to look out into the night. She could see dark outlines of trees in the back yard, faint movement as they bent slightly in the wind. She heard a dog bark somewhere down the street. She let the curtain fall.

"What do you want to do tomorrow?" Sister asked. "Shop? You have to do some shopping when you come to Memphis."

"Yes, I need a few things. And maybe a visit to the beauty parlor. I'm thinking about cutting my hair."

"Oh my." Hands on her hips, Sister eyed her critically. "A bob's the latest thing. But your hair, Isabel. I would give anything to have your hair."

"It's a nuisance. I wear it up all the time anyway, and it's hard to take care of."

"If you insist. I'll call the beauty parlor in the morning."

Isabel woke the next morning to the sounds from Sister's kitchen, Caroline's chattering, Hasty's low response, chairs scraping on tiles. She smelled coffee and bacon, heard the telephone ring and Sister's voice when she answered. It was raining. Drizzling, more like it. She lay in bed in the early morning gloom, watching rainwater run down the windowpanes. The bedroom was cool, the darkness close and inviting. She closed her eyes and drew the covers tight around her.

She had dreamed the night before about Edward, and about Kane. Like many of her dreams, this one was shocking. She was standing somewhere in her nightgown and Edward stood a few feet from her, naked and erect. A woman she didn't know stood beside him, fully clothed. Edward walked to Isabel and took her hand, and she stroked him the way he wanted until he spent himself in her hand. Isabel went to the woman, who had watched silently, and wiped her hand on the woman's shoulder. "My husband's seed," Isabel said. Then she felt her nightgown being lifted and turned to see Kane behind her. Kane pushed inside her and she wrapped her arms and legs around him, aroused from what she had done to Edward, pulling him fiercely to her and rocking hard against him. As she thought about the dream, longing hit her in a wave, stronger than it had been for weeks, and she groaned and opened her eyes. *It must be because I know he's somewhere near*, she thought. She pushed the covers aside and got out of bed.

Sister appeared at the bottom of the stairs as she stepped into the hall.

"You don't have to get dressed for breakfast," she said.

"I'll be right down." She went to the bathroom, then back to her room to get her robe and, wrapping it around her, padded down the stairs in her bare feet. "Where's Caroline?"

Hasty lowered his newspaper. "Playing with a neighbor girl. Sleep well?"

"Very well, thank you."

"You look better," Sister said. "I was worried about you last night – you were so pale."

She set a plate in front of her – biscuits and gravy – and Isabel suddenly was hungrier than she'd been in a long time. She picked up her fork and ate, stuffing large bites of biscuit dripping with gravy into her mouth as fast as she could chew and swallow. Hasty folded the newspaper and set it on the table, Sister sat down with a cup of coffee, and the two of them watched while she ate. She sopped up gravy with the last biscuit until the plate was clean, then looked up. Sister and Hasty were still watching her. She flushed.

"More biscuits?" Hasty said.

She shook her head and stood up to take her dishes to the sink.

"You sit," Sister said. "Read the newspaper." She brought the coffee pot to the table and poured. "I got an appointment for you at the beauty parlor. Four o'clock. We'll shop first."

"That sounds fine." Isabel turned a page of the newspaper and caught her breath. On the inside corner was a small advertisement. "The Time of the End," it read. "You soon will have to face God." <u>Services Tuesdays, Thursdays, and Sundays at Full Gospel Tabernacle, Nina Pressler, Pastor, with a special message from Reverend Micah Kane.</u> "Everybody Welcome."

"What is it?" Sister asked, looking over her shoulder.

"Just a name I know." She tapped the paper lightly. "A preacher by that name came through town last summer. Edward let him hold a revival up by the pecan grove."

"That's him," Sister said. "Doc told me about him and I went to see him one night."

"Who's this Nina Pressler?" Isabel asked.

"Well," Hasty said, settling back in his chair. "She's caused a little stir around Memphis. Her daddy was a real estate developer, made a lot of money after the war. He died a year or so ago and left Nina and her mother well off. No one knows quite why Nina decided to take up the ministry, and her mother's apparently not happy about it, but she's gotten quite a following."

"Has she," Isabel said.

"I don't think Kane's been with her long," Sister said.

"Probably not. It's just been a couple of months since he was at our place."

"Would you like to see him while you're here?"

She folded the newspaper and drank the last of her coffee. "No." She carried her cup to the sink and went upstairs to get dressed. She collected her hairbrush and satin bag and set them on the edge of the sink in the bathroom, then turned on the water in the bathtub, slipped off her robe, and drew her nightgown over her head. There was a long mirror on the bathroom door, and she stood naked in front of it, examining herself while the bathtub filled. She had lost weight, but she wasn't thin. She turned and looked over her shoulder. It wasn't vanity so much that made her look. More curiosity. It had been a long time since she'd seen herself like this.

The tub was almost full. She turned off the faucets and lowered herself through the steam into the water, which was perfect – not like at home where she could never get it the right temperature. She stayed in the bath until she thought Sister might be wondering about her, then brushed her teeth, put on a little rouge and powder, dressed, and went downstairs.

Sister was waiting. "Hasty's out in the car," she said, pulling on her coat. "He'll drive us downtown unless you want to try your hand at driving in the city."

Isabel shook her head. "I'm not about to. Not that you'd ever talk Hasty into it anyway." She followed Sister out the front door.

"Look at that," Sister said. Hasty's Packard sat gleaming in the driveway and his legs stuck out from under it, knees bent toward the sky. "He loves his fool cars more than anything. I never know when he'll come home with a new one. He'll show up honking and grinning all proud, and I'll have to come out and see."

Hasty rolled out from under the car and raised himself to his feet. "I need a fancy car for driving pretty ladies around."

Sister looked pleased. Isabel was amused. Pushing seventy, both of them. There was a time when she'd thought she and Edward would be that way when they got old. Hasty opened the door for Sister and Isabel crawled into the back seat.

She watched the sights out the window as they drove and wondered what it would be like if she lived in the city, married to a man like Hasty, in younger days of course, and didn't have to get up every morning before dawn for chores. Looking after a house while the boys were in school didn't seem like enough to keep her occupied. She'd have to find something else to do to keep her busy and out of trouble. She smiled to herself. *I stirred up some trouble without even having time to do it,* she thought. *No telling what I'd get myself into in Memphis.*

As he always did when she came to visit, Hasty took Isabel on a short tour of downtown, pointing out the office buildings under construction, the new Lowenstein's store being built where the old Peabody Hotel had been, the Loew's State and Pantages theaters, and the Piggly Wiggly. After Sister complained that Isabel hadn't come to Memphis to look at real estate, Hasty dropped them in front of Goldsmith's department store at Main and Gayoso.

"Pick us up at Miss Vi's at five o'clock," Sister said, and slammed the car door. Hasty saluted, then eased the Packard back into traffic. Sister took Isabel's arm and guided her through the front door of the store, where she soon lost herself in the merchandise. She looked at silk stockings but settled on four pairs of cotton for 99 cents, less than the cost of one pair of silk. She bought two blouses, one voile and one suzette, and splurged on a pair of $2.98 leather pumps with one-button straps. Her greatest pleasure was lingering over the underclothes without the watchful eye of Wally Lambert, who was known to discuss his customers' purchases with the town at large. There were satin camisoles, and lace brassieres, and drawers that barely covered any leg.

Sister led her through the dresses, pulling one after another off the rack and Isabel shaking her head each time.

"Just try one on," Sister said. "It won't hurt to try one on."

She finally relented and found a dress that had caught her eye earlier. A salesgirl carried it to the dressing room and Sister followed her in. Isabel waited until the salesgirl left, then went into the room and set her packages on the floor. Sister settled into a chair in the corner. Isabel hesitated, then turned away and began to unbutton her blouse.

"For heaven's sake," Sister said. "I don't care what you look like with your clothes off. A sight better than me, that's for sure."

Isabel blushed. She shrugged off her blouse and stepped out of her skirt, handing them to Sister, then took the dress off its hanger and pulled it over her head. She smoothed it over her hips and let Sister fasten the buttons down the back, then stepped to the mirror for a look.

"Beautiful," Sister said.

It was. Ivory georgette for spring, sleeveless, with a scooped neck, embroidery and a silk sash at the waist, and a hemline that stopped just below the knee. The sight of her arms and legs so exposed was shocking.

"I think they ran out of material," she said. She looked at Sister and they began to laugh.

"Dresses get shorter every year," Sister said. "It's hard to imagine they could get much shorter."

Isabel put her hands on her hips and strutted around the tiny dressing room.

"I could cause a commotion in this dress."

"It sure would make Edward sit up and take notice. He'd send you to Memphis more often if you came home looking like that."

Isabel stopped short. She turned her back to Sister. "Undo me."

Sister pursed her lips and reached for the first button.

"Did you see anything else you might like to try on?"

She shook her head. "Edward bought me a new dress when he was here last summer. Another one would be too much."

Sister hung the dress back on its hanger and carried it out to the sales-girl while Isabel dressed. They went from Goldsmith's to Lowenstein's, then on to Kress's, where Isabel bought new rouge and lipstick. By mid-afternoon she was exhausted. Sister appeared unfazed.

"We have just enough time to stop at Britling's to get a bite to eat," Sister said. It was getting colder. Head bowed against the wind and clutching her thin coat tighter around her neck, Isabel was beginning to regret their decision to do anything but go on to the beauty parlor when Sister pointed with her elbow at a sign just ahead on the other side of the street. They crossed at the light and, ducking between people hurrying in the other direction, opened the door to the cafeteria and went inside. They walked past a long counter to the last booth in a row only half occupied, put their packages on the floor under their feet and sat down to lamb stew, chocolate pudding, and large glasses of Coca-Cola. Isabel insisted on paying for their meal.

Miss Vi's Beauty Parlor was down a few blocks and around the corner. A bell chimed when they stepped inside to smells of wet and shampoo and curling lotion. Miss Vi fluttered a howdy do and said to set themselves down while she finished an ample woman planted firmly in a swivel chair facing a large mirror. They waited politely while the lady complained about her daughter-in-law and Miss Vi brushed and patted and hummed sympathetically. Just when Isabel thought there was nothing more to be done to the woman's hair, she found another little spot that needed adjusting. She didn't appear to feel pressed by other customers waiting.

Miss Vi finally eased the woman towards the door, apologizing afterwards while she swept the floor around the chair.

"She's your customer today," Sister said, pointing at Isabel. She made introductions and Miss Vi patted the seat of the chair. Isabel sat down, and Miss Vi positioned herself behind her.

"What are we doing today?" she asked, unpinning Isabel's hair and running her fingers through it as it fell down her back.

"I'd like a bob."

Miss Vi looked at her in the mirror and lifted the long, luxurious locks. "It'll be quite a change."

"I'm ready for a change."

"Of course you are. We'll cut it, then wash it. It'll style real pretty with all this curl in it."

She made a part in the middle, separated a strand of hair on the left side of Isabel's face, then picked up her scissors and snipped. When she made another cut and the strand fell just above Isabel's shoulders, Sister drew in a sharp breath.

"Too late to go back now," Miss Vi said.

"No reason to," Isabel said. She watched in the mirror as Miss Vi worked her way from the left to the back to the right of her head, separating strand after strand and cutting. Hair floated to the floor, the long black curls discarded, their familiarity lost already as they settled on the linoleum in a cloud around her chair.

"We could stop at this length," Miss Vi said, finishing the first round of cutting. "You can still pin it up, but it won't be so hard to work with."

"No. Keep going."

She started on the left side again, pulling a strand of hair firmly between her index and middle fingers and cutting at the jaw line. She worked methodically, quicker this time, pulling and snipping and gently pushing Isabel's head into position. She finally stopped and looked up.

"Now the wash. Then I'll trim it up a little bit." She led Isabel to the wash basin in the corner. Isabel eased her head back into the basin and closed her eyes, falling into a trance as warm water flowed through her hair and firm fingers scrubbed her scalp. A warm rinse, then the water stopped, and Miss Vi wrapped a towel around her head. Isabel sat up groggily.

"It's the best thing in the world having someone wash your hair for you. Some of my ladies come in every week just to have me wash their hair."

Isabel sat in front of the mirror again. "Every week?" She was shocked at the thought of the expense. "I can't imagine it." Miss Vi pushed her head forward and the snipping resumed. "Then again," she said, chin to her chest, "I might be able to imagine it."

"Of course you could, honey." She put her scissors down and picked up a jar of pomade, rubbing a little into her palms and then through Isabel's hair.

"A few minutes to dry and you'll be set." She took Isabel to sit by a pot-bellied stove, then went to visit with Sister. Isabel couldn't hear what they were saying, but she could see they were chatty, drawing their heads close together and laughing. Occasionally they would look out the window at someone passing by, then bend to each other again for more talk. *Sister made a place for herself in Memphis*, she thought. *Nobody looks at her like she's country come to town. If Sister could do it, why can't I?* She shook her head. *What's gotten into me? Edward would never let me take the boys, and I could never leave without them.*

They seemed to have forgotten she was there. She felt her hair and shook her head until Miss Vi finally noticed and jumped up. "I didn't mean to roast you," she apologized, seating Isabel in front of the mirror again. Sister stood by Isabel's chair while Miss Vi finished styling. Then both women stepped back.

Isabel stared at herself in the mirror. Her hair fell in short waves just below her ears, a few strands curling to the right across her forehead. The short cut made her eyes appear even larger, her jaw more angular. She felt lightheaded and free. She wanted to laugh and run her fingers through her hair and shake her head wildly from side to side. *They'd think I was crazy*, she thought, *even crazier than they probably already think I am.* She turned her head to the left, then to the right, and rubbed the back of her neck. She grinned.

"I like it."

Miss Vi beamed. Isabel got up from the chair and found her purse. While she was counting out the money for the haircut and thanking Miss Vi for fitting her into her schedule, a horn sounded outside.

"No trouble at all," Miss Vi said.

The horn sounded again.

"If Hasty doesn't stop with that fool noise," Sister said. Miss Vi saw them to the door. Hasty got out of the car and Sister fussed at him for honking instead of coming inside, but Hasty paid no attention. He looked at Isabel, walking in a circle around her so he could see her from every side.

"My, oh my," he said.

"What do you think?"

"Makes you look ten years younger."

She felt her face and neck turn red. He helped her and Sister into the car and started the engine. Isabel looked out the window as they drove away from the beauty parlor. "It feels good," she said. "Not ten years younger. But good."

Hasty dropped them at home, then went down the street to fetch Caroline from the neighbor's house. The girl was fascinated by Isabel's hair.

"Why'd you do it?"

"I'm not sure."

"Fashion," Sister said. "A woman has to keep up with fashion."

"The boys won't like it," Caroline said.

"They may not. We'll find out when we get home."

Caroline's chatter died, and she was quiet during supper.

"How was your day, Caroline?" Hasty asked.

"Fine."

"Do you want to play dominoes after supper?"

"I don't feel like it."

"I guess we're all tired," Sister said, "everyone's so quiet."

Caroline set her milk glass down hard on the table and looked at Isabel accusingly. "When are we going back?"

"In a day or two."

"I won't ever see Ruby Anne anymore, will I?"

Hasty and Sister and Isabel looked at each other. "Maybe someday," Sister said.

"Ruby Anne's her friend," Hasty explained.

Isabel stood. She hadn't met Caroline's granny yet, but she knew the part of the country where Caroline was going to live and a little about the life the Piggotts left behind when they came down from the hills. It wasn't likely Caroline would end up in the company of girls raised in the Annesdale Park section of Memphis.

"We'll be sure you have time to say goodbye," she said.

Caroline jumped up. "I don't like your hair," she screamed. "It's ugly and hateful and so are you."

Isabel went to the kitchen, poured soap into the sink and turned on the hot water, watching steam rise and cloud the window as Caroline ran up the stairs.

Sister woke everyone early the next morning. Isabel could hardly stay awake during church as the pastor droned on about God's plan and the need for faith, wondering how many times in her life she'd heard that popular theme. It didn't seem to do her much good, no comfort in the notion that God had a plan to kill thousands of young boys or rape a little girl. She stifled her yawns, fidgeted with the satin cuffs on her gray dress, shifted uncomfortably on the hard wooden pew and hoped she wasn't embarrassing Sister.

The smell of pot roast and potatoes cooking slowly in the oven greeted them when they returned home. Hasty loosened his tie and rolled up his sleeves and Sister sent Caroline to change clothes. Isabel set the table in the dining room, using the Sunday china and silver. She admired how easy it was to cook on Sister's new gas range, then helped her put the food on while Hasty and Caroline hovered about and asked how soon it would be ready.

Caroline disappeared after dinner to play with Ruby Anne. "Quiet play only," Sister reminded her. "No loud shouting or running on the day of rest."

Hasty went upstairs for a nap. Sister and Isabel went to the living room, where after a few attempts at conversation, Sister dozed off in her chair. Isabel lay lethargically on the sofa, thumbing through <u>McCall's</u> and <u>Modern Priscilla</u> magazines, riding the surface of sleep, aware of the soft chimes of the clock on the mantle and Sister's occasional snort. After a while she pushed herself up and crept softly up the stairs, took off her dress, and climbed into bed. Without the constant battle of chores and the farm and Edward, her weariness seemed to have over-taken her. She sank into unconsciousness.

She was sweating when she woke, arms leaden at her sides. She pushed the covers aside, sank back again, then forced herself to get up. She put on her robe and went down the hall to use the toilet and when she emerged, Sister was standing at the bottom of the stairs.

"Put on your gray dress," she said. "Holler when you're ready and I'll come up and pin it. Won't take me long this evening to fit it nicely."

Isabel wanted to tell her it didn't matter what the dress looked like. But Sister was proud of her handiwork, so she nodded and went back to her room. She straightened the covers on the bed, took the dress out of the closet and put it on, called down the stairs to Sister that she was ready, then sat on the side of the bed until Sister appeared.

"Stand up straight." Isabel complied. Sister worked quickly, her mouth full of pins, scratching Isabel once in a while and saying she was sorry. Then stepped back.

"Turn around." Isabel did.

"Better," Sister said.

"Take up the hem a little. It's too long."

"Short hair, short dresses."

"Not short like that one yesterday. Just a little shorter."

Sister pinned the hem, then asked if she wanted to look in the mirror. Isabel said no, it was fine. Sister told her to watch the pins when she took the dress off and to bring it downstairs when she came.

Hasty and Caroline were playing dominoes by the fire when she went downstairs, the dress draped carefully over her arm. Sister took it and carried it to her sewing room off the kitchen. Hasty looked at Isabel in her robe and said she must be ready for an evening by the fire. The living room suddenly seemed oppressive to her, with its dark, heavy furniture and dim lights, the fire too hot, the clock ticking on the mantle too loud, the clacking dominoes too monotonous.

"Actually, I was thinking I might go out to church again tonight," she said.

Hasty looked up from the domino game. "You didn't get your fill of Pastor this morning? Sunday morning and Wednesday evening is about all Sister and I can take anymore."

"I was thinking I might go hear Reverend Kane speak."

"Who's Reverend Kane?"

"We were just talking about him this morning," Sister said, coming back into the room. "That preacher Isabel knows from last summer. Holds services at the Full Gospel Tabernacle with Nina Prosper."

"Pressler, not Prosper," Hasty said. "You should remember that. Pastor mentions her by name in his sermons when he's all worked up over women's place in the church. Her claiming visitations from the Holy Ghost is downright blasphemy to him."

"Prosper, Pressler," Sister said. "If Pastor doesn't drop that topic for a sermon, I'll give him a piece of my mind."

"I'm happy to ride the streetcar," Isabel said.

"You'll do no such thing," Sister said. "Hasty will drive you. He'll be out of here for a drive pretty soon anyway. Just let him know when you're ready."

Isabel stood. "I'll get dressed. I think the paper said the service starts at 7:30."

Her hair was flattened by the nap, so she wet it again, and while it dried she applied her new lipstick and rouge. She put on one of the blouses she had bought the day before and was slipping into her skirt when she heard the telephone ring and the muffled sounds of Sister's side of the conversation, then footsteps from the kitchen and Sister calling up the stairs.

"Isabel. The telephone's for you. It's Edward."

Her heart beat rapidly for a moment. "Edward? What's Edward doing on the telephone?"

"He went to Doc's to call you. I told him you'd be right down."

She fastened her skirt and walked slowly down the stairs.

Sister smiled broadly. "I'll shut the kitchen door so you have some privacy."

Isabel walked into the kitchen and picked up the telephone, waiting until Sister had shut the door to speak. "Hello?"

"Isabel?" Edward shouted.

"Yes."

"It's Edward."

"I know. You don't have to talk so loud, Edward. I can hear you."

He lowered his voice a little. "I was just wondering if the trip went all right."

"Yes, it went fine. How are the boys?"

"They're good." They were silent for a moment.

"Are you still there?" he said.

"Yes."

"Are you coming home tomorrow?"

"No, not tomorrow. Maybe Tuesday. There's still a little shopping I have to do."

"Shopping? Sister said you went shopping yesterday."

"I'd like to find some books. For the boys and me." She could almost hear him thinking about that one.

"Books can be expensive," he said.

"I know. I'll look for used books. Say hello to Doc and the boys for me."

"All right. Isabel?"

"Yes."

"You sound real natural on the telephone."

"I'll let you know when I'm coming. Goodbye, Edward."

"Goodbye."

She hung up the telephone, walked out of the kitchen into the hall, and saw Sister and Hasty looking at her expectantly from the living room.

"Everything all right at home?" Sister asked.

"Fine. Everything's fine."

"Good. I didn't spoil your surprise."

"Surprise?"

"Your hair. Did you tell Edward you cut your hair?"

"Oh. No. No, I didn't tell him."

Isabel was late getting to the service. Hasty dropped her in front of the Tabernacle and they agreed he would return at 10:00 to collect her. He wrote their address and telephone number on a scrap of paper, and she tucked it in her purse. She could hear a sermon in full swing before she even opened the door. The Tabernacle was packed with people, still dressed in their Sunday best. She stood uncertainly in the vestibule, glancing around the crowded pews for a place to sit, but unable to focus on the crowd because of the man at the front.

He looked a little more well fed, more prosperous than the last time she'd seen him. He still wore a dark suit and white shirt, but even from a distance she could tell that the fit of his clothes was a little finer. He moved back and forth across the stage in subtle, studied rhythm with the cadence of his voice and the music accompanying him. His voice started low and soft, the congregation straining to hear him, then rose, little by little, gaining in urgency, until he reached a peak of momentum and ecstasy and the congregation cried out and raised their arms and swayed in rapture. He let them go on until they realized he was silent. Then, like him, they fell silent, too. He looked at them, looked around the room until it was hushed, waiting in anticipation. He smiled. A little knowing, loving smile. "Can you say amen?" he said softly. "Amen," the congregation shouted. And he began again.

Isabel felt herself go weak. *He has the power to sway people*, she thought. *And he knows it.*

A deacon approached her from the side. "Would you like to join the worship service ma'am?"

"Yes," she said. "But it looks like there's no place to sit."

"Come with me. We'll find you a place."

Head down, she followed the deacon into the sanctuary, relieved that he stopped at the last pew in the back. He leaned over and whispered, and the people shifted to make a place for her. As she sat down, the crescendo of Kane's voice faltered. Just for an instant. He looked at her. Then he went on.

There was a woman sitting on the platform behind Kane, whom she assumed was Nina Pressler. She half listened to Kane's words and took a good look around at the crowd, but mostly she watched Nina Pressler. Isabel was surprised she was so young. She was not surprised that Miss Pressler appeared captivated by the Reverend Kane.

Kane finally finished, and when he sat down Nina Pressler leaned over and took his hand and whispered something. Isabel felt a stab of jealousy. Then Miss Pressler got up to speak, moving gracefully across the stage, wearing a white robe that fell to the floor.

"This is the day that the Lord hath made," she said, her voice strong and clear. "Rejoice and be glad in it."

"Amen," said the congregation.

She was good, Isabel had to admit. She didn't have the fire in her belly that Kane had, but she was charismatic and well-spoken. Isabel could see that the two of them made a strong combination. Kane nodded along and said an occasional amen or praise the Lord, sitting in what appeared to be rapt attention to her words except for the times his gaze wandered to the back pew where Isabel sat. She tried to avoid looking at him, but their eyes met more than once. *I should be ashamed for what I'm thinking in a house of the Lord.*

An altar call, and the service ended. Kane and Nina Pressler walked together down the center aisle, touching outstretched hands and blessing people as they went. Nina passed by only a few inches from Isabel, between her and Kane, and Isabel caught a whiff of light perfume. Isabel looked at her pocket watch and saw that it was a little before nine. She felt a mild rush of panic. Hasty had thought the service would be over much later.

As the crowd left the Tabernacle, she hung back, moving into the vestibule and watching through the open doors as Kane and Nina shook hands and chatted and appeared to give counsel to some of their flock. When only a few people were left outside, she knew she couldn't stay in the vestibule any longer. She started toward the door, then stopped when Kane stepped back inside.

"Mrs. Fuller."

"Reverend."

"What are you doing here?"

"Micah. What kind of question is that?" It was Nina, appearing in the doorway behind Kane. *She calls him by his given name,* Isabel thought.

He turned to Nina. "I'm surprised, that's all. This is Mrs. Fuller, the kind lady who provided us a place for the revival in New Caney last summer. I didn't expect to see her in Memphis."

Nina came to Isabel and held out her hand. "Micah has told me about you."

Not everything I'm sure, Isabel thought as she shook Nina's hand. "I'm here visiting friends," she said. "I saw your meeting notice in the newspaper and thought I'd pay my respects to Reverend Kane. I didn't get to spend much time at the revival last summer and now I see why it was so successful."

"Yes," Nina said. "I feel God move through him when he speaks."

I'm sure you do. They both smiled at Kane. Isabel observed his discomfort with some satisfaction.

"I'm afraid I'm in a pickle," she said. "My friends aren't picking me up until 10:00. They didn't realize the service would be over this early."

"We'll take you home," Kane said. "There's a telephone in the office. We'll call and tell them there's no need to come." He turned to Nina and suggested she see after the collection plates while he and Isabel went to make the call. He led Isabel to the back of the sanctuary and opened the door to a small office. They stepped inside and he closed the door behind them. Isabel took the scrap of paper from her purse and gave it to him. He recited the number for the operator, then handed the telephone to her, sitting on the edge of the desk and watching her while she called. Sister answered.

"Isabel! What's wrong?"

"Nothing's wrong," she assured her, explaining the problem. "Reverend Kane and Miss Pressler will bring me home." She told Sister it was fine, no trouble at all to the Reverend, then hung up the phone.

"You have a car now?" she asked.

"It's Nina's. She has two. She lets me use one."

"Do you live with her?"

"No. There's nothing between us." He stood. "We'll take her home first. So we have a chance to visit."

Nina wasn't happy about that, she could tell, no matter what Kane said. Nina had taken off her robe and was smartly dressed in a wool suit and patent leather shoes. She had put on lip color and wore jewelry that Isabel hadn't noticed before. It looked expensive. Kane said little on the drive to Nina's. Nina, however, seated in the front next to Kane, had a number of questions for Isabel.

"You're married?"

"Yes, I am."

"Your husband is still living?"

"He is."

"Praise the Lord." Nina smiled broadly. "Children?"

"Three boys, ten, eleven, and fourteen."

"Do you get to Memphis often?"

"Not often. I don't often have the time."

"I'm sure it's busy down on the farm. All those pigs and cows and things to take care of."

"Yes, it is."

At last Kane pulled to a stop in front of a large house where, Nina explained, she lived with her elderly mother. They all got out of the car and Nina invited them in for coffee, but Kane declined.

"Stop by and visit before you leave if you get the chance, Mrs. Fuller," Nina said brightly. "We're not far from the zoo. They have animals there. You might like to see them."

Kane walked Nina to the door while Isabel waited by the car. When he returned, he opened the front passenger door for her. She thought she saw the curtains in the front room move as they drove away.

They drove in silence, Isabel studying his profile in the dim waves of light from the streetlamps, Kane glancing at her every so often, taking his eyes off the road to meet hers for brief moments. She felt the tension between them mounting. There were things she wanted to ask, but she couldn't seem to make herself formulate the questions. They drove down streets she didn't recognize, and after a while he pulled to a stop in front of a dark, two-story house in a slightly run-down neighborhood. They sat for a few minutes in the car.

"You cut your hair," he said.

"Yesterday."

"It looks nice."

"Thank you. This is your house?"

"Mrs. Kincannon's. She takes in boarders. In her seventies, deaf as a post and forgetful. My rooms are in the back, with my own entrance off the porch. It's a good arrangement – meals when I want, and I come and go as I please."

They sat a little longer.

"I hope I haven't offended you by bringing you here," he said quietly.

"No. You haven't."

He got out and opened her door and held out his hand. She took it and they walked to the rear of the house. He pulled a key from his pocket and unlocked the door, and they stepped inside to a small sitting room, the bedroom visible through an open door. The furnishings were worn, but clean. He took off his coat and hung it on a hook. She unbuttoned hers and handed it to him.

"There's a bathroom down the hall," he said. "She won't hear you. She's asleep by eight o'clock." They walked softly to the bathroom, and she went inside, Kane standing guard outside the door. When she came out, he went in. She slipped back to his rooms and sat down, waiting for him to return. When he appeared in the doorway, he seemed larger than she remembered, more in control. He moved deliberately toward her, and she panicked for a moment, thinking she should tell him to take her to the Walkers' now. Then he pulled her to her feet and began to undress her with such urgency, his mouth everywhere on her, that she knew she'd never had any real intention of telling him to take her home.

He stripped her so fiercely that she was afraid he would tear her clothes. When she was naked, he pushed her down into the chair and knelt in front of her. He put his hands on her knees and spread them, then ran his fingers lightly up the insides of her thighs. Then he put his hands under her hips and pulled her to the edge of the chair, tracing her thighs with his fingers again. Isabel felt the blood pounding in her head and heard the short rasps of her own breathing. She closed her eyes and groaned, clutching the arms of the chair and thrusting herself toward him.

She had never felt so completely exposed – not only in her nakedness, but that he could see her need so clearly. She burned with shame, but then she was beyond shame and did what he wanted. She rode wave after wave, each one stronger than the next, until she begged him to stop, but he wouldn't until finally he pulled her down onto the floor on top of him and put his hands on her hips and shoved her against him again and again until he was finished.

She collapsed onto the floor beside him. The room was cool, but she was covered with sweat. She felt Kane's heart pounding and heard his deep rapid breaths.

"I thought I'd never see you again," he said. "Thought I'd never be with you like this again. How have you been?"

"I've been all right."

"How are things at home?"

"About the same." She pushed herself up onto her elbow so she could see his face. "I was surprised to see you with Nina Pressler. I didn't know you were making such a name for yourself."

"Not much of a name yet. I'm still second fiddle to Miss Nina." There was an edge to his voice. "But that's all right for now." He turned his head to her. "What are you really doing in Memphis?"

She stood up and began to dress. For some reason she didn't want to tell him about coming to fetch Caroline. "I told you. Visiting friends – Sister and Hasty Walker. Shopping for my family. I've known Sister a long time. It's not the first time I've been to Memphis."

He laughed and got up. "I didn't mean to insult you. I'd put you up against these city women any day."

She finished buttoning her blouse. "In what way?"

He pulled her to him and kissed her, long and deep, and she felt herself go weak again. "In every way."

"You'd better take me home."

Kane talked while he drove this time, telling her about how Nina had been to hear him preach one day and offered him a place with her at the Tabernacle. That he was still thinking about enrolling in the university to study theology and the ministry.

"You still feel the call?"

"Stronger than ever."

They pulled up in front of the Walkers' house.

"I'll walk you to the door," he said.

"No. Sister's likely waiting up for me. It might be best that you didn't."

"I want to see you again. How long are you staying?"

"I haven't decided. Another day. Maybe more."

"I'll come for you tomorrow. We'll spend the day together." He drew her to him and kissed her gently. "Stay awhile. Stay as long as you can."

"I will," she whispered. "I will."

CHAPTER

17

SISTER WAS WAITING UP. ISABEL TOLD HER THEY'D HAD coffee at Miss Pressler's house and got to talking and forgot the time. She waited until the next morning to tell Sister and Hasty that Reverend Kane had offered to show her a few of the sights and would be picking her up.

"That's mighty nice of him," Hasty said. "Sister and I are happy to take you anywhere you want to go."

"I reckon the Reverend wants to show his gratitude for last summer," Sister said.

"That must be it," Isabel said.

He came for her late that morning, and the next day, and the next. They left each day on the pretext of a visit to the zoo, a drive in the country to see horses for sale, services at the Tabernacle. Kane called Nina Pressler and told her he was sick. "Fevered," he said into the telephone, and Isabel covered her mouth so she wouldn't laugh. Nina wanted to come see him, but he said no, he thought he was contagious.

Monday afternoon they went to a used bookstore, where they browsed for several hours, and Isabel bought books for herself and the boys. They went on to Dinstuhl's Candy Shop, then, famished, stopped at a café for an early supper. She stepped inside first, the customers looking up as the bell over the door rang. Kane, behind her, ducked his head to remove his hat, then quickly jammed it back on again, turned abruptly and bolted outside. Isabel, face burning under the quizzical gazes of the now quiet diners, hesitated for a moment then turned and walked out.

Kane was almost to the car, which was parked several blocks away. Isabel, furious, hurried to catch up. He was behind the wheel by the time she reached the car. She got in, slammed the door, and he took off.

"Two women from the Tabernacle," he said. "At the corner table. I don't think they saw me."

After that, they wandered aimlessly in the countryside and small towns on the outskirts of the city, Kane concerned that someone might recognize him and cautious about where they went. When the cold, early nights fell, they crept to his rooms, not lighting a lamp until Mrs. Kincannon had gone to bed. He took her home later and later, Isabel letting herself in and slipping furtively up the stairs and into bed, exhausted and sore. She forced herself to get up for breakfast each morning, which she ate under the increasing silence and averted eyes of Hasty and Sister, pulling her robe up tightly to hide the marks on her neck.

She told herself each morning that she would put an end to it. The daylight hours dragged a little more each day. She had hoped to see a motion picture or have dinner out, do something interesting while she was in Memphis. Instead, she took in scenery not that much different from home as she discovered that she and Kane actually had little to say to each other. What conversation they had usually turned to the subject of Kane – his ministry, his future. How the congregation reacted on various occasions to his message, how well he thought he could read an audience.

But as each day wore on, he would do something – a look, a whisper, a hint of something he had for her – to make her desire return, crawling slowly under her skin and burning until he could touch her. Edward called again on Wednesday. She wasn't there when he called.

Late Thursday evening they lay spent in a tangle of sheets, on the edge of sleep, when they heard a soft knock at the door.

"Micah?"

It was Nina Pressler. Isabel sat up in a panic. "Sshhh," Kane said, pushing her back down.

Soft tapping again. "Micah?"

"I have to answer her," he whispered. "She won't go away until I do."

Isabel pulled the covers over her head. *This is it,* she thought. *The moment we're discovered. I'll live with this shame and regret it for the rest of my life.*

He rose, found his trousers on the floor, pulled them on and fastened his belt as he crossed the room. He opened the door a crack.

"I'm sorry, Nina. I'm not dressed."

"How are you? I've been so worried about you."

"Better. I'm still sleeping a lot. Fighting it off."

"I'm sorry if I woke you. But I thought I heard voices. You must not have heard me knock the first few times."

"I must have been dreaming. Talking in my sleep."

Nina craned her neck, attempted to look inside. "I brought you some soup." She held out a jar.

"Thank you. I would ask you to come in, but I'm not dressed. And it wouldn't be proper for you to be here alone."

He cracked the door a bit more and she handed him the jar.

"Will you be able to preach on Sunday?" she asked.

"I'm sure I will."

"Good. I've been pondering a topic for the sermon all week and only one keeps coming to mind."

"What's that?"

Nina paused for emphasis. "'For the wages of sin is death.' I think that would be appropriate, don't you?"

He nodded solemnly. "Always appropriate, Nina. Always appropriate. Thank you for bringing the soup. It's just what I needed." He closed the door quietly.

He set the jar on a table and sat on the edge of the bed. Isabel lay quietly under the covers. She sat up when he pounded his fists on the mattress. They looked at each other but neither spoke. Then she rose, and they dressed in silence.

"I'll go out first," he said. "Walk down the street a ways, just to be sure she's gone."

He returned a few minutes later and she followed him to the car. When they pulled up to the Walkers' house, he parked the car but left the engine running. He turned to her.

"I'll pick you up tomorrow. But I think it should be the last time."

"Yes," she said. "It's time for this to be over."

It was a little before midnight when Isabel turned the key quietly in the Walkers' front door. She took off her shoes and padded in her stockings toward the living room to turn off the light Sister had left burning, but a few feet from the door, she froze. Someone was in there.

"Isabel."

She jumped. It was Doc. Heart pounding and hands shaking, she walked into the living room, where Doc was sitting in Hasty's chair, his feet propped up on a footstool. She went to him and bent to kiss his cheek, holding her body as far away from him as she could, knowing that every inch of her smelled like Kane, his skin and shaving lotion and semen and sweat. His potions, she thought. He pours his potions on me and in me until I'm drugged and he does whatever he wants. She sank wearily on the sofa and focused her mind back on Doc.

"What brings you to Memphis?"

He looked at her sadly. "I think you know."

She rested her head on the back of the sofa and stared at the ceiling. "No, Doc. I don't know. Why don't you tell me?"

"It's time for you to come home. I told Edward it might be best if I was the one came to tell you that."

A jolt of anger shot through her. Her knee began to twitch, and then bob up and down as her heel tapped the floor. "Don't say. The two of you put your heads together and decided who'd come fetch me?"

"It's not like that."

"Oh, I think it is, Doc."

Doc pushed himself up straight, his feet on the floor now, his hands gripping the arms of the chair.

"You have a family. Your boys need you. Your husband wants you home."

"Maybe he wouldn't," she shot back. "Maybe he wouldn't want me home if he knew some things."

He sighed and rubbed his face. "He knows, Isabel. He knows, and he still wants you to come home." He slumped back in his chair. "I don't know many men could love a woman like that. Then again, I don't know any women like you. At least not since your mother died."

Her throat tightened. She blinked back tears and swallowed several times until she was sure she could speak. "You don't know me anymore, Doc. I don't even know myself."

"I can't know what it's like to be you. But when I look at you, I see Isabel. She's got near forty years of living inside her. She's got a hole in her heart her mother left, and a bigger hole Carl left. She's the same Isabel. She's just different now."

She looked at him. "I reckon if I think about that long enough it'll make some sense."

He laughed softly. "Might. Might not. If it ever does, come tell me. The more I know about life, the less I understand it."

She stood. "Sister didn't tell me you were coming," She paced around the room.

"I told her I'd just surprise you."

"Well, I'm surprised."

"Not often I get to do that. After knowing you all these years." He watched her pace. "Sit down. I'm going to tell you a story you've never heard before. About your mother."

She sat back down on the sofa. "If it's about my mother, I've probably heard it."

"No, you haven't. I'm the only one she told." He settled back in his chair.

"It was late one night," he said. "Not long after your daddy died. There wasn't any food in the house, and she'd put you and your brothers to bed hungry. She was darning socks by the fire when a stranger came to the door. She hadn't heard him coming, no sound of a horse or footsteps. For some reason she wasn't afraid – he looked familiar to her, and kind.

"She asked him how he'd got there, and he said he'd walked. She asked him in, but he said no. He was carrying a box, and he handed it to her and smiled. 'The children will be fine,' he said. She looked in the box and there was bread and ham and some dried apples. When she looked up again, he was gone, without a sound. She put the box in the kitchen and went to bed.

"That night she dreamed she was lying in bed, sick, and you were sitting beside her. You were a woman, still young but married, and she was in your house. She heard someone at the door, and then the same stranger who had brought the food came into the room and held out his hand. 'The children will be fine,' he said. She knew then who he was. It was her granddaddy, although a younger man than when she'd known him. So, your mother got out of bed and went with him, knowing it was the last time she would see you. The dream upset her so much she woke up. It was still dark, not quite daybreak. Thinking it all to have been a dream, she went to the kitchen, not expecting the box to be there."

"Was it?"

"Yes," he said in a hushed voice. "Ham, bread, and dried apples – enough to feed the family for a week."

"The day she died," Isabel said, "she heard someone at the door. I was sitting beside her, and she asked me who was there. I told her no one. Then she was gone."

They sat quietly for a while.

"If you ever think about giving up on life, you remember that story. You remember what you came from. Not the poverty – the power. And you remember what your mother did for you and your brothers, what she would expect you to do for your children."

She got up and knelt in front of Doc. She put her arms around him and laid her head on his chest and wept silently, her tears spilling onto the front of his shirt. He stroked her hair and patted her back, then reached into his pocket and took out a handkerchief. He wiped his own eyes and then hers.

"We'll go home on Saturday," he said. "It's time you go home."

She got to her feet. "I'll go with you, Doc, but I can't promise I'll stay. I want my boys. But I don't know where home is anymore."

She helped him out of his chair. "The Reverend's coming for me tomorrow. Do you want to see him?"

"No. I've got nothing to say to him. And it's best that if Edward ever asks me, I can tell him I never saw you with him. That I never saw the man at all."

Kane was late. Isabel put on her coat and gloves and sat outside to wait for him. She sat on the front steps under a slate gray sky for over an hour, chilled to the bone by the time he got there. When she saw him coming, she walked down to the street without saying goodbye to anyone in the house.

They drove south of the city, until he finally turned off the road and parked the car on a bluff overlooking the Mississippi River. He seemed distracted. Isabel cracked a window open for some fresh air and rested her elbow on the car door. She turned to look at him. This was the last day they would spend together, and she realized that he had never really known her at all. She wondered if he was even interested.

"Have you ever known someone with the sight?" she said.

"You mean someone who has visions?"

"That's part of it."

He stared out the window. "Yes," he said finally. "I know someone like that."

"Who?"

"Me."

She thought she saw a little smile of what – modesty? satisfaction? – on his face.

"What kind of visions do you have?" she asked.

"They come on me sometimes when I'm preaching – when I'm on fire. One time I was preaching about Joshua and the battle of Jericho, and for a minute I *was* Joshua. I heard the priests sounding their trumpets, the shouts of the righteous as the walls came down. Another time I was baptizing a man and I knew what it was like to be John the Baptist just as surely as if Jesus was standing in front of me, asking to be baptized. When it happens, I see and understand things more clearly than ever before."

She contemplated him for a moment. The thought flashed through her mind that for the first time in a long time, she was bored. "Do you ever feel like you're Jesus Christ?"

He reddened. "You're mocking me."

"It wasn't my intent to mock you."

He reached into the back seat for a picnic basket and pulled out bottles of tea and sandwiches wrapped in paper. He handed her a bottle and wolfed down a sandwich.

"My mother had the sight," she said. She took a sip of tea. "I have it, too."

He unwrapped a second sandwich and offered it to her, but she shook her head. He took a large bite and chewed vigorously, then swallowed.

"Well," he said. "You both were from the hills."

"What do you mean by that?"

"Conjuring and magic. Haints in the graveyard, lights in the woods. Panthers following you home at night. I've heard those tales my whole life."

She was instantly furious. "My mother wasn't like that, and neither am I. I have visions and dreams. Sometimes I see things before they happen. Other times there are messengers, pointing me in a certain direction. It happens in different ways."

"What kind of messengers?"

"Lately it's been crows. And my mother coming to visit."

He paused, sandwich at his mouth, but instead of taking another bite he set it on the paper, then re-wrapped it. She thought he might ask her for more details, but he just sat silently, looking out the window.

"Do you have anything to say about that?" she said.

He pinched the bridge of his nose and pursed his lips. "I think the past few years, since Carl died, have been very difficult for you. Grieving people imagine all sorts of things."

"Imagine," she said. "Well. Suppose it is just imagination. Or conjuring and magic. How is that so different from what you were talking about – imagining you're fighting the battle of Jericho?"

He smacked the steering wheel with his palms.

"Matters of the spirit are not conjuring and magic. They are not imagination. And that is why matters of the spirit are peculiarly within the knowledge and understanding of men – not women."

She gaped at him in disbelief.

"I wonder what Nina Pressler would have to say about that."

"Nina Pressler is young in years and in wisdom. I expect her to mature as time goes along – which I also would have expected from a woman your age."

Well, there you have it, she thought. *A woman my age. Truth is, a woman my age should have more wisdom.* She looked at the bottle of tea in her hand. Her fingers itched to dump its contents in his lap. Instead, she screwed the lid back on the bottle. "I think it's time you took me home."

Kane stopped the car. Isabel looked up at Hasty and Sister's house, quiet and dark in the settling dusk. A light went on in the kitchen. She couldn't remember anything about the drive – how long it had taken them to get there, or whether he had said anything more to her on the way.

"Doc's here," she said.

"Who?"

"Doc Walker. From New Caney. He came to Memphis yesterday. He's at the house."

"Ah, Doc Walker."

"He came to take me home. Caroline and I will be leaving tomorrow."

"Caroline?" he said quietly.

"Caroline Piggott. You remember her from last summer. She's been staying with Hasty and Sister and now her granny's coming to New Caney to get her."

"I remember very well." He cleared his throat. "Is there some reason you didn't tell me that's why you came to Memphis?"

"You know why I came to Memphis. Someone else could have come to fetch her. Edward. Doc. Or Sheriff Dennis for that matter."

His eyes narrowed. "The sheriff's got no need to come back to Memphis. He's found out all he's going to find."

She felt sick to her stomach. "What do you mean?"

"He was here not long ago. Asking if I knew anything about Piggott's murder. I asked him if he even knew when the man was killed and he said no. I said I wasn't in New Caney long, so there wasn't much chance I'd know anything about it."

"Why would he even come looking for you?"

He shrugged. "I was a stranger in town. Piggott said some things. About me, about his little girl." He paused. "About you."

Her nausea grew worse.

"I told him a man like Piggott's got a better chance than most of getting himself shot. Even by someone otherwise considered an upstanding member of the community."

"How did you leave it with him?"

"He told me to stay away from his town and never come back. I said I hadn't been run out of a town since I was saved, but I had no intention of passing his way again." He looked up at the house and then back at her. "I got the impression the murder wasn't the only thing on his mind when he told me that. And I got the impression he didn't care about finding out who killed Piggott so much as he wanted the whole thing forgotten."

It grew colder inside the car. Her breath fogged the window. He took her hand and lifted it to his lips, then rubbed it between his palms. His lips felt like rubber to her, his palms like sandpaper irritating her skin.

"This isn't good. Nina at my door last night. Doc coming here. And a sheriff who could make trouble for me if he wanted. He'd have no reason to, but he might if he knew I was with you."

"Well, we certainly don't want to cause you any trouble."

He shifted uncomfortably in his seat. "This hasn't been easy for me, Isabel. A man in my position."

"What position is that? A man kept by a rich young woman preacher? Do you talk about salvation when you're together?"

He reddened in anger. "You're one to talk, being a married woman. We knew there was no future in this."

"We didn't talk about the future that I recall. And pay no mind to what my life may be like when I get home."

He sighed. "I don't want to leave it this way between us, Isabel. There were times last summer I thought I would give up everything to be with you. But I'm on a path now to serve the Lord in ways I never imagined. I'll never be able to do that if people know me as a man who broke up a home and took another man's wife."

"You prefer to do your sinning in private."

"No," he said quietly. "That's not what I meant at all."

She pulled her hand away. "It's all right. I knew there was no future in this, too. And truth is, I don't recall ever thinking that I would give up everything to be with you." She got out of the car. She went slowly up the walk to the front steps, then turned and sat down, her feet on the step below and her knees pulled to her chest. She could see only a shadowy figure inside the car, and it was impossible to tell if he was looking at her. He waited a few minutes more, then started the car and drove away. She watched him disappear around the corner.

She sat on the steps for a long time. Lights came on up and down the street as darkness fell. Every once in a while a car passed, but none stopped. A man went by on foot, walking his dog, the dog's panting breath trailing in puffs behind them. Flurries of snow danced in the light of the streetlamps, and the cold from the stone steps seeped through her clothes. She hardly noticed when the porch light came on and the front door creaked open. Doc closed the door behind him and lowered himself slowly onto the steps beside her.

"No stars out tonight," he said. He put his arm around her shoulders, and she realized she was shaking. She pulled her knees tighter to her chest.

"Winter's coming, Doc. It'll be here before we know it."

"I know," he said. "I know."

It was still dark when they rose the next morning to catch the train. Isabel wore her gray dress for the trip home, pulling the matching hat down over her hair. Sister packed a bag of food and offered to fix breakfast before they left, but Doc and Isabel said no, coffee for them and a cold biscuit or two for Caroline would be fine. The sun was just coming up as they drove to the train station, Doc in front beside Hasty, and Caroline wedged between Sister and Isabel in the back seat. Isabel insisted on paying for the three tickets, pulling the money from her purse and handing it to Hasty, who went to stand in line at the ticket window. Sister sat on a bench with Caroline, holding her hand and murmuring to her softly. A whistle blew and it was time to go.

The five of them walked together to the train. Isabel stood back while the others embraced, Caroline clutching Sister and Hasty fiercely and both of them wiping their eyes. Doc held out his hand to Caroline, but she clasped her arms around Sister's waist and shook her head.

"I ain't going," she said. "I ain't going."

Isabel went to Caroline and dropped to her knees. Caroline buried her face in Sister's skirt and said something, her words muffled and unintelligible.

"I'm sorry," Isabel said. "I can't hear you."

Caroline looked briefly at her, then turned her head away. "My daddy ain't dead. You say he is, but I know he ain't."

She stroked the girl's hair. "He is dead," she whispered. "He can't hurt you anymore."

Caroline's shoulders heaved, and Sister patted her back while she sobbed. Isabel let her cry for a moment, then took her hand.

"It's time to go. We don't want to miss the train."

Caroline released her hold on Sister. Isabel turned to leave, feeling too ashamed to say anything else, but Sister pulled her arm and then wrapped her in an embrace.

"Come back soon," Sister said. "When you can bring Edward and the boys with you."

"I will. Thank you for all you've done – for Caroline and for me. And I'm sorry. Really sorry for all the trouble I've caused you."

"You haven't caused me any trouble. I think you caused yourself some, but you're the one who has to live with that."

Isabel smiled slightly. At least you always knew where things stood with Sister. She kissed her on the cheek and said goodbye.

Doc and Caroline ate some of the food Sister had packed, then slept most of the way home. Isabel tried to sleep but couldn't. Eyes fixed unfocused on the passing scenery, thoughts of what she and Kane had done raced through her mind like some demon she couldn't escape. She shifted restlessly in her seat, legs cramping, arms itching.

The closer they got to home, the more she felt a rising sense of panic and dread. She wanted to see her boys, touch their skin and hair, smell the sweet, stinky musk of boys. She would wrap her arms around them, the good mother who missed them, come home again to take her place at the center of the household. She was afraid that when she did, they would sense the evil and lust running in her veins, whispering to them to watch out, she wasn't what they'd always assumed. Edward and Doc knew about her and Kane, and Sheriff Dennis obviously did, too. What would she say to her boys if they found out? Her arms and legs twitched more violently, and she felt as if her flesh were splitting apart as the train hurtled toward home.

The next stop was theirs. She woke Doc and Caroline when the train began to slow for its approach into the station. They braced themselves for the lurching stop, then collected their coats and bags. Doc and Caroline made their way down the aisle first. Isabel lingered behind to brush crumbs off the seats and retrieve a scrap of butcher paper that had fallen into the aisle. She pulled her hat down further over her hair and picked up her things. Then she stepped off the train into the raw November wind.

Edward and the boys were waiting. She dropped her bags and held out her arms. Ben and James bumped heads, trying to be the first to kiss her and she rubbed their noggins and laughed, then Samuel picked her up and twirled her around. They fought over who would carry her bag, asked to see what she had brought them from Memphis, and she told them they would have to wait. Edward hung back, hat in his hands, face reddened and chapped by the wind.

"Take the bags to the car, boys," he said. "Doc's and Caroline's, too." They headed off in a noisy procession, Doc and Caroline following, leaving Edward and Isabel facing each other across the platform.

"Welcome back," he said. He stood stiffly, holding his hat in his hands behind his back.

"I've only been gone a week," she said, "but the boys look like they've grown a foot."

"Eight days to be exact."

"I missed them."

"It's good to hear that, Isabel." He put on his hat. "I knew you forgot you were a wife. I was afraid you'd forgot you were a mother, too."

She was suddenly very tired. She turned and walked slowly to the car.

They dropped Doc off then headed for home. Samuel drove and Edward sat stone-faced beside him. The younger boys were unusually quiet, glancing from Edward to Isabel to Caroline, trying to determine the source of their father's unspoken rage. Hawks circled over the fields, their shadows from the cold sun gliding swiftly, silently across the ground until they rose, disappeared, then turned and swooped again. A rabbit made its escape across the road, barely missing the car, and jumped, trembling, into hiding again. *He'll wait a while to come out,* Isabel thought. *Then he'll think it's safe, hop out of that hole and end up nothing but a hawk's supper.*

They passed their property line, Isabel's return greeted by rows of cotton stalks picked bare and dying, waiting to be burned and plowed under. She saw the remains of the brush arbor in the distance, the tall poles still standing, patches of brush here and there still hanging from the roof. "Cotton's all in, Mama," Samuel said. "We made a good crop this year. Started cutting wheat day before yesterday." Ben and James nodded wisely, relieved that Samuel had the courage to speak.

"That's good to hear," she said. "Everybody's been working hard." Ben and James nodded again. Samuel turned the car into the lane and parked at the back of the house.

"Put your mama's bag in Carl's room," Edward told the boys. "Caroline can sleep in there, too."

Isabel followed them into the house. There were piles of dirty clothes on the back porch, a stained tablecloth on the kitchen table. The floor looked as if it hadn't been swept since the day she left. The dishes were washed, but still sat on the counter where they had been left to dry. She took off her coat and hat, hung them on a peg by the door. She ran her fingers through her hair.

"Oh my goodness!" Ben had stopped short in the doorway between Carl's room and the kitchen. "Look at Mama's hair!"

The other boys came to look, and they took turns ruffling her hair and patting her head. James said it looked funny and Samuel said it looked nice. Edward said nothing. He turned away, his lips curling slightly in contempt.

"All right," he said. "Get your chores done and we'll go to town." He paused at the back door. "Me and the boys will eat supper in town," he said to her. "I don't reckon you need to go – all the time you spent in the city lately. Give you time to clean this place up a little." He went outside, letting the screen door slam behind him.

She went to Carl's room to change clothes. She had forgotten about Caroline. The girl was waiting in the bedroom, sitting on the old suitcase Sister had given her. She'd hardly spoken a word since they'd left Memphis. Isabel knew leaving Sister was hard on Caroline and tried to think of something to say to reassure her. She helped her unpack the suitcase, emptying one of the bureau drawers for her clothes, then changed into trousers and an old shirt, went to the kitchen, and told Caroline to sweep the floor while she killed some chickens for Sunday's dinner.

She made a pallet of quilts on the floor for Caroline not long after Edward and the boys were gone, and the girl fell right to sleep. She finished preparations for Sunday dinner then scrubbed the kitchen. She worked until she couldn't work anymore, the dull aches between her shoulders and in the small of her back returning to remind her that she was home. It was well after dark when she went quietly into Carl's room and changed into her nightgown. She found her suitcase and carried it to the kitchen table and opened it. She pulled out her dirty clothes and pressed them against her face, breathing in Kane's fading scent. The books and bags of peanut brittle they had bought together one afternoon were at the bottom of the suitcase. Kane had read over her shoulder as she browsed through the bookstore, pressing up against her and breathing in her ear until she told him to stop. He had whispered shameful things to her at the candy counter, and she had paid for the candy with trembling fingers, afraid the clerk would hear in her voice the thickness of her desire. She had left the satin underclothes he'd bought her in his rooms, where she had put them on and taken them off as he demanded. Tiresome as he had become at the end, she wondered how long it would take until she couldn't remember how he smelled or how his skin felt against hers – how long until the things they had done were buried in her memory rather than playing over and over in her mind while she cooked and cleaned, not even conscious of what she was doing. She looked around the kitchen and tried to imagine the future. It was no use. She tucked the clothes under her arm and took them out to the porch.

She waited up for Edward and the boys. The boys weren't excited about the books but were happy to get the peanut brittle, and she let them eat some before bed. James asked her to lie with him and sing, and she said she would. Samuel and Ben called him baby, but when she lay down and began to sing softly in the dark, she knew they were listening while she sang "Amazing Grace" and her other favorite hymns until Ben and James were asleep. She pushed herself up.

"Mama." Samuel spoke quietly in the dark. "When Caroline goes home are you still going to sleep in Carl's room?"

"I'm not sure. I know you want that room."

"I do want it. But that's not the only reason I'm asking."

"What's the other reason?"

"I'm almost fifteen, Mama. And I'm not stupid. I see how it is between you and Daddy."

Her heart began to pound in a moment of panic at what Samuel might know. She took a deep breath. "It's complicated, Samuel. Sometimes a husband and wife –" She heard him turn in his bed, punch his pillow.

"No it isn't," he said. "It's not complicated at all. Carl's gone. But we're still a family and nobody in this family has the right to bust it up."

"Samuel."

"If Daddy leaves, I'm going with him."

"Samuel!"

"I don't want to talk about it anymore," he said, his voice muffled.

"We can talk about it tomorrow."

"I said I don't want to talk about it anymore."

"Well, good night then." She waited a few moments, but he didn't respond. She closed the door gently behind her.

Edward, sitting at the kitchen table reading the newspaper, didn't look up when she came into the room. She put the candy away then stepped to the table. The few items still left in her suitcase were in disarray. Edward had been through her things. She clicked the suitcase shut.

"Me and the boys'll head to the fields as soon as it's light," he said. "We'll want breakfast before we go."

"Tomorrow's Sunday."

"I know what day it is. We'll rest when the work's done. You saw that mess of dirty clothes on the porch."

She heard the accusation in his voice, the implication of a long list of unspoken grievances. She wondered where on his list not doing the wash would fall. "I saw it. When did I ever not see it." She picked up her suitcase and went to bed.

CHAPTER

18

THE WEEK WENT BY IN A BLUR, ONE DAY FADING INTO the next. Isabel was up every morning before daylight and went to bed after midnight, welcoming the exhaustion that left her near crawling to bed each night, too tired to think. There was no word from Caroline's kin. She tried to put Caroline to work, but it was more trouble than it was worth as the girl drew more and more into herself, finally not speaking to anyone, not even the boys. She left the house each morning with a doll Sister had given her and stayed away most of the day. The first time it happened, Isabel went looking for her after a few hours. She found Caroline in the pecan grove, lying hidden on the cold ground under a honeysuckle bush, where she had hidden last summer. The next day Isabel gave her an old blanket and some food to take with her, asking if she stayed warm enough. Caroline nodded and seemed content, so Isabel let her be.

She felt Edward watching her for a sign of penitence, his anger mounting as the week went on and she refused to show him any. He gave her orders like he did the boys, telling her what needed to be done as if she hadn't been doing it every day since she'd married him. She turned her back on him and held her tongue, knowing that if she uttered one response there would be no stopping what would be said between them and what would be said could never be undone. She thought she could wait him out, that if she just waited, one day they would sit down and talk civilly to each other about how they would manage until the boys were grown. She was wrong.

It was mid-morning on Saturday. Edward and the boys had left early for the fields and Caroline was off playing. Isabel was ironing the last of the week's wash when she heard a horse outside and footsteps on the porch. Edward opened the back door. She looked up at him, puzzled.

"I forgot something in the barn," he said. "Thought I'd get me something to drink while I'm here."

She went back to her ironing. "There's a jug of sweet tea on the porch."

"Why don't you get me a glass," he said, sitting down at the table.

She flushed with anger. She set the iron carefully on the stove and folded the shirt she was ironing. She set the shirt on top of the stack of clothes she had already ironed, went to the cabinet and got a glass, went outside and poured tea into it, then came back inside and set the glass in front of him. She took the iron off the stove and started on another shirt. He watched her while he drank.

"You might as well stay home again tonight," he said. "While me and the boys go to town."

She smoothed the shirt collar and applied the iron. "I don't plan on doing that. I've been wanting to see Doc. Caroline can go with us."

He set his glass down. "I'm telling you to stay home."

The shirt collar began to scorch. She watched the white cloth turn brown and the steam rise, letting it scorch until it started to smoke. Then she lifted the iron and threw it against the wall. It stuck briefly in the wallboard, then thudded to the floor. She wadded up the shirt and threw it in Edward's direction. He jumped up from the table, ducking instinctively, his chair crashing to the floor.

"Is that what you want?" she yelled. "A woman who'll bring you food when she's told, and clean your house when she's told, and wash your stinking clothes when she's told, and spread her legs when she's told? Is that what you want?"

"What I want," he said, his fists clenched and his face red with rage, "is a woman who won't spread her legs for every man that comes along."

"It wasn't every man," she shot back. "It was one. One man who made me feel something again."

"One man or ten. You're still a whore."

"Better a whore than a murderer. Better to love like a whore than to murder your own son. Did you murder Piggott, too, when he mouthed off about you not being the man you think you are?"

He came toward her. "If I was a murderer, I'd kill you right now and not a jury in this county would convict me. I'd tell them what you did and that would be the end of it."

She leaned back, her head and shoulder blades pressed to the wall. Her knees went weak, and she slid down the wall to the floor, squatting with her head in her hands and her elbows on her knees. "Then do it," she said, tears streaming down her face. "Do it. Being dead has to be better than this."

He took another step toward her. She saw the frayed cuffs of his trousers, the worn-out boots caked with mud from the fields, and waited for the blow to come from fists raw and hardened from years behind a plow. Edward loomed over her like the burden of death he carried on his shoulders. Then he turned away from her and walked out the door.

Isabel huddled on the floor for a long time after he'd gone. She gulped and wiped her eyes and nose on the hem of her shirt, thinking she had herself under control. Then the sobs began, racking her body like convulsions, until she was so tired, she wanted to lie down and sleep. Finally, she forced herself to get up and go outside. She took a long drink of water from the pump, scrubbed her face and hands, then went back inside and finished the ironing.

Around noon she found Caroline and brought her back to the house. They dressed to go to town and went to sit in the living room, Caroline playing on the floor with her doll while Isabel sat in her rocking chair, darning socks and waiting.

Edward and the boys came in mid-afternoon. Edward stood in the doorway to the living room, silently taking in what she was wearing, made no comment when she rose and headed to the car. It was a quiet ride. Edward was subdued, the boys were tired, and Isabel thought they all should have stayed home and gone to bed, although she wouldn't have welcomed the thought of facing Edward across the supper table. When they got to town, he gave the boys a little money and told them to watch out for Caroline. They spoke politely in front of the children about what time they should all meet back at the car. She bought sugar, flour and oats at the store and put them in the car, then walked to Doc's house. The days were getting shorter, and it was dark when she got there.

"I thought that might be you," Doc said when he opened the door. "Come in this house."

She followed him to the parlor, his feet shuffling slowly in worn leather slippers. He put another log on the fire and wrapped his sweater tighter around him.

"I'm not looking forward to winter," he said. "Seems like every year my blood gets a little thinner and the winters get a little colder."

She told him to sit and that she'd fix him some tea. "You need to watch yourself, Doc," she said when she came back. "Don't go chasing around after patients in the wet snow this winter." He pretended to agree, but she knew he wouldn't pay any mind. He'd gotten sick several times in the past few years and last winter he'd come down with pneumonia. She had nursed him for weeks and seen what the sickness did to him. She didn't know if he was strong enough to survive it again.

They talked about the weather and the crops. He asked if there was any word on when Caroline would be leaving, and she told him there wasn't any news. He said he'd heard a bobcat the night before. Shep had heard it, too, and got to howling, so Doc made him come inside. "That dog's too old to be taking off after a bobcat," he said. They sat and rocked quietly by the fire. She thought he dozed off once or twice, but he roused himself with a question.

"How are things between you and Edward?"

"About as bad as you could imagine." The floorboards creaked under her chair. "You said he wanted me to come home, Doc. I don't think that was true."

"Oh, it was true. He wanted you home. I just think he didn't know how hard it would be on him to live with you when you got there."

She winced. "You don't blame him, do you?"

"I don't blame either one of you. What's the use of blame? There's enough hurt between the two of you to last a lifetime. The question is whether you let it or whether there's enough feeling left so you can find a way to live with each other. Maybe even love each other again someday."

She got up and put another log on the fire. She stood with her back to the fireplace, letting her clothes heat before she started the cold walk back to the car. She couldn't remember the last time she'd felt strong for Edward, or when the thought of loving him had even crossed her mind. It was years ago, she knew that much. She tried to think of it now; what loving him might mean. All she could call up was the flat image of his face, like a photograph of someone she didn't know. She couldn't get her mind around the idea of loving Edward at all.

CHAPTER

19

"CAROLINE," EDWARD SAID. THEY ALL WERE SEATED at the kitchen table on Monday morning, finishing breakfast. "Your granny will be here mid-week to take you home."

Caroline looked up from her plate, wide-eyed, a look of alarm on her face.

"When did you hear this?" Isabel asked.

"Saturday night. Sheriff told me her kin had contacted him."

"I don't want to go with my granny." Caroline pushed her plate away. "I like it here. Why can't I stay?"

"Boys," Edward said quietly. "Go hitch up the wagon. Your mother and I need to talk to Caroline for a minute."

The boys jumped up, relieved to be excused from the conversation. "You can have one of my marbles," Ben said to Caroline as they hurried to the door. "A shooter. A going-away present."

Caroline didn't respond. The three of them sat for a while without speaking, Isabel at one end of the table, Edward at the other, and Caroline in the middle, the clinking of Edward's spoon against his coffee cup the only sound. He finally spoke.

"It's been a real pleasure having you, Caroline. We hope you know that we'll always care about you and your well-being. But truth is, you have family. And if your family wants you, we've got no right to keep you here."

Caroline turned to Isabel. "But you made me a dress. You said I looked real pretty."

Isabel stood, reached for the plates the boys had left behind. "You did look pretty," she said. "You're still pretty. But there's nothing to be done. You've got a life ahead of you and it's time to get on with it. I'm sure your granny will do her best."

Caroline looked as if Isabel had slapped her. She pushed away from the table, tucked her doll and blanket under her arm, and slammed out the back door.

"That was harsh," Edward said.

"Maybe it was. But what else is there to say? The past is past. She'll at least keep some good memories of the time she spent here."

He shook his head, then stood. "Maybe it's time for all of us to get on with it. Let go of the past."

She carried the stack of plates to the sink. "What do you mean by that?"

He reached for his hat and coat hanging by the door. "I'm not sure."

Isabel poured herself another cup of coffee and sat quietly for a moment, thinking about the coming winter. The wheat would be in before long, and the boys would go back to school. There were clothes to try on and let out, pencils and books to buy. It wouldn't hurt to review arithmetic before school started, although convincing the boys of that wouldn't be easy. She would have to come up with some projects for herself, too, to keep her busy. Maybe make new curtains, like she'd thought about earlier in the fall, with a pretty fabric, not just flour sacks.

She got up and finished cleaning the kitchen, then collected Caroline's clothes to wash for her trip. The sheets hadn't been washed in a while; she stripped them off the beds, pulled on a jacket, and carried them outside.

It took most of the morning to get the sheets washed and rinsed and put through the wringer. Her arms felt like lead as she carried them to the line to dry. She threw the first sheet over the line and was pinning it in place when she smelled smoke. The wind was blowing from the north. She stepped from behind the sheet and looked out over the cotton field. The smoke was coming from the brush arbor.

She squinted her eyes against the weak November sun. She saw figures in the distance and could tell that the brush arbor had been torn down. The fire was catching hold, the blaze visible from here. *It must be Edward and the boys,* she thought. She shook her head. *Letting the crops sit in the fields while he tries to burn down memories of something that can't be forgotten. He'll set the whole pecan grove on fire then complain when there's no pecan pie anymore.* She turned back to the sheets.

A few minutes later, she heard the first explosion. *Damn him,* she thought. *He knows I don't want him using dynamite around the boys. There are only a few stumps up there, not even worth fooling with, and he can get Everitt to help him after the boys have gone back to school. And they better be watching out for Caroline.*

Her fingers froze on the clothesline. Her thoughts flashed back to the vision she'd had standing at the kitchen window last summer. Flames leaping from the brush arbor, an image of someone running toward it in a panic. Being filled with dread, and the certainty that something terrible would happen there.

Caroline, she thought. *I never told any of them about her hiding place. They don't know she's there. All that brush will catch fire and she'll never open her mouth, curling up to die like some mute, suffering animal and it will be my fault.* She dropped the wet sheet to the ground. When she heard a second explosion, she started to run.

She ran through the field, the cotton stalks grabbing her dress and the damp earth slowing her down, cursing herself for not being kinder to Caroline, for not keeping her close to the house. She threw off her jacket as she ran and held her dress up to her thighs to get it out of the way. She stumbled as she jumped from one furrow to the next, and finally fell. She thrashed on the ground, kicking off her loosely tied shoes, scrambling up again and running in bare feet, aware in some far corner of her mind of the pain as the dry stalks and hulls cut her over and over again. The flames of the brush arbor rose higher. Smoke drifted in her direction and seared her lungs. She saw Edward and the boys running to the creek bed to shelter themselves for the next charge. She screamed, but they didn't hear her.

She skirted the blazing brush arbor and drew up short, struggling to breathe. The honeysuckle bushes were on fire, the trunks of the pecan trees beginning to scorch. Smoke and heat hit her from all directions. She doubled over from the pain in her side, then struggled upright again. She drew in as much air as her burning lungs would hold, and screamed again, a hoarse wail of desperation. Her cry was answered by the third explosion. *A fitting message,* she thought as she fell, *from an angry God.* It was the last thing she remembered.

It was dark when Isabel woke. She was roused to consciousness by the suffocating stench of death in her nostrils, the groans and cries of the near dead ringing in her ears. She opened her eyes slowly and looked up the walls of a narrow trench into a cloudy night sky. She was lying on her back in muddy water a few inches deep. She raised her head painfully, and saw bodies stacked around her in the trench, some with legs or arms or faces blown away. She lowered her head again and closed her eyes, sickened by what she had seen. Someone was lying next to her, pressed against her right side, and she pushed her arm in a feeble attempt to make him move. He moaned with pain. She turned her head to look at him.

It was Carl. His chest and belly were ripped open, his flesh exposed in a caking mess of blood and dirt.

"My God," she said. "My God." She rolled over on her side, put her arms around him and pulled him to her, and began to cry. "Carl. My baby. I've missed you so. Not a day goes by I don't think about you."

"Mama," he said. "I've been calling you. I was starting to think you wouldn't come."

"I'm here, baby. I'm here."

They held each other for a long time. Isabel stroked his hair, kissed him and told him over and over that she would never leave him. Carl finally pushed himself up onto an elbow.

"We have to go," he whispered. "It's time to go."

"No. It's too dangerous. And you can't walk – you're hurt."

"I'm fine. You're the one I'm worried about."

She tried to sit up but fell back with a moan. Bolts of blinding pain shot through her head, and she almost lost consciousness again. Carl got up on his knees, then braced himself against the side of the trench as he stood. He bent down and picked her up. *When did he get so tall and strong?* she thought through a haze. *He's a man.*

He lifted her over his head, rolled her onto the ground outside the trench, then jumped up beside her and gently lifted her into his arms again. She saw the sun coming up, and heard the battle begin not far from them, the whine of mortar shells, booming artillery and relentless machine gun fire, screams when the ammunition hit its target. They were surrounded suddenly by silent, grim-faced soldiers running in the opposite direction, hundreds of them, carrying bayonets and smelling of gunpowder, rancid clothes, and fear. She wanted Carl to hurry, to get away from them, afraid they would drag him into the battle again. The ground was rough, and he stumbled every once in a while, but at last they were clear.

"Carl."

"Sshhh," he whispered. "Don't talk." He smiled down at her. "We're walking on hallowed ground, Mama. We're walking on hallowed ground."

She looked down. The muddy battlefield was behind them. They were in a cotton field, the fat, white cotton bolls drooping on their stalks, the smell of bursting ripe cotton heavy under the rising sun. She heard mockingbirds calling, a dog barking, and the faint sound of a screen door slamming in the distance. She turned her head and saw their house. Then she looked up at Carl. She could see it in his face. He was happy to be home.

He carried her up the steps of the back porch, through the kitchen, and down the hall to her bedroom. He laid her on the bed then sat beside her, the bedsprings creaking under his weight. Isabel sat up.

"Carl," she said. "Do you blame us?"

"Blame you for what, Mama?"

"For not stopping you. For getting you killed in that godforsaken war."

He shook his head. "I don't blame you, Mama. Or Daddy either. You raised me to live my own life. Make my own decisions and hold myself accountable. You raise a son like that, you can't go back on it, Mama. I almost got myself killed once or twice before I ever went off to the war. I just didn't tell you and Daddy about it."

"But you were so scared. The night before you left. And at the train station the next morning."

"Of course I was scared. I wasn't stupid. I knew what I was doing."

She began to cry. "I've been so angry with your daddy. And I've asked myself every day, what more should I have done to keep you from going. I wondered if you hated us for what happened."

Carl smiled. "Hate you and Daddy? How could that ever be? There's so much love in this house I don't hardly know how there's room for anything else. It started with you and Daddy, and the two of you gave it to me and the boys. It's tied us all so tight we'll be together forever."

He laid his head on her shoulder and she rocked him in her arms, swaying gently from side to side.

"Do you want some supper?" she said.

"No, Mama. I'm just passing by."

He kissed her on the lips like he did when he was a boy. Then he was gone.

Edward thought he heard Isabel stir. For two days he'd sat in a chair beside the bed, until Doc insisted he get some sleep or he'd be of no use to any of them. He finally agreed to make a pallet on the floor beside her, where he slept fitfully, waking at any sound, not sure whether he had heard it or dreamed it. Now he rose and looked at her. If she had moved, he couldn't tell. He looked at the clock beside the bed – two o'clock in the morning – and felt her face. The fever was rising again. He went to the bureau, dipped a fresh cloth in the basin of water, and wiped her face, careful not to touch her too hard. He set the cloth down and picked up a cup of water that sat by the bed, then spooned a little between her lips. Most of it ran down her jaw, and he dabbed it with the cloth. He set the cup down and took the cloth back to the basin.

He knew he wouldn't sleep again that night, so he rolled up the quilts that made his pallet and set them aside in the corner. Then he pulled his chair up beside her and sat down.

Swelling on the brain, Doc said. A rock hidden under the stump had shattered, a lump the size of a baseball hitting her in the head. They'd know in a few days. Nothing Doc could do for her. Nothing any of them could do but wait. And pray.

She must have seen the fire and heard the dynamite and come running for Caroline. There was no need. James had spotted Caroline under the bushes – he was off playing like he usually did, while Edward and Samuel and Ben tore down the brush arbor and built the fire. They'd taken her down to the creek bed, well out of harm's way. They'd set the third charge and were waiting for it to blow when Samuel heard something. He poked his head up over the bank in time to see Isabel scream and then fall. Samuel's face had twisted in terror, his own screams matching his mother's as he scrambled over the bank to get to her. Edward had told the other children to stay back.

Samuel reached her first. He picked her up and carried her all the way to the house, like he was possessed with the strength of the Furies, his tears dripping silently on the front of his mother's dress. He carried her to the house and laid her on the bed, and by the time Edward and the other children got there, Samuel had run to the barn to get Blue. He hadn't bothered to saddle the horse, just jumped on and whipped him with the reins, cutting through fields and riding as hard as he could to get Doc.

Edward shifted in his chair and cursed, blaming himself for clearing the brush arbor. He had left the house Monday morning not sure what he'd meant about letting go of the past, not sure what he wanted for the future. Then he had looked out over the field and seen that brush arbor, mocking him like some evil skeleton spoiling his land, and he knew the first thing that had to be done was to get rid of it. He should have known no good could come of that brush arbor from the beginning. It had no business being there, and Kane had no business being there, and then Edward had no real business being there on Monday morning. There were more important things to occupy his time than that. That's when trouble starts – people doing what they have no business doing. That's the makings of trouble.

He rose and paced slowly around the room. He thought back on Saturday, when he'd stood over his wife with his fists clenched while she slumped on the floor and told him to kill her. As if he could ever raise his hand against her. Folks would say he had a right to, no doubt. But he'd walked out of the house and gone back behind the barn and lost his breakfast, sick to his stomach with the force of his anger and disgust with himself.

There was no excusing what she'd done. There was no excusing some things he'd done, either. She'd called him a murderer. Maybe she was right. Carl had come to him one night, late. He'd gone out to check on a sick mule before turning in and Carl had followed him outside, wanting to talk about something on his mind. He was thinking about joining up, he'd said. A chance to serve his country. Edward had heard him out and knew Carl was waiting for what he had to say. He had also known with certainty that if he'd told him not to join up, that he needed him on the farm, Carl never would have gone. But he didn't tell him that. He couldn't remember now what he'd said. Something about a man owing a duty to his country, and how he understood Carl wanted to be a man. He couldn't remember exactly what he'd said, couldn't remember saying that Carl should go. The one thing he did remember, though, was the look on Isabel's face when they stepped out of the mule's stall and saw her standing in the doorway of the barn. She'd come out to see what they were doing and had heard it all.

Tell him not to go, she'd said. Tell him not to go. But Edward had refused. After Carl died, he knew she'd been right. Leave it to women and there'd be a lot less killing in the world.

"Isabel," he croaked hoarsely in the dark. There were things he wanted to say, but he couldn't seem to put the words to them. She was the one good with words. She'd gone so quiet after Carl died that he'd almost forgotten how she could talk. Not silly talk like a lot of women, but something funny she'd seen, or something sad, or just something she'd noticed about folks. A gift with words, that's what it was. Carl had it, too. When her and Carl got going at the supper table, you'd never heard anything like it. Edward would sit back and drink his coffee and listen to the two of them and think there wasn't a man alive he'd trade places with.

"Isabel," he said hoarsely again. He cleared his throat. "You remember the first time you made me a birthday cake? You couldn't believe I'd never had a birthday cake before. I thought it was a lot of trouble for nothing, but you made me a cake and we had a party, just you and me." He felt foolish, talking to himself in the dark, but he went on. "You always had a way of making the least little thing seem special."

The words came slowly, haltingly at first, but then they kept on coming, pouring out like he couldn't stop them. He told her how he hadn't paid her any mind for years, she was just a scrawny little kid, and there was plenty of skirt to chase and keep him otherwise occupied. Then she'd shown up at school one year grown up all of a sudden. She'd walked through the door of the schoolhouse and his heart had leaped to his throat and he'd known then he'd have her if it was the last thing he did. It took two years of waiting, watching while she turned down every boy and man for miles around. Then he'd presented himself at her door one day and told her and her mother his intentions. He didn't plan on staying in the hills for long, he'd said, and was already saving to buy some land. He'd give Isabel things no other man would be able to give her. He'd asked if he could come calling.

Mary Clara had looked him square in the eye the whole time he was talking, taking his measure. When he'd finished, she sat quiet for what felt like a long time. He'd wiped his hands on his pants legs and hoped Isabel and her mother didn't notice how he was sweating. Then Mary Clara spoke. "It's up to Isabel whether you come calling," she said. "Then it's up to you to convince her you're the man you seem to be." Isabel had said yes. Edward courted her for a year, and then they were married.

"I thought I'd never love anyone as much as I loved you," he whispered in the dark. "Funny how I was wrong. Carl came along, then Samuel and Ben and James. Every one of those boys special. It was like the love kept growing, there wasn't no end to it." His voice broke.

"Things end though, don't they? In ways you'd least expect. Something died in both of us when Carl died. I could see how you were suffering, but there was nothing I could do about it. Because it was eating me up inside, too, Isabel. Every day, eating me up inside."

He knelt beside the bed and reached for his wife's hand, rubbing it between his. "It may be over between you and me, Isabel. I might be able to live with that someday. But let me tell you, there's one thing I don't think I can do. I don't think I can walk down that hall and tell those boys we got to bury their mother." He pressed her hand to his lips. Then he laid his head on the bed and cried.

Someone was crying. It was a terrible sound, like sorrow itself had found a human voice. The cries washed over Isabel like waves, loud sometimes like they were crashing into her, then faint as they faded away. Stop crying, she wanted to say. Stop your crying right now.

She had called and called, but Carl wouldn't come back. She sobbed and grieved that he'd left her again, then her grief turned to anger, and she fussed at him when she called, fussed and scolded until she heard the tone of her voice. Then she was chastened and told him she was sorry. It wasn't him she was angry with, she explained. It was the pain that was making her act that way. Come back, she said in her sweetest voice. Your mama needs you. Fussing and sweet, back and forth, and always fighting the pain. Come back, Carl. Come back. He wouldn't come.

"I heard you calling for Carl." Mary Clara pulled a chair up to the side of the bed and took her hand.

"Go get him," Isabel said. "Tell him he has to come here right now."

Mary Clara shook her head. "I can't do that."

"Then you're not being very helpful, Mother."

Still holding Isabel's hand with one of hers, Mary Clara stroked her cheek, then her hair, with the other.

"Are you in pain?"

"Yes."

Mary Clara picked up a wet cloth lying on the bedside table and pressed it gently to Isabel's forehead.

"I saw him," Isabel said. "He was so beautiful."

"He always was a handsome boy."

"Where is he now? What's he doing?"

Mary Clara appeared thoughtful and looked around the room. "Where, I can't say. But what he's doing – he's learning. Learning to be patient. And other things."

"That makes no sense, Mother. You say these things, but you never really explain anything."

Mary Clara smiled. "I know. But even if I explained them, you wouldn't understand."

"You used to have a higher estimation of my intelligence."

"It has nothing to do with intelligence. You'll see. Someday."

Isabel was becoming increasingly agitated with her mother.

"I've waited so long for him," she said. "Sometimes I thought I heard him singing or whispering a few words. But I could never see him, so I thought I must have imagined it."

"It wasn't your imagination," Mary Clara said. "He comes around every once in a while."

"But why doesn't he visit me like you do? It seems the least he could do is come and talk, tell me how he's doing."

"I don't know that either," Mary Clara said. "But it might have something to do with Edward."

"Edward."

"Yes. It wouldn't be fair to Edward. Edward was crazy about that boy. And Carl felt the same way about his daddy. Still does. They were so much alike."

"I always thought Carl had a lot of me in him," Isabel said.

"He did. But he reminded me more of Edward. Samuel's the one who favors you the most."

Mary Clara reached for the cup of water sitting beside the bed and spooned a little between Isabel's lips.

"I'll always be grateful to Edward," Mary Clara said.

"For giving you grandsons?"

"That. But also because I didn't know if there was a man alive that could live with you. Sure enough, though, he's done it."

"Am I that hard to get along with?"

"No. But most men would be hard-pressed to keep up. Edward was willing to let you be, and he never let his pride get in the way of loving you. He showed you a lot of respect over the years."

Mary Clara set the cup down and leaned back in her chair. "I don't have many regrets. But I do wish I could have grown old with a man.

With your daddy. Or with Doc. What a fine life that would have been. And then taking care of each other as the end drew near."

"Doc loved you so much. He still does."

"It was mutual. But no stronger than the feelings between you and Edward."

"There's a lot of anger between Edward and me."

"Yes. But people can forgive. Under that anger, the love is still there. You think about that, Isabel. And set your mind on growing old with Edward."

Mary Clara stood and let go of her hand.

"Don't leave, Mother. Please."

"It's time."

"If you're not going to help me find Carl, I'll do it myself."

"You can try, but you won't find him."

Isabel groaned. "I'm tired, Mother. I'm so tired."

"I know," Mary Clara said, and leaned to kiss her. "But you have a lot of living to do yet. You'd hate to miss the years that are coming. Listen… You hear that, don't you? Someone's crying. I know you hear it."

Isabel turned her head to the sound. *All that suffering,* she thought. Quit crying, she wanted to say. Quit your crying, I need some sleep. If I can get some sleep, it'll come to me where Carl is and then I'll find him again. The crying stopped. Too late. She was never going to get any sleep around here. Isabel opened her eyes.

Edward raised his head when she moved. He wiped his face with his shirt sleeve and tried to calm himself. It was almost daybreak, her pale face on the pillow taking shape in the morning light. Taking her hand, he watched her intently. He was looking right at her when she opened her eyes. He thought he'd say good morning, or we didn't know if you would make it, or the boys have been worried sick, but all that came out was a sob that sounded like a cough. He laid his head down on the bed again.

"Sshhh," Isabel whispered, stroking his hair. "Don't cry, Edward. Sshhh. Don't cry."

"How are the boys?" she asked.

"Worried sick about you. They said to wake them if there was any change."

"Not yet. They need their sleep."

He nodded. "Caroline's fine, too. We found her before starting the fire. Her granny came to get her yesterday."

"What was she like?"

"A thin-lipped woman."

She sighed. She was very tired. He told her to get some sleep.

It was four days before she felt well enough to get out of bed. The boys came in and out of her room, checking on her and not wanting to let her out of their sight. Hazel Matthews had organized the ladies in town to bring meals and Edward taught the boys how to make breakfast. Samuel carried her to the outhouse when she needed to go.

On one of the trips back from the outhouse, Samuel stopped short of the porch.

"Mama." He squeezed her tight, struggling to get the words out. "I said some things to you. About Carl. About you and Daddy. I shouldn't have said them."

She touched his cheek. "Don't, Samuel. You were carrying a burden you should never have had to carry."

On the fifth day she felt well enough to come to breakfast. Samuel made biscuits that were a little flat and gravy that was a little thin and she said they were the best she'd ever tasted. Ben poured her coffee and James spooned canned peaches into a bowl. She sat at her place at the end of the table, drawn and worn, and smiled when anyone looked at her. She ate as much as she could, and when she set her fork down the boys urged her to eat more.

"She has to go slow," Edward said. "Don't want her to overdo."

The boys cleared the table and washed the dishes, and Edward told them to get on with the chores. They kissed her and told her they'd be back soon, while she stroked their cheeks and told her she would miss them. When they had gone, Edward poured himself another cup of coffee and motioned with the pot to Isabel. She shook her head. He put the pot back on the stove and sat down across the table from her.

"You should be getting the wheat in. Instead of worrying about me."

"Everitt and the hired hands can take care of the wheat."

He poured coffee from his cup to his saucer to cool, then back to his cup again.

"There's something I want you to know," he said. "You can think on it, but no need to make a decision until you're ready."

She drew her shawl closer around her.

"Old man Coggin finally agreed to sell me his acreage down by Floyd's Landing," he said. "I gave him a little money down while you were in Memphis."

"It's good land. You've been wanting it a long time. You'll have to hire more help to work it, though."

"That's true. I've been thinking on how we'd manage it." He took a drink of coffee and cleared his throat.

"One thing I've been thinking is I could build a little place down there for me to live. You and the boys could stay here, and I'd still be close. I'd take care of anything you need."

She stared out the kitchen window. The sky was gray and cold. It looked like rain.

"Is that what you want?"

He shrugged. "I don't know what I want. The only thing I know for sure is I never thought I'd be sitting here saying something like that to you."

She smiled sadly. "There's a lot of things we never expected, did we Edward?"

"That's true."

They fell silent for a while.

"It would be hard on the boys," she said.

"It would. But I'd come see them every day."

"I expect so. You're a good father, Edward. You were a good father to Carl."

He looked away. She could see his lips trembling, his Adam's apple bobbing up and down as he gulped, and the sudden redness around his eyes.

"I saw him, Edward. I saw Carl."

He didn't speak for a moment. Then he whispered, "How was he?"

"He was our beautiful boy, Edward. Our beautiful boy. He doesn't blame either one of us."

His chest heaved. He rested his elbows on the table and rubbed his eyes.

"I wondered if he'd come to you over the years – you with the sight and all. Wondered if you weren't telling me."

"No. This was the first time since the night he died."

They fell silent again.

"I need to know something," he finally said. "I need to know if it's over between you and Kane."

"It's over. It was over when I came back from Memphis."

He seemed to accept her answer.

"I need to know something from you," she said. "Did you kill Piggott?"

He shook his head. "Naw, I didn't kill him. Sheriff put a lot of pressure on the boys down at Smitty's and one of them finally confessed. He and Piggott got liquored up one night and got to arguing over a card game. He followed Piggott later and shot him and stole the two dollars they were fighting about." He stirred his coffee and took another sip.

"I'll tell you, though," he said, his voice low, barely above a whisper. "I almost killed a man once. The day me and Samuel came back from Memphis. I told Samuel to go on home, and I went to see the sheriff, and after we'd talked awhile, I borrowed his horse. I loaded my pistol, and I went down to Floyd's Landing."

She drew a sharp breath.

"I snuck up on Kane from the riverbank. I had him in my sights. I knew then that I could kill a man. I could have killed him and walked away and never thought another thing about it." He paused. "What stopped me was I knew if I killed him, you'd never come back to me. I'd lose you forever."

She swayed in her chair. He leaped up and came to her, picked her up, and carried her to bed. He laid her down gently then pulled his chair up beside her.

"Do you want me to go?" he asked.

"No. You can stay."

She closed her eyes, sinking into sleep, and thought she caught a glimpse of Edward standing at the bureau, opening the drawers and removing his underclothes, pajamas and work shirts, stacking them on the bed in preparation for leaving. She asked him where he was going but he wouldn't answer, his face stony, indifferent, as he moved to the closet for his hanging clothes. She was overcome suddenly with loneliness and loss, and she began to cry. She woke then to Edward sitting beside her, watching her.

"Are you hurting anywhere?" he asked.

"No. Why?"

"You were whimpering in your sleep. Like you were in pain." They were quiet for a while and then he remembered something he'd wanted to tell her.

"The day you were hurt. It was the strangest thing."

"What?"

"You got hit on the side of the head. There was a cut – not much of one. But there was blood all over the front of your dress. It was an awful mess, blood and mud, wet in some spots and caking in others. When Doc got here, he ripped your dress open, expecting to see your insides torn out." He got up and paced the room a few times before he went on. "There wasn't a scratch on you, Isabel," he said in a hushed voice. "All that blood, but there wasn't a scratch. Doc doesn't know what to make of it."

She shook her head, tears dripping into her ears and onto the pillow. "I don't know what to make of it either. It's hard to say."

She closed her eyes, she wasn't sure for how long. He was still sitting beside her when she opened them again.

"You can do what you want, Edward. Build you a house down at Floyd's Landing. But wait a while. It might not be necessary."

He took her hand. "No need to be hasty," he said. "If you think it will be all right."

Isabel felt his rough hand on hers, the soft quilt covering her bed, the feather pillow under her head. She felt herself drifting off to sleep again.

"Yes," she said softly. "I think it will be all right."

ACKNOWLEDGMENTS

Many people generously gave their time to read and comment on early drafts of this book, for which I am deeply grateful.

Special thanks to Jacqueline Simon, whose instruction in the art of creative writing gave me the courage to begin the book, and whose critical eye was invaluable throughout.

Special thanks also to Laura Wimer Jewell and Gabe Jewell for applying their incredible talents when needed.

Thanks to Zach Jewell for being an abundant source of inspiration.

And to my husband David, for his unwavering support, insight, and encouragement. The time and space to write has been a true gift of love. Thank you.

ABOUT THE AUTHOR

Karen Jewell is a former trial attorney and author of numerous pieces of nonfiction. She has an undergraduate degree in English, a Master's in Business Administration, and earned her Juris Doctorate degree at the University of Michigan. Karen lives in Houston, Texas, with her husband. *In the Garden of Sorrows* is her first novel.

CPSIA information can be obtained
at www.ICGtesting.com
Printed in the USA
LVHW040751190523
747462LV00001B/266